LEVIN, Betty

The sword of Culann. N.Y., Macmillan [c1973]
280p.

DISCARD

1. Space and time - Fiction 2. Ireland -
Hist. - Fict. I. tc.

M9397-15 CS

THE SWORD OF CULANN

THE SWORD
OF CULANN

BETTY LEVIN

MACMILLAN PUBLISHING CO., INC.
New York
COLLIER MACMILLAN PUBLISHERS
London

Macmillan Publishing Co., Inc., 866 Third Avenue, New York, N.Y. 10022
Collier-Macmillan Canada Ltd., Toronto, Ontario
Library of Congress catalog card number: 73-583
Printed in the United States of America

1   2   3   4   5   6   7   8   9   10

Library of Congress Cataloging in Publication Data

Levin, Betty.
    The sword of Culann.

    [1. Space and time—Fiction.   2. Ireland—History—Fiction.]   I. Title.
PZ7.L5759Sw   [Fic]   73-583   ISBN 0-02-757340-0

FOR KITTY HEALY BECK

The fort opposite the oakwood
  Once it was Bruide's, it was Cathal's,
It was Aed's, it was Ailill's,
  It was Conaing's, it was Cuiline's
And it was Maelduin's—
  The fort remains after each in his turn,
And the kings asleep in the ground.

—TRANSLATED FROM OLD IRISH
BY KUNO MEYER

PART ONE

ONE

Dickon could not open his eyes. Not yet. He tried to let his lashes veil the brightness, but all was glaring white.

It wasn't until he heard the rustling just a few feet away that he forced himself to look. Through the fringe of lashes he could see the foal thrashing in the beach grass. Then he closed his eyes again, lowered his head until his face was resting on the sand. He could hear the quick rasps, not quite snorts, from the struggling animal. He groaned.

He tried to tell himself that he had survived, that by some miracle the violent surf had cast him onto Sable Island alive. A freak of fortune had saved him from the sea and this spit of land that had claimed so many ships and men through the centuries.

He knew about the Sable Island ponies, the herd that must have started in the sixteenth century from a few that had been stranded, just as he was. But what about this little one? Had its mother grazed too close and been caught by one of the combers during the storm? Spikes of dull green beach grass pierced the dunes. Perhaps she had waded after some seaweed and been caught in the fierce undertow.

Dickon looked again. "There," he whispered. "There now. You're hurt. Don't be afraid." He began crawling toward the little beast, which thrashed frantically, its eyes staring with alarm. "There," Dickon told him, crooning, finding he could slither forward like a worm. But he had to clamp his teeth together to stifle a groan. He felt bruised, pounded. "There," he murmured, reaching out his hand.

The little foal drew back, bared its teeth.

"No," cried Dickon-Claudia, "you're curious. You're in conflict. You have to show it by stretching toward me. Timid but curious, terrified but drawn by some mysterious—"

The foal leaned toward Dickon.

"It's two things at once," Dickon-Claudia instructed. "Don't you get it?"

"I want to go see if Tim's home yet."

"But we're right in the middle of this. Listen, Evan, your part's about to begin."

"He must've come by now." The foal sat up. "Later, Claudia. I want to see Tim."

Claudia brushed the pine needles off her front and got to her feet. Sable Island was gone and she was looking down at a different coastline, steep rocks, green-black trees rearing up from the edge of the bay.

She'd make the best of Evan running out on her. She'd finish composing the story tonight. Once she was in bed, she'd pull the covers over her head and become Dickon again and work out more of the details. She'd be sure to give Evan more to do so that he'd stay interested.

She wasn't surprised that Tim's homecoming had lured him away. For Evan, theirs was all one single family, not two halves joined by Susan's and Phil's marriage. Susan, who was Claudia's and Tim's mother, was re-

3

garded by Evan as mother of them all, Tim as oldest brother. Claudia could understand that, at least where the kids were concerned. She tended to think of Evan as her little brother, though he really wasn't, and lumped all the older ones together as "the others." That was how she thought of them now as she started off after Evan to join them in the house.

She stopped at the kitchen doorway, taking in the family group, brother and little stepbrother, stepsisters, her mother and Phil. Only Doug wasn't there; he was still away being a junior counselor.

Tim had a milk bottle in one hand, a cigarette in the other. Claudia was instantly put off by the cigarette. It wasn't Tim's style at all. "Why are you smoking?"

"Just, well, just because of what happened. Got to get adjusted to life here again. I can't explain. Only it gets on your nerves."

"He's had a harrowing time," Rebecca explained for him. Her eyes were glowing. "He's just been telling us. Lost in fog. They had to row all night, and he's starved, and everything."

"What did they do to you?" Claudia hadn't figured on abuse. This survival training had been something he'd wanted to do so badly he'd worked for half the tuition.

Tim puffed nervously. "It's not what *they* did. It's what the elements did. Or were. It was . . . oh," he sighed with exasperation.

Susan said, "Was it fun, though, dear?"

"Fun!" Tim exploded in smoke. "It wasn't exactly a cruise. You . . . you and Phil, I mean even when you camp out or get caught in a storm . . . I mean this was really do or die." His voice dropped. "Sorry, Mom. I

4

guess I've got to get used to civilization again."

Susan smiled at him. "We're all dying to hear about your adventures."

He gave another impatient sigh. "You make it sound like one of Claudia's stories. It was real." He turned to Phil. "Two of the guys crapped out on us. You know, really blew it. Couldn't take that kind of beating. I mean, it was an ordeal like they have in primitive cultures."

"Sounds like a lot of chauvinist nonsense," Maddie declared. "So you went out in an open boat in the fog at night and finally got to your island and lived on a lot of junk that no sensible person would feed to a cat. And that makes you a man. Thank God women don't try to prove themselves with anything that phony."

"Why don't we give Tim a chance to clean up," Phil suggested. "Then we can hear all about it at dinner."

Maddie muttered something about merely having an inferior type job to have to go to. Nothing dramatic that cost hundreds of dollars. She merely earned money. Waiting on tables.

Tim heard enough to respond, "They also serve who only stand and wait." He turned to Claudia. "I thought you'd come to meet me."

"I forgot the time."

"She was being Dickon," Evan supplied.

"Who?"

"Nothing," Claudia cut in. "Evan, it's just between us."

"I didn't tell him about the shipwreck. I didn't tell him what we were doing."

It was better to shut up. Evan, having no capacity for embarrassment, had no powers of concealment.

5

"Sounds pretty wild." Tim was teasing. "You were having your own private ordeal, huh? Who's this Dickon?"

"A character," Maddie retorted. "A character from *The Secret Garden* who has a special way with animals and nature. Now leave her alone."

"It would," Tim threw back as he started up the stairs, "be good to get Claudia into the real world once in a while."

"It would," Maddie flung after him, "be good to engineer a Terrible Ordeal Against the Elements for her to realistically cope with? Is that what you mean?"

Phil said, "Let me remind you, Maddie, that it was your idea to be a waitress at the inn this summer. No one made you."

"I'm not jealous, if that's what you think. Only thing I mind is the way he's blowing himself up. Besides," she added, "I'd already decided to quit at the end of the week. I've even told them."

"Oh, good, dear. Maybe we can have a last cruise. Or do you want to see if Roy can come?"

"I don't know yet. I don't know what I want to do. But if Tim doesn't stop all this nonsense about his Great Ordeal, I'm going to go somewhere else. Far away."

"Give him a day or so. He'll unwind." Phil smiled at her. "Besides, he may have had a really cataclysmic experience. We haven't heard the details yet."

"Yes," Rebecca offered. "He may have been in a really cataclysmic tight spot."

"Where he had nothing to eat but starfish," Maddie elaborated with a giggle.

Evan asked, "Will Tim tell us what starfishes taste like?"

"He'll probably feed them to you if you show enough interest," Maddie warned him.

"And would they grow back their arms as you ate them? So that you'd never run out?"

Maddie laughed. "Maybe we should go and find out for ourselves. What about it?"

Claudia recognized the tone of determination beneath Maddie's joking. When Tim came back to recount his arduous weeks surviving off the Maine coast, Maddie listened, quiet and thoughtful. Claudia could tell that she was up to something, but it wasn't until much later in the evening that Maddie finally announced her decision: "An island. But no phony nonsense. We'll do it naturally, and not just taking care of ourselves. Women traditionally take care of others. Of children, for instance. So we'll take Evan."

"Oh, I don't know, dear," Susan began.

"How about the aged?" Phil inquired. "I'm beginning to feel left out."

"They don't take care of them, Daddy," Rebecca declared with a laugh. "They expose them on the hillside. When they stop being useful, that is."

Maddie just plowed right on. "We'll take Evan and plenty of supplies for him in case he doesn't like our survival diets."

"And plenty of paper and pencils and crayons for him," Claudia joined in. "Just for Evan. No one else will be allowed to borrow."

Tim began to laugh. "I can see you all now. A trunk

full of games, picture puzzles, corned beef hash and instant milk and pancakes. A tent, no doubt. Soap. Toilet paper. You better begin making the list. It'll take two weeks just to write all that stuff down."

"That's not the way we're going to do it," Maddie countered. "We'll just have things for Evan in case he needs them. Otherwise we'll have no more than you did per person. And we'll stay longer."

"I'm not sure about Evan," Phil cautioned. "For your sakes as well as his."

"Oh, don't leave him out," Claudia cried.

Now Rebecca spoke up. She thought it would complicate things if Evan were along. She and Claudia argued until Rebecca accused Claudia of wanting Evan so that she could use him for her story-making.

Claudia felt her face growing hot. Rebecca's charge was unfair simply because it took a part of the truth and turned it into something that wasn't true at all. Sure, Evan was suggestible, but that was because he had the imagination an artist. It was too bad for Rebecca that she couldn't see how unique he was, that she could only think of him, like Claudia, as different.

It was hard for Claudia to know whether being considered different was the same as being different. All she knew was that things that seemed natural to her always turned out to be embarrassing for Rebecca. Becca couldn't stand the way Claudia always wanted to know what happened next after a story was finished, or what it was like before, and even before that.

Claudia had found a book in the town library by someone Phil said was a nut that gave a complete description of the Red Paint People who were the first inhabitants of

Maine. Rebecca, overhearing Phil's comment, had observed that it took one to find one.

Ignoring Becca's jibe, Claudia had defended the book. "How can you be sure he's a nut?" she had argued.

"Because there's only the slightest evidence, not enough to come to all those conclusions. It's romantic conjecture built on a few hard archaeological facts. Listen, Claude, the world is full enough of nuts like that. Don't you be one."

Now she began considering what it would be like to act out natives and explorers on this island Maddie wanted them to go to. "Vikings," she found herself mulling out loud. "Tim could be the Indian chief because he knows the most."

"We're not playing games like a bunch of kids out of one of your idiot stories," said Rebecca.

"Anyhow, the Vikings landed on the coast of Newfoundland," Tim added.

"But some of them could have come here too," Claudia countered.

Susan said, "We're not having any unsupervised landings."

Phil said, "Don't forget the Vikings didn't have charts. All those navigation aids we depend on are relatively modern. The compass was still something of a recent innovation in Columbus's time."

Maddie dismissed all ideas of historical reenactment. If Claudia and Evan wanted to play games, that was their business. As for the boat, the parents could keep it, just drop them at the island. "What we really have to settle is whether if Tim comes he's going to think he's in charge and try to throw his weight around."

"If he's a Viking," Claudia put in, "then someone would have to be his thrall. Becca. I guess that would be Becca."

"You don't even have to stick to Vikings," Phil remarked to Claudia. "Some people think that Irish monks may have crossed the Atlantic even earlier."

Susan stopped him. "Don't encourage her fantasies. Tim's right. She needs more real contacts. A good reason for letting her go. Though I'm not sure about Evan."

"Evan can be my contact with reality," Claudia promptly suggested, and was rewarded with a smile from Phil.

"Remember," he told her, "lord or thrall, Evan's younger than any of you. You'll have to watch out for him, keep him gooed up. You know how badly the sun gets him."

"If we ever see the sun," put in Tim. "Out there it's mostly fog."

"Out where?" demanded Susan. "What island do you have in mind?"

"Probably one of the outer ones. Right, Maddie?" And finally they were in agreement, rallied against the cautious older generation. "All right, near enough so that if we have to send up a flare, someone will see it. But definitely one of the outer islands." Away from you, his tone declared.

"Away from civilization," Maddie supplied.

That launched them into more negotiations. The fire died down. Claudia's head drooped. The voices fell away from her so that she barely heard the next compromise: Thrumcap Island with that old fisherman's shack in case they needed shelter, though everyone would pretend it wasn't there. They would be on their honor not to use it.

"Except Evan," Susan interjected. "You kids will have to exercise some judgment and flexibility."

Rebecca asked, "Doesn't someone use that shack? I've heard them talking down at the wharf about an old man who stays there sometimes. They always expect to find him dead."

"Then we won't be alone," Maddie objected. "We'll have to choose another island."

"Don't worry," Phil said with a laugh, "you will be. From what I hear, he's a senile recluse who comes and goes. At least he won't be there mentally."

Claudia, her head swimming with vague, unfocused islands, was tempted to ask about this man so that she could fit him into the picture. But she was on her way to bed now. Downstairs they were still at it, hashing out their ideas and plans. Besides, she didn't know where to put any more characters. Vikings and monks, Indians and stranded ponies merged into a single image like a double exposure and faded slowly into sleep.

TWO

EVAN was already scrambling along the rocks that led out to the point. He was like a little goat, elastic and sure-footed.

If he were going around the point to wave off the parents, Claudia supposed she would have to keep an eye on him. She hated the way she would look to the others as she clambered clumsily after Evan.

She would never wear shorts or even cut off her dungarees until she had lengthened or thinned or whatever it was that needed to happen to her body so that she would stop being the round-square peg of the family.

Claudia saw Evan begin to wind down through the rocks just before the point. Something had caught his eye, and now he seemed to have forgotten about running out to wave off the parents. He was an avid collector. Beachcombing drew him at every picnic, and on foggy days he could always be found down along the wharves at low tide, stooping like a shore bird picking at leftovers.

The boat had reached the open water. They could hear the boom being freed. Suddenly the parents were really leaving them, the sails, fuller now, pushing the boat toward and beyond the point. They all called and waved their good-bys. Claudia saw Evan raise his head and squint vaguely in their direction. The parents were already out of his mind. He had new business to attend to there among the weed-covered boulders.

Claudia cupped her hands to her mouth, really to remind him they were here. "Evan. Any mussels over there?"

"That's my girl," Tim laughed. "Food first, no matter where you are or what you're doing."

Rebecca said, "Honestly, Claude, you'll never lose any weight if that's all you can think of."

But Maddie's laughter was for Claudia, so that Claudia could join in and not just stand sullen and hurt. "First you complain because she's not reality-oriented. Then when she shows she's more with it than the rest of us, you jump on her for that. Weren't you warning us that we should take advantage of every sunny moment to acquaint ourselves with the island and all its possible food?"

Standing in the lee, the sun high and hot, it was hard to reconcile this atmosphere with what they had prepared for. So now, on this rare, picniclike day, they agreed to let the supplies remain for the time being while they searched out their home for the next week.

The island was bigger than they had guessed from the chart. It had low-lying promontories that looked like separate islands, satellites to their own, until they discovered that at low tide they could be walked or waded to.

Claudia and Evan found the first of these just beyond the point that Evan had been heading for. They also found the fisherman's shack set back above the next cove on a high-level plot, turf-covered and tracked with paths leading inland to the only wooded area on the island. "Sheep," Claudia remarked. "I didn't know there'd be sheep here." They peered into the hut, but the brightness outside made it impossible to see the dim interior.

Evan wanted to explore everything, but it looked creepy to Claudia. She said, "Let's see where those paths lead to," in a voice meant to convey all kinds of mysteries. "We're cast ashore," she told him. "Slaves. So we can barely walk, because we're shackled, see. Evan, you have to walk like this." She showed him how the shipwrecked slave must stumble and lurch along the path. "We know nothing about this place, so we hope that the path means something, a woodsman or a fisherman who'll feed us. Or treasure. Or a spring with fresh water."

What they found was the carcass of a sheep that had been dead for some time. It smelled no worse than the seagulls that strewed the windward side of so many of the islands they'd visited. But its upthrust head bespoke a death throe, and Claudia could not bear to look at it.

She turned along the darkening path where the trees and brush were thick and the moss hung down in shreds like dull green cobwebs. "Mushrooms," she called. "Look, Evan, poisonous mushrooms." The promise of the deadly drew Evan from the dead, but he trailed a long, yellowed strand of fleece that he'd pulled from the sheep.

They had appointed Claudia Keeper of the Log because it made sense that the one who watched over Evan should also take charge of the paper supply. But she knew that they were giving in to her weakness. "Only no indulgences of imagination," Tim had warned. "Straight reporting is what we want."

She made her first entry there beneath the hanging moss surrounded by the dusty orange of the mushrooms she must not touch. There was a faint odor of decay in

14

this small primeval forest. "We found a dead sheep which had suffered. Evan took some wool." She began to tuck away the little notebook, then pulled it out again. "Claudia," she added, "would not eat any sheep, no matter how fresh."

The path kept forking. Here and there they came across more tufts of wool, not long strands like Evan's, but fluff stuck to twigs and brambles. They found raspberries in a sun-filled glade, and then were back in darkness on a wooded slope that turned to brush and thistle and then led to a marshy place covered with rotting logs and slime.

Finally they were climbing again and in open sweet grass with only an occasional thistle, the sun still hot, the wind beginning to creep round to them, waking them from the darkness and stench, so that suddenly they realized they were hungry. And then they remembered that there were no sandwiches to return to or hot dogs to cook on sticks or lobsters to rake out of steaming seaweed.

"What I want," Evan informed her, "is a marshmallow."

It was late in the day before they had their first meal, consisting of clams and mussels.

Claudia said, "Evan's going to run out of cans of drink."

"Tell him he has to conserve them."

"You tell him."

Evan was off again, drawn to the dead sheep, the position of which had been one of the determining factors in selecting a camp site. Far enough from the smell, they had agreed. And then, after some discussion, far enough from the fisherman's hut to ensure privacy in case the old man showed up. Also to put off temptation for shelter.

15

"Out of sight, out of mind," Tim had said.

They subsided into private thoughts of dessert until Rebecca broke the silence. "How are we going to keep Evan from eating all the berries?"

"Vigilance," Tim suggested.

"No one can be that vigilant." Claudia laughed, recalling Evan's red-smeared lips and cheeks, his raspberry fingers. She reached for her notebook.

"But it's not fair, when he has chocolate and all. He has to stick to the rules about island food."

"Our camp site is protected from the southwest," wrote Claudia, "but Tim says we'll have to move if we get a northeast storm. Tim says you have to stay fluid. But Maddie would like to make a real home. She dug a drainage ditch around her sleeping place and it looks like a little room. Evan has chocolate on his sleeping bag already. Has used two cans of ginger ale. We've had one cup of water each from the drinking supply."

Claudia stopped because the subject had changed to one of vital interest to her. It was prompted by Tim stopping Maddie from tossing out the shells.

"But we've got to keep up with our own mess," Maddie was protesting. "We have to keep our environment clean."

"All wastes have to be thoroughly disposed of. You've got to wait for half tide."

"Evan's been going in the bushes," Claudia informed them.

"And I," Tim replied, "am going to dig a latrine pit before anyone else goes his way."

Rebecca grumbled, "The worst thing about camping," but then she ran after Tim to help.

16

"We are going to use the earth for a toilet," Claudia wrote. "Maddie wanted to use the sea, but Tim won't let her."

Thinking Rebecca would do anything for Tim, even digging a toilet she hated the very thought of, Claudia turned to Maddie. "Shouldn't we dig pits for storing things too?" There was the emergency box wrapped in plastic, medical supplies and flares. "Let's go find some digging stones. Come on, Maddie. What if it rains?"

They looked out at the flat bay, islands riding the surface like plump, charred dumplings. All Claudia's thoughts turned to food, and they hadn't even gone through their first day. Three shags flew low and black just above the glinting surface. She could hear the flapping of their wings.

Evan returned with a picture of the dead sheep. He had done it from an inland vantage point, so that out beyond there was a glimpse of water on which he had sketched a boat of some sort. It had been erased several times before he had finished with sharply curving lines.

That was how she learned they were no longer alone on the island.

"He's in the hut," Evan told her. "Let's go."

"We're supposed to pretend he isn't here."

Evan shrugged off that foolishness. "We're already friends. He smells. Only not as bad as the sheep."

Claudia waited. She knew there would be more.

"He's got this crow," Evan finally continued. "This crow he talks to and it knows everything he says. He's going to teach me to talk to it too."

Much later, after they had crawled into their sleeping bags and were lying quiet for a while, Claudia whispered

17

to Evan, "What else about the old man? What else is he like?"

Evan was already asleep, a small lump of darkness in their already dark tent. Claudia wondered about the sheep lying so near the hut, about how it might have met its death. She imagined the old man luring it with food, clubbing it or casting a rock. And then what? Not eating it. Certainly not skinning it. She rubbed at the image as Evan had rubbed at the lines he had first drawn on his picture.

Always accurate, he had settled on a fair depiction of the little double-ender now lying at its mooring halfway round the island, snug behind a curving point that reached out like a hook to a grassy knoll rising up to miniature cliffs and a scattering of rocks. Just beyond, the water moved swiftly down between the islands, this side of Moosebec Reach. There was always a sound of surf, even on a quiet night like this, while over on this end of the island, you could only hear the lapping of a placid sea, the droning of a mosquito coming and going in its own quest for survival.

Now the insect circled her head. Live and let live, she thought, burrowing into her sleeping bag.

Moments later, close by, she heard a slap, a second slap, and Tim's voice pronouncing, "Yessir, the first law of nature. Kill or be killed." And laughter.

Way in toward the heart of the island a sudden screeching. It was like an echo of his mirth, or else a death cry. Then silence again. Owls, she thought. And then, on the edge of sleep, Or that crow, the old man's crow.

18

three

THEIR waking was like a chain reaction. All except Evan, whose sleeping bag was empty. Of course he would be off already, the first to sleep, the first to rise.

Maddie and Tim decided to catch some mackerel for breakfast, but an hour later all they had were three small pollock and a crab.

"You need an earlier start," Rebecca advised.

"I didn't know fish could tell time," Maddie rejoined. "Anyhow, you can dig some clams while we start the fire."

When they were nearly finished eating, Maddie began to wonder about Evan, but Tim figured he'd be back when his stomach told him it was breakfast time.

As if to prove Tim's point, Evan came down from the rocks along the path. He was mumbling to himself, absorbed, as if he could hardly care where his wanderings took him.

They showed him the fish they were saving for him. He looked down with interest, but no apparent eagerness. "What is it?"

"Pollock."

Evan shook his head.

"Beggars can't be choosers," Tim warned. "We eat what we can get."

Evan shook his head again. "I had breakfast. Long time ago." His breakfast had consisted of mackerel fried in oatmeal, a kind of hard pancake or biscuit cooked in the same pan, and milk. He had to repeat this remarkable menu for them.

"Evan, you can't do pretends about important things like meals." Maddie's voice had the tone of one of those phony nurses on television that the patient falls in love with. Claudia couldn't stand it. "Or else this island thing won't work, and we'll have to use one of the flares and Susan and Daddy will come and take you home."

Evan had the look that said he couldn't be bothered with a bunch of dumb kids like these.

Claudia offered the obvious explanation. "The man with the crow?"

Evan nodded. "And you know what? He just swears at it. All the time. Lots of swears. He doesn't really talk a special language. The crow goes to the bathroom indoors under the window."

They spent the rest of the morning collecting useful drift on the windward side of the island. They found one really good crate for hauling clams and mussels, numbers of plastic bottles and cartons, lengths of pot warp, not all of it rotten, and various other twentieth-century artifacts. They talked about looking inland for a spring, or even a well. Tim reminded them that many of these islands had had little farmsteads back in the eighteenth and nineteenth centuries; once they had discovered the foundations of a house and barn on Seal Island.

Passing the cove with the double-ender, they stood for a minute, admiring the outhaul arrangement that let the old man pull it safe beyond the rocks.

"I suppose it wouldn't hurt to call on him," Maddie considered.

Claudia guessed what was on her mind. "So long as you don't talk like Mother about hoping Evan won't make a nuisance of himself."

Maddie was surprised. "What's wrong with saying that?"

"He's Evan's friend."

"Well, we'll say a friendly hello," Tim mediated. "That can't hurt."

"And see his crow," Claudia agreed, now that Maddie had been warned.

"And his sheep," Evan added.

"His pet dead sheep?" Rebecca sounded half revolted, half amused.

"The sheep he milked for breakfast. It doesn't want to be tied, but it'll stand for him, and then he feeds oatmeal to it, same as he puts on the mackerel. He's a good cook."

"Sheep's milk, yuch." Rebecca made a face.

The door swung part way open, but they could see nothing within. It was Evan who stepped onto the rough granite threshold and pushed through.

"See if it's all right," Maddie whispered. The nurse voice again. Claudia decided it must be a sign of nervousness with her.

Evan reappeared. "He's asleep, but he'll wake up soon. He sleeps a lot. Fell asleep making breakfast. He calls it going away."

"He'll go away in smoke," Tim observed, "if he falls asleep over the stove."

Evan ducked back in. They heard voices, some squawks, the rattling of metal. He called them.

"You were nice to give Evan breakfast this morning," Tim began. "I'm afraid we overslept." Tim's voice was overloud. "Hard on Evan. But yesterday . . . ." He faltered.

Maddie picked up for him. "Anyhow, we're not really sticking to any schedule." She smiled beautifully.

The old man was looking them over. "You hungry too? The boy can fetch the pan."

They thanked him, protested, tried to explain. The man rocked back against the wall and said no more. He was dressed in a dark, discolored jacket, grime-creased pants, heavy boots, and wore a sort of hunter's cap. Claudia thought she could see at least two other shirts beneath the outer one, but his face bore no sign of discomfort or any sense of heat or cold. His skin was a mass of dark wrinkles. Only the eyes, light as shallow water under a high sun, seemed ageless, set deep under furrowing brows, like embers buried beneath a heap of cold white ash.

Claudia began to notice her surroundings. There was a wisp of stinky smoke from the stack above the stove. Beside the stove, heaped in even lengths, were squared-off blocks that looked like rotten timber. Nothing else in the hut was neat. Objects seemed to cling miraculously to the few slanting shelves. Even the hearth in the crowded fireplace sloped steeply, the flags separated. A table, tilting precariously, was propped against one wall. The place had the look of a storm-tossed boat, and yet there was a quality of permanence about it, almost like tranquillity.

"Here, you bastard," Evan crooned. As the crow fluttered toward his outstretched hand, he picked a bit of biscuit out of a rusty can and glanced at them over his shoulder, announcing proudly, "See, he already knows me."

The hut was sour with a strange burning odor. The stove was smoking from a crooked pipe, cracked at most of its joints and held together by wire. There was wood and cardboard tacked around it where it went out through the roof.

Evan gave Claudia some biscuit and told her how to let the crow come to her. She spoke to it, barely aware of the limping conversation behind her. There was Maddie's voice, then Tim's, Maddie's again. And the old man grunting briefly, never saying anything for long.

She called to the crow, offering the tidbit, praising its glossy feathers, its bright suspicious eye. Slowly its beak opened, but it did not come forward.

"Swear at him," Evan instructed.

She said "damn" to it several times in a pleading tone. Behind her they were stumbling over the old man's name, hard to get from his nearly toothless mouthing, and gleaning information about how he didn't go out with the seiners no more, had a few of his own pots set around these ledges, mended nets some, and come here some ways back with his daddy from Grand Manan down Fundy Bay. Expected to die here too, right on this island, why not, and, no, he weren't the owner, didn't know who was, but never had no trouble about it, didn't expect any.

"Are the sheep yours?" Claudia asked, suddenly distracted, turning toward the others but with her hand still out to the crow.

"Might say so," the old man answered. "Raised up that ewe myself when the dam fell off the cliff t'storm.

23

They used to come and cull 'em and clip 'em, but not these many years back." This was his longest speech, and he seemed exhausted by it. His eyes began to close, then opened briefly, sought out Evan. "These all your brothers 'n sisters?"

"You might say so," Evan responded, his accent echoing the old man's.

Claudia knew it was too complicated for Evan to explain that his mother was dead and he really regarded Susan as his mother. For Claudia it was different, because her father came around once in a while and made everything about as confusing as things could get. "Some more, some less," she added for Evan, and then, feeling the dry rake of the beak, shut up so as not to scare off the crow's first advances. The crow swallowed hard, poked again into her palm. Like one already at home, Evan poured some thick yellow milk into a cut-down can and placed it beside her. The crow shuffled over, swaggering a little.

"Well, you son of a bitch," the old man gummed. "Taking up with strangers."

Claudia couldn't tell whether he was expressing pleasure or displeasure. His words filtered off like wisps of smoke and disappeared in their midst. His head slid back, his mouth dropped open.

They tiptoed out, Rebecca gasping for breath, Maddie squinting in the brightness, Tim declaring the old man a rare character, real local color, and Claudia blissful because the crow had approached her and eaten from her hand.

Only Evan stayed behind.

24

FOUR

Finding the well in a swale of sweet grass that looked almost like a farm field, they postponed their return for pot warp and a bottle, because there growing with the thistles were more raspberry suckers, the fruits so plump and sun-warmed that they all fell to, since after all Evan had done that yesterday and anyhow had ginger ale and peanut butter and raisins and chocolate set aside for him. Below this western slope more and more rocks showed as the tide ebbed. Not too far out they could see seals, one to a rock, sometimes two, each a shiny torpid king of its castle.

Eating, they talked of food, deciding that next they would look for beach peas.

"I wonder," Claudia mused, "what sheep's milk tastes like."

"Don't they have to be tested for some disease?"

Claudia giggled. "You can't go into the wilderness and expect pasteurized milk."

"But sheep's milk—"

"Romulus and Remus drank wolf's milk, and look what they started. Rome."

Maddie said, "That's legend, not history."

"How do you know?" Claudia rejoined. "How do you know that those legends weren't the kind of history they had before people wrote things down?"

"If they were people like you, O Keeper of the Log, history would get so bogged down—"

They scrapped amiably, eating all the while, their greed taking them deeper and deeper into the thistles.

"Water's a different color," Rebecca observed, looking down at the rocky inlet.

It was. Now as they made their way back through the woods they could feel the change in the air, the wind not so much strong as heavy with moisture.

It was a real fog rolling in from the Bay of Fundy, the kind they had learned to respect. They knew enough to dive for their warm clothes and to cover up with foul-weather gear. Claudia got out Evan's and started off for the hut. The others were sheltering driftwood piles, pulling bundles into Evan's tent. They stooped over, avoiding the drift that spun like a fine rain, groping for objects they had carelessly laid aside that morning.

Claudia felt exhilarated. Now it would really stop being a picnic. Anything might happen, and yet nothing really bad, because after all they weren't lost on the bay, but safe and snug. Tonight they would make a fire and boil up a chowder with sorrel and jewelweed.

When she first looked inside the hut, she thought it was empty. Perhaps they had gone down to get something from the double-ender; maybe the old man was letting Evan help him with the outhaul.

A sudden flapping brought her up short. It was the crow, as startled as she, rising to the low ceiling and then descending with a clatter. From the darkest corner

26

heaped with sacks and rags, the old man stirred, swore, subsided.

"Where's Evan?" she asked, then again, louder, and a third time.

The old man raised himself up on an elbow. "The boy? Took him off."

The crow was opening its beak, begging. She guessed it must be perpetually hungry and cast about for crumbs or something to throw it.

After a while she shouted into the dark corner, "Where did he go?"

"Other place." The old man raised his arm; he seemed to be pointing. "Just a look, I told him. You don't linger."

She went to the door, stared out and saw nothing but a solitary fir tree misshapen by winds; she saw a few bushes, a pile of rocks. The cove was swallowed by the fog, the islet a slightly darker mass, or maybe not even that; it could be only her knowledge that it lay off to the east like a left arm cradling the cove that made her think she could see it.

She called. She shouted Evan's name. She heard the querulous muttering of the crow, the slapping of the sea against the shingle. Again she called, and this time she heard his voice. Complaining.

"Where have you been?"

"Out there. He calls it the Other Place." Evan indicated the direction of the islet. "Why do you have to come after me just when it gets interesting?"

"The tide's coming. Do you realize you might be cut off?"

"He says it's the fog you've got to watch."

27

"Well, I'm glad he warned you, but, Evan, you shouldn't go out there alone."

"I wasn't alone." He held up something to her. "I had the man. He says you've got to have the man to get there, at least in the beginning. He says he can go there any time now, just closing his eyes. But that's after years and years." He thrust the object at her.

She was surprised at its weight. It was some kind of heavy metal, a figure of a man, with rounded knobs for hands and feet and a head with a real face on it. She could hardly distinguish between scratches and lines, but she could see remnants of some design, intricate curves and an X with scrolls at the ends on the back. In the middle of the side with the face there was a round hole, but it didn't go all the way through.

"Where'd you get this?"

"He keeps it under a stone in the fireplace."

They went into the hut.

The old man grunted. "She come looking for you."

"I didn't stay long. Anyhow, I could hear her."

"Longer you stay, less you'll hear. Mind that fog."

"Mind the fog," Evan snorted. "At home it's watch out for the sun. Always something."

"It's his skin," Claudia explained.

"Liken that's why he got through so easy. I'm that way about the sun too. Remember."

"Remember what?"

"Why, to mind the sun. I just said."

"No, you didn't," Evan told him. "You said to mind the fog."

"It'll be the same. A touch of the sun, and you be caught. So you mind the fog. Keep this side of it. Sun

28

burns off the fog and happen you're there, then there you will stay."

"That's silly," Claudia exclaimed. "If anything, the sun makes it easier for you to see your way."

He eyed her. "You'd be tempted to stay too, with that way of looking. Just remember, you stay with the sun, and it's *them* that'll be seeing *you*. Once I got the temptings there because it was like my dad's telling of the place he come from." He seemed to be drifting off.

"What happened? Did you stay?"

"Run into a patch of fog. Like a wall of wet cobwebs. Stuck to me too till I was back here safe. And the sun hot as iron on the anvil, burned that fog right up around me. Even singed my damn beard." He rubbed his stubbly chin and wheezed in merriment, his mouth like a wet black stone.

"I'm not sure I'll go again anyhow," Evan declared casually. "It wasn't very interesting. Just a whole lot of people wearing bathrobes."

"What?" yelled Claudia. Between the old man and Evan, she was reeling. She turned to the old man. "Will you please explain? You see, my little brother—"

"He's too tired," Evan informed her. "He talked a long time already. To me. I can explain, Claude. This man he let me hold is something his father left him. It comes from a long time ago. It's something like how it wants to go back and find something. So if you hold it, it'll take you, except it only works when you can't see. He says if you forget and stay after the sun comes out, you can't come back too easily. Or something."

"So who are the people in bathrobes?" Claudia was so mixed up that she didn't know whether she was being a skeptical older sister or an indulgent grownup.

Evan shrugged. "They have swords and spears and things, though. And great big gold pins to hold their bathrobes on with. I couldn't see whether they had anything on underneath."

The crow rattled its feathers, stepped over to its window area, tilted its tail, and deposited a wet-sounding dropping. Claudia felt oppressed by the sourness of the air filled with a smoke that had none of the freshness and toastiness of the fires she was familiar with. She found herself wondering whether the old man ever washed or changed his clothes, and shuddered at the thought of crow muck and sheep's milk and the black frying pan upended on the hearth. And that heavy figure that was kept beneath a stone like some magic charm. Claudia was certain that she did not believe in magic, at least not this kind, all encrusted with filth and age and silly notions about people in bathrobes sitting on a fog-bound islet.

"I don't think you should spend so much time here. He's filling you full of nonsense."

"At least I don't have to pretend it, the way I do with your stories."

That stopped her. She wondered if she was going through one of those spurts of growth that had hit Rebecca last year. She said, "Would you like to show me those people in bathrobes?"

He gave her a quick glance. "Why are you talking like that?"

"Like what?"

"Sweet."

"I was trying to be considerate and generous," she snapped.

The crow let out a single croak, as if speaking for Evan.

"Anyway," Evan went on, "he says it's few can get to the Other Place. You have to be the right person. He didn't tell me about any girls going there." Evan paused. "Though there are girls in the Other Place. One I saw up close, she had these three braids with a sort of glassy bead holding them together at the ends. I've never seen hair in three braids before. Come to think of it, one of the men had braids too. That is, I think it was a man."

In spite of herself, Claudia was drawn in. "Are the girls in bathrobes too?"

"Sort of. And you know what, Claude, some of the men have necklaces. They dress funny."

Claudia reached for the metal figure. "How do you do it?"

Evan led the way off the turf bank, sliding down to the shingle and across the stony bar that connected the islet to the main part of the island. She kept falling, slipping on round, wet, seaweed surfaces. The tide was flooding, and they had to pick their way from rock to rock.

"We can't stay long," Claudia panted. She wished Evan would slow down.

Once they were on the other side, he waited, holding out his hand, taking the figure and then carrying it before him like a flashlight, as if it could cast a beam that would show him the way.

The islet seemed to hump at the center. They scrambled upward and seaward toward the farthest promontory. It was like walking on the back of a giant turtle. They had clambered on at the tail, the tip of bar that trailed into the water. Up from the tail took effort, and then they were aloft on the dull green carapace. They followed the ridge at the center of this turtle, on toward the promontory that was its head. Coming toward the drop, the cliffs and rocks that studded the steeper shore, all they could hear was the wash of the bay and the screams of birds they could not see.

Claudia wanted to caution Evan. In this fog you could step right into a crevice. But he seemed to realize this, because he was standing now, staring into nothingness. She caught up with him. "Now what?" she asked.

"Ssh," he whispered. "I'm trying to hear."

She listened. The gulls screamed, the terns gave their hollow cries as they came darting down across the promontory. She could hear their wings, the whistle of their flight. Automatically she put her hands over her head. She didn't want them dive-bombing her out here. It was one thing in the sun, with a dazzling bay, when you could laugh and wave at them or fling yourself down. It was another out here in this dripping blindness, with only a sense of how the land was dropping away from you, of jagged rocks and surging tide.

"See them?" he was whispering.

She thought he meant the terns. "Where?" She looked skyward.

"No." He pointed. "Down there."

She tried to go along with him. "Where exactly are we?"

He seemed to be examining his surroundings. "A kind of balcony, I guess. Look down there, across the way. It's

32

a cow and a calf. See? And the man feeding them something. Oh, boy, now I can see what they wear underneath."

"What? Where?"

"See, Claude?" He laughed, but kept his voice low. "Miniskirts. That's what they're wearing." He turned. "And I guess that room's a kind of kitchen. See the girl with the braids? She's making cakes or something. That must be her mother. I guess only the men wear miniskirts." He looked at Claudia. "What's the matter? Can't you see?" He sounded disgusted with her. "Boy, does it smell good. Even with that cowflop."

"I don't see anything but a lot of fog."

"Well, you're right with me on this kind of balcony, and if you'd just open your eyes—"

"Did the old man tell you about this place?"

"Sure, he's seen it lots of times." Evan considered. "I haven't seen any of those fights yet. I might just keep coming till I see one."

Claudia was silent. It was obvious that Evan was having a hallucination. She didn't want to contradict him or get into a hassle out here where he might run off and get hurt.

"Here, Claude." He was holding out the metal figure the way he would proffer binoculars when they were taking turns looking at birds or seals. "Hold it like this," he instructed, "head pointing away from you. No wonder you can't see anything."

She obeyed.

"Well?"

"I still don't see a thing."

"That's funny. I do. There's a man, really old-looking,

33

with long white hair and a long white sort of nightgown on."

"How do you know he's a man?"

"He has a beard. He's talking to a guy wearing one of those miniskirts. You know what that guy has on? It's like a collar or a . . . a bib, only sort of gold and very fancy. Ssh, the old man in the nightgown is turning our way. I think he sees us. Ssh, Claude."

"I'm not saying anything."

Evan grabbed her. "He's staring right up here."

"What's he doing?" Claudia whispered.

"Nothing. Only staring. He knows we're here. Oh, and his face, Claude. His face."

"What about his face?"

Evan was shaking his head, mesmerized.

"Come on, Evan, we have to get back now. Tide's coming. We have to get this thing back to the hut. Maddie'll start worrying." She tugged at Evan, who seemed rooted. The old man in the nightgown appeared to exert some kind of power over Evan. Not that she believed in him. But Evan did. And it was weird the way he seemed to resist her, as if someone or something were holding him, drawing him away. "You promised," she shouted into Evan's face. "Promised to come right back." He tried to shake her off, but she was yelling, and then she began yelling into the fog. "Go away. Leave my brother alone. Stop staring. Mind your own business." She shook Evan's arms, and then dropped the figure between them.

All at once Evan was himself again, though cross because she had gone and spoiled everything. They were both tired and hungry. By the time they found the figure

34

and got it across to the main island, they were soaked to their knees and cold as well.

It took a while to warm up, even after the chowder. Claudia was curled into a tight knot, her feet wrapped in her sweater, her sleeping bag up to her ears. Evan looked like a snail. They giggled at each other. They could hear the sounds of older conversation, boring but reassuring, outside their tent.

Claudia longed to pick up her Sable Island plot, but Evan's experience kept intruding, disturbing the rhythm of her thoughts. Finally she gave in. She considered Evan's vision, wondering how she could free him from it so that he wouldn't be tempted to go out there again and be caught by the gaze of some old man in a nightgown. Probably it had something to do with the man in the hut.

"Did the old man in the hut tell you a lot of things . . . about himself?"

"He's a fisherman," Evan answered. "Name's Colman Something, but I call him Mr. Colman, and it works. His father came from some island across the ocean. He's kind of mixed up when he talks. It's like a whole bunch of stories cut into pieces and then taped together any old way. So I couldn't get it all." Evan's voice fell away.

Quickly she asked, "And did he describe the things, well, that you saw?"

"Yes. No. Not all."

"What does that mean?"

"And more. Maybe I'll go back tomorrow. I don't get any story there yet."

"Evan, remember when we did that game about being in a caravan on the desert?"

"Um."

"Remember about the mirage? You were the camel. Remember?"

"It was stupid," he murmured. "It didn't have any ending for me. I just stood over your body keeping watch. There was no ending."

"Eventually you died too. Defending my body from wolves. Or jackals, I guess it was. I'm not sure they have wolves on the desert."

"What Mr. Colman didn't tell me," Evan volunteered, "was about the man with the white hair and the beard."

"The man in the nightgown?"

"His face wasn't . . . wasn't what you'd expect."

Claudia waited. "Not what he led you to expect?" she prompted.

"Mr. Colman didn't tell me what to expect."

That had been too blunt. And she had failed to make her point about the mirage. "All right," she said, willing to hear whatever his imagination or Mr. Colman's yarns might supply.

"His face wasn't old at all. It was . . . well, fierce like some bird, an . . . eagle, only so smooth it was almost, well . . . ."

"Almost what?"

Evan changed his mind. "You don't believe me anyway. Why should I bother to tell you?"

"But I'm trying to. Come on, Evan. It's not my fault if I couldn't see what you saw."

Evan heaved himself over, sleeping bag and all. His voice came to her muffled and faint. "Either you see it or you don't."

"Well, I want to. We'll try again tomorrow. O.K.? It

36

isn't fair if only you see those people with robes and spears and things. I'm the one that wants to live in olden times. I do all the reading to find out what they were like."

"You sound," he mumbled, "like you're talking about going to the movies. Like you've got a right to go since you read the book of it."

Claudia stretched out. Her feet were unthawed finally, but she felt that she would never get to sleep now. "Tell me more about what you saw. About the way things looked."

"It's round," he responded drowsily.

But when she pressed him for an explanation, she could get nothing from him but a gentle snore that reminded her of Phil asleep. Only a faint reflection of Phil, like the hint of an echo.

FivE

THEY were all up early. With no moonlight and lots of wetness, the only thing that had made any sense the night before was getting under cover. They had ended up in sleeping bags long before their usual time.

Tim and Rebecca went to the great flat rock where he had fished the previous morning. They came back with four mackerel, soaking sneakers, and dungarees sopping to the knees.

Then it took a long time to get the fire started. Evan grew tired of waiting. He knew where there was a fire that never went out. Off he went, leaving Claudia torn between her hunger and loyalty to the communal breakfast and her envy of Evan. She didn't want Mr. Colman to be all talked out before she could get there.

And Rebecca was keeping an eye on her. "You going to spend a lot of time up there today just because Evan is?"

Claudia shrugged.

Maddie and Tim were crouched over the fireplace trying to get a flame. Without lifting her head, Maddie said she supposed it would be good to keep Evan engaged up in the hut on a day like this.

It was a good moment to point out the drawbacks. "It's stuffy," Claudia reminded them. "Smelly. Just because

38

Evan's there," she began, letting her words trail off. Later she would just sort of wander up that way and check in on him.

The fire caught, and they all stood around it extending their wrinkled fingers, drawing from it the smell of warmth and dryness they couldn't really feel through fog-laden clothes.

Maddie had a surprise for them. She had picked rose hips while Tim and Rebecca were fishing. They had fruit for breakfast.

When Claudia was finally able to get away to the hut, the sheep was still hanging around the door, nibbling something. She slowed, but at the last minute it dashed out of her way and stood off at a distance, nearly swallowed by the fog, while its lamb gave in to curiosity and stepped toward Claudia on sharp, tentative hoofs. The crow flapped to the door, its appearance so sudden and clamorous that the lamb shot straight into the air before retreating behind its mother.

"Damn you," Claudia said to the crow. He seemed to consider this an appropriate greeting, for he walked right up to her dragging his wings carelessly, stretched with open beak in her direction, and then fell to pecking what the sheep had been nibbling.

Inside, Mr. Colman sat in his usual place by the cast-iron stove. Evan was at the window, stuffing pieces of rag around the frame.

"Helping me," Colman remarked.

Claudia wasn't sure that sealing the cracks was much of a help. The hut seemed dense with smoke and all the smells of closeness she was beginning to associate with being inside here. But the old man had spoken to her first, which meant that he was not only awake, but perhaps more ready to accept her, so she plunged right in with her questions. "Do you often go to that other place? How did you find out about it? How did you get there the first time?"

"His father told him," Evan grunted, jabbing something into a space where the wood was deeply split. "His father went there a lot. That's why he knows about the sun. His father got caught there. Says it changed everything, what he learned."

"Please, Evan, I was asking Mr. Colman."

"He's right," the old man told her. "My daddy, he brought the bronze man all the way from his home to Birsay. Thought he'd get him wonderful things. He told me. But he got pulled in. After my mam died, he went a bit gormless, stopped work in the smokehouses. Seining, he did, and me along, but off with that man whenever he could. All over he went. It was here it took him, here to the Other Place. Told me all the strange things. Look, when you stay, when you go through into the sun, then you hear their talk. Only it's like the herring weir for catching you up, and I never had that tempting like my daddy. It was part of his queerness. . . ." Mr. Colman rambled on. Claudia could scarcely follow. Mr. Colman was saying, ". . . things some fierce there, wouldn't want to be in it . . . ."

"But you go all the time, you said."

"Not like my daddy after that time."

"What happened to him?"

"Come back talking queer. And stranger yet how he had to keep on going back, and warning me off. And

40

going back. Got to be like a man without his wits. Ever seen a man like that?"

Claudia shook her head.

"And nearly lost the bronze man, so witless, wanting to put it away there, back, he would say. But you know, girl, he couldn't do that, for he found it himself when he was a boy, and that was across the ocean, before he come to Grand Manan to settle. That was long ago." His voice was drifting, fading.

"And you've seen the man with the white hair?"

Mr. Colman nodded. He leaned forward, and with an iron poker lifted the slab and reached for the metal man. He stared at it a moment. "And this very man, I think, in that one's hands. He knows what it can do. More than I know. A handle for him. And gold it is, not green like this, and with a blade you'd not want to feel." He was shaking his head, musing.

Claudia was afraid he would fall asleep. "What is it used for?"

The old man gave her a wide, toothless smile that sent shivers down her back. His mouth was a gaping hole with a small, discolored tongue. "Strange things. I've seen more heads stuck on the carts than all the barrels of herring salted down at Seal Harbor when the seiners leave their catch."

"What kind of heads?"

"People heads," Evan called from the window. "He says they cut off the heads and tie them. Like balloons. Do you believe that, Claude?"

Mr. Colman held the man out to her. "You want to see?"

She looked uncertainly toward Evan. "Uh, thank you very much. We're . . . my brother and I appreciate . . . appreciate . . . ."

"You won't be setting there too long. Watch for the sun. I know. I go for a look, but I can't make any sense of it. I tell you, I don't believe there's any sense to be had, except the kind my daddy had, and that was the biggest foolishness, that sense he made of it."

From the window Evan said, "Claude, want to taste the pudding he made?"

Claudia was glad to be able to turn away from Mr. Colman, but she accepted the metal man before joining Evan at the crate beside the door. Inside the crate, under the lid, was a chipped enamel pan with something in it that looked like creamy jello that hadn't quite finished hardening.

"What is it?"

"It's from the milk and some special seaweed he picks that makes it get lumpy." Evan stuck his finger in; the yellowy-white stuff that coated it looked like curdled milk.

"Is there a spoon or anything?"

"He drinks it. He said I could have all I wanted. He saved some milk to soak his biscuits in. He doesn't chew so good, but he eats all right."

The pudding tasted awful. Things that were milky and thick made her expect sweetness, a dessert. This was not only salty; it had a faint flavor of iodine. She lurched to the door. She was still feeling a little unsure of her stomach when Evan passed her and beckoned her on toward the islet.

The tide was barely low enough. He had the metal

42

figure by the leg, hanging down like Winnie-the-Pooh being hauled up to bed. But once they were down by the bar, Evan was in command and holding the figure properly.

"Let me hold onto him too," Claudia insisted.

Evan shared it with her, though that made climbing the bank on the other side awkward. Evan slipped, pulling her down with him. They laughed at this, feeling like dominoes set up for the purpose of being toppled by an invisible finger.

The fog was as thick as the day before. Claudia kept imagining she could make things out—a boulder, waves well out to sea, birds. But really she could see nothing but Evan beside her. Now he went still, just as he had yesterday, staring, looking blind and lost. He whispered something.

"What?"

"Ssh. They're having a fight. Wow. There's this one boy. Smaller than me, and they're all ganging up on him. He's doing all right, though. All those kids. What's the matter, Claude, can't you see?"

Claudia strained frantically. "There isn't anything there. If there were, I'd see it. I know I would. Are you still on that balcony?"

Evan shook his head. "But I think I can see where that balcony is. Inside a big round wall. There's a kind of roof with hay on it. And something like a road that slants up to the gate. Boy, is it big. The men . . . they must be standing on roofs inside. I can't get over the way they carry those great big spears and wear little tiny dresses." His head turned slightly. "That kid's something. He's beating them all up."

43

Claudia tried to follow the direction of his gaze. "Where? Where are you now?"

"Still out here. It's like a big football field, Claude, and all those kids are having some kind of fight, and, oh, look, there's someone coming. Wow!"

"Stop saying wow. Describe it. Tell me exactly what you see."

"I don't know why you can't look for yourself."

"I'm trying," she wailed. "I'm trying and trying."

He was staring open-mouthed with wonder. "You won't believe this," he whispered. "The fanciest cart I've ever seen. Circus horses, with gold and colored stuff on their harnesses. Boy, would I like to get close to those horses." He started forward.

"Don't you dare." She grabbed him.

"I guess they're ponies," he amended. "He has this stick thing to make them go." He turned. "There's so much to watch, you don't know where to look."

Claudia peered into the thickness. It was impossible not to believe in Evan's hallucination. Whatever it was that Evan was seeing was the result of the power of suggestion. He had spent hours listening to old Mr. Colman and so he had a precise idea of what he was supposed to be seeing. The trouble was that she hadn't had the benefit of all that description. She needed to have Evan do for her what Mr. Colman had done for him, and of course the best way for Evan to get something across was with his drawings. "Let's go back for a while, Evan. There's plenty of time. We can visit again. Even on this tide. Come on back now. Probably they want us for digging clams."

Claudia was right about the clamming. They worked

like demons so that there would be time to get back to the islet before the tide was too full.

"I want to see what happens to that kid," Evan told her.

"What?" said Rebecca.

"It's a game we're playing," Claudia supplied. Then she said to Evan, "I can finish here. Why don't you get back and dry off for a while."

"I'm not too wet."

"Well, rest."

"I'm not tired."

"Evan, remember what I asked you, about drawing me some pictures?"

"You want me to do that now?"

It was a good thing he got the point when he did, because after he left, the others cautioned her against mothering him too much.

"Though it's great the way you're looking out for him," Maddie added generously, and Tim said. "Yeah, you're doing all right, Claude."

When her clam hole began to fill with water and she straightened up from it, spattered and aching, she was glad to be treated like a younger child and be told to go off with Evan again.

He had forgotten to wash off the mud, so it was a pretty smeary picture he presented to her. She traced the outlines with her finger. "That right?"

He nodded.

"What's that?"

"A mistake," was the answer.

"Only two wheels?"

He nodded again.

45

"You know what a chariot is?"

He shook his head.

"Evan, you'd better go down to the beach and wash that stuff off. You've got it all over the paper and on your jacket and gear too." While he was gone she stared some more. It wasn't one of his better efforts. She could see where he'd started to draw the football field and then given up. The perspective was wrong. But she got a real sense of that two-wheeled chariot, the ponies in elaborate harness, and two men—unless that was a mistake too—the driver with an odd stick sort of thing, and the other with a shield on his back, and all decked out, hair flying like the ponies' manes, a kind of wildness to all of it like the force of a gale out of the northwest.

"Tide's coming," Evan called, scrambling up from the beach. "We'll hardly have time."

"Then you've got to promise to quit the minute I say so," she warned.

He ran ahead to fetch the figure of the man. She had to pick her way to avoid the freezing water. "Ten minutes at the most," she declared as he passed her with running leaps, then waited impatiently at the base of the turtle's tail.

This time he stopped even sooner than before. "Oh," he gasped, and was silent. It was as if he had turned a corner and run full tilt onto a stage. He had that look of someone half embarrassed and half delighted who has awakened to find himself in the middle of a play.

"What is it?"

At first he couldn't speak. Then he said, "Claude, Claude, can't you smell it? I bet you can smell it if you shut your eyes."

46

Claudia closed her eyes and breathed in through her nose. At first she could only smell the familiar odors of the coast made heavy by the fog. A little of the mud flat lingered, the scent of the firs from behind and above where they stood at the crown of the island. She detected the slightly spoiled smell of stranded starfish and sea urchins, mussels dropped by gulls, the acrid remains of old nests and spattered rocks. Then, while she squeezed her eyes shut against the wet gray air, another smell was carried to her, tickling her nostrils, half pleasant and half sour.

Her heart sank. It was nothing but the smoke from Mr. Colman's hut. That fire he kept going all the time with its dank blue smoke and its special scent of earth. She was so disappointed she forgot to keep her eyes closed, and when she opened them she was looking into a fire in the center of a round building and watching the steam rise from an immense cauldron hanging from a chain over that fire. She had to step back because a girl, no older than herself, came past on bare feet carrying a board with a loaf of bread on it that smelled of honey and butter. While it was carried across to a man dressed in a crimson tunic who sat in a kind of stall or box, two younger men approached the fire and reached with fork-like sticks after whatever was in the cauldron. That seemed to anger them both, because they drew themselves up and glared at each other.

Claudia heard Evan whisper something about a fight, but she was concentrating so hard on what everyone wore that she hardly heard him. She was sure that the shiny neck things were made of gold. And the men wore bracelets on their lean, muscled arms.

47

She watched as the two young men stepped back and approached the one in the crimson tunic. Then she was distracted for a moment by another man who stood beside the box, his brilliant purple cloak flung back from his shoulder and held by a circle of gold pierced through the center by a bar that was decorated with shiny coils of blue and purple. He stood tall and proud, and appeared larger than the red-clothed man on whom he seemed to wait. The two youths now stood before the box and addressed the man in red, who responded with a kind of stern authority.

But it was the man in purple at his side, the great proud-looking man, who held Claudia's attention. There was something disheveled about him, his hair like a shaggy mane or a golden sunburst, while his face reflected something troubled as he took in the youths and their argument.

As she gazed at these people and the general scene with its dogs and maidens, shields hanging on the wall beside spears so gorgeous she could not imagine them to be deadly, she noticed on the farther side of the box a tall ancient-looking person with flowing white hair and a long white beard. There was a look of frailty about him; though he was covered from neck to toe in folds of white, she had the impression of a skeleton. She could almost see the contours of his bones, the whiteness heightening the cold, spare look of him. Even his eyebrows, she could see now that he was beginning to turn, were long and white. All was white except for a golden buckle at his throat, a buckle more elaborate than any of the other gold things she had seen, though the tracery was simply a pattern of interwoven lines, gold upon gold as white upon white.

He was turning with the movements of the very old, now to the man on the enclosed platform, and now to the two young men who had confronted one another at the cauldron.

"Quick," Evan was whispering. "Before he sees us."

"But they can't. You know that."

"*He* can," Evan retorted. "Come on."

As the old man turned, his eyes swept everything they passed. For the briefest instant he paused, staring at Claudia as if marking her, marking Evan. Claudia gasped. She had expected an old man's face, a face like Mr. Colman's with its little hole for a mouth and squinting, watery eyes. The face of the man in white was smooth and hard as marble, except that it was living, not stone, and the eyes were the deepest blue she had ever seen.

"Come on," Evan repeated.

She could feel him tugging at her, but those blue eyes held her fast. And then it was as if the old man had released her. He was attending to the two young men, trying to settle whatever dispute there was between them, and Evan was able to pull her back.

Crossing the bar, she stumbled, gasped again, this time with the shock of the freezing water that surged all the way to her waist.

"You can dry at Mr. Colman's," Evan encouraged her as she came out shivering, grabbing onto rockweed, careless of the sharp little barnacles hidden under the green. "Then you won't have to explain why you got wet."

It was good enough justification for using the shelter and the stove. While she warmed up, she thought about their shared hallucination: it hadn't been prompted by either Mr. Colman's talk or Evan's picture. She almost said out loud that of course they had responded to the power of suggestion that hunger held over them, but something kept her from asserting the sensible explanation. It wasn't those baking and cooking smells, though she could still almost summon them again simply by recalling how real, how delicious they had seemed.

It was something else: the intensity of that look she had received, the depth of blue of those bright-dark eyes that had seen her as she had seen everything in that strange round building.

She turned her back to the stove to toast the other side, and began to feel herself again. The acrid smoke brought tears and made her sniffle. But she felt good. She didn't really mind the smoke.

It wasn't until much later, when she was at another fire, toasting her feet this time and listening to a not very interesting discussion about the kinds of greens they might try in tomorrow's stew, that it suddenly came to her that the smoke inside Mr. Colman's hut was not only unlike the smoke from this or any other fire she had known. It was also like the smoke that had curled back from the hole in the roof of that round building in the Other Place. That smoke had been less dense, probably because the hole provided pretty good ventilation. But there amidst the juicy, meaty, brothy smells from the cauldron and the honey-butter aroma of the bread had been the pervading odor of earth and roots, the kind of smell that made you wrinkle your nose and sniff a little even when it wasn't all around you.

six

"IF YOU were home now," Rebecca began, but they wouldn't let her finish. It would weaken everyone's morale, they claimed. It would allow subversive thoughts to creep into their midst.

"Think," Tim laughed, "what you would do if this were a three-day snowstorm, not just fog."

"Talk about dangerous ideas," Rebecca answered.

They all laughed, but it was an effort. They were tired of being wet. When they covered up, they got clammy, sticky. But it was easy to find themselves suddenly chilled, and then the careful fires, lit only for cooking their monotonous meals, just barely got them warm again.

"The funny thing," Maddie pointed out, "is that the one we were most worried about is getting along the best."

Tim agreed, and he mentioned the way Evan had pitched in yesterday with the food gathering when they had all worked right through the whole of low tide.

Maddie wanted to know what kind of seaweed Evan had been telling them about, the kind that turned milk solid. She was all for experimenting with new foods. She had found patches of orach nearby and had cooked it up into a limp, spinachlike mash of greens which Claudia

51

rather liked and they had all hungrily devoured. So why not seaweed?

"Probably what they call Irish Moss," said Tim. Some of the guys had used it on their solo survival stints. He and Maddie went off to hunt for some in the coves beyond the hut.

Claudia was wondering whether she should tell Rebecca about the Other Place beyond the fog, when Rebecca broke the silence. "Now that they're not here, what would you be doing? If you were home."

To her surprise, Claudia had no ready answer. What would she do on a foggy day? Read, maybe. Or conjure up one of her dramas with Evan.

She tried to picture home. Phil typing with the door closed. Mother working on one of the manuscripts the office sent her when she came to Maine, and probably with something burning in the kitchen. Becca would either be watching television or trailing after Maddie. Next came Doug, but he didn't fit into this picture because he'd been away all summer. That stopped her cold. She heard Rebecca repeat her question on a note of urgency; it was like an appeal. "I don't know," Claudia told her, thinking poor Becca was at a loss, having no fun at all, just wishing she were home in front of the television brushing her golden locks. Or picking her feet. "Becca, want to come with me and Evan this afternoon? We've found this place to go to where there are, I don't know what you'd call them, but people from . . . from some other time. They've got chariots and gorgeous—"

"Oh, for God's sake!"

"But you like jewelry, don't you? You'd love—"

"Cut it out, Claude. Why don't you grow up? No one

52

else I know your age is so out of it. You're as bad as Evan."

Claudia stalked off to the shack sooner than she had meant to. She realized how much she needed to talk to someone about what she had seen. Her head was buzzing with questions, and all she had was Evan, who had no information at all to go on, and old Mr. Colman, who was clearly too far gone to provide any reasonable explanations.

Still, she found herself questioning him all over again. She didn't like the way he grinned and seemed to challenge her, but there were times when he sounded almost glad to be asked, pleased to be invited to share his impressions and experiences.

It was like doing a picture puzzle without any idea of the image to be completed. She wasn't good at puzzles like that. She preferred to read about people and places and then use her imagination to make them come alive. With puzzles there was this mechanical business of fitting together the hundreds of pieces, which didn't seem to her to take any imagination at all, only the kind of eye that people who are good at numbers and fixing radios have.

But she listened, as now when he repeated his warnings, telling once more how he had never stayed past the lifting of the fog, for you couldn't just retreat then, if you let the sun come out on you in the Other Place; that he knew from his daddy, because his daddy had had that happen, and not once, oh, no, but more, and each time deeper in than the time before, till he had turned all queer and forgot what he'd been after.

"But he came back. You said that if you waited too long then you couldn't come back."

He leaned forward, so that she guessed he was going to impart something crucial about this mystery. "The year out it was. Their year. But when he come back, it was no more than the changing of the tide here. And still a full season where he'd been."

Evan was sitting on the crate eating out of a pan like Little Jack Horner. The crow squatted opposite him, its beak wide, waiting for a share, and Evan was obliging. "I told you," he said. "It's the only way you get to talk to them. His father, he talked to a man, then he got to drive the ponies for him. But he had to do everything they said. And there was lots of fighting. He could've been killed." The crow tipped its head to receive the milky finger. "Look, Claude, it's being careful not to bite."

Claudia had been making friends with the bird too. She had discovered that if you talked to it without swearing, it responded just the same. But Evan went on calling it names. "You're supposed to," he'd declare to no one in particular whenever one of the words seemed to hang over-bright in the silence.

"Is there a way," Claudia pursued, "to go just part way? I mean, so you can understand them, but they can't . . . ." She faltered. Colman was giving her that vacant grin that made her feel shivery. He seemed to be egging her on.

"My dad, he could after he come back. A few times yet he could hear some, and then it would be just the ordinary way."

Later, when the tide was low enough to cross over, Evan remarked that Mr. Colman had indicated there might be different times and locations in the Other Place.

54

"Told me his father once went to where he lived when he was a kid. Only it was before that time, way before."

Unprepared for this confusing possibility, she had to reject it. "Evan," she explained in the tone of a patient older sister, "when people get old, they imagine all sorts of things. Especially about being back in their childhood."

Evan sent her a look that reminded her of the crow. "When they get old, huh?"

"Well, it's different from our kind of imagining." She wasn't sure of this, so she added for emphasis, "Really it is."

Since they were crossing at dead low tide, they were able to run across the bar. Claudia thought she must be getting more sure-footed. She could almost keep up with Evan and still avoid the slippery rocks. Then it occurred to her that the reason she could run to the islet now was because she was getting used to the way. Even in the thickest fog you could learn the route, like going to the bathroom in your own house in the middle of the night.

Up the turtle's shell they climbed. She didn't have to reach blindly for roots to haul herself by. She knew where they were. No, that wasn't it. She could see them.

"Evan, it's lightening."

Evan only grunted. He was leaving her behind again.

"We'll only stay a minute," she pronounced in her big-sister voice. She felt her way after him, reassured now that the fog seemed thicker again. She stretched out her hands and called him softly, till she found him trembling, altogether unlike himself.

"What is it?"

She peered into the gray void and could at first make nothing of the gray figures. There was running, some kind of excitement, and an ugly hot smell.

Evan said, "I don't want to stay. I don't like that boy."

"Wait a minute."

"No. I'm quitting. He . . . he killed that dog. Awful. It was awful. I'm going back."

She could see the blood that she had smelled. A powerful man with a grizzly beard was standing over a little boy. Ranged behind them were some familiar figures, the man who had seemed so important the day she had seen him in his enclosed platform at the feast, the man in purple, and the man in white. And many others, who looked like warriors, all talking at once, arguing, exclaiming. One of these bent over the remains of the dog, his face registering amazement.

The powerful man addressing the little boy looked baffled. He shook his head. Now the white-haired ancient was speaking. Everyone paid attention to him.

Evan said, "I'm going to throw up."

"No, wait."

"You didn't see it happen, or you'd be sick too."

The man in purple was lifting up the little boy. He hoisted him easily onto his shoulders and turned toward the entrance of the round building behind them. There was a ramp that sloped up beyond a deep ditch that surrounded the whole circle of stone. Now she could see men standing on the inside along the top of the wall looking down on the scene. They held shields and carried spears, but at this moment they looked more bewildered than fierce.

56

"Here." Evan thrust the metal figure into Claudia's hands. "You can stay if you want."

She didn't want to stay without him. With one backward glance which told her they were all going inside, the little boy riding atop the purple-clad shoulders and clutching the great yellow mane, she turned and followed Evan through the dense atmosphere into the lighter fog along the bar.

She scolded him all the way. They had seen the same people again, which meant there might be a story with characters you could recognize, and here he was copping out. "We may never have another chance."

"You can have a chance any time you want to." He was over the shakes now that he was away from that place. She heard him mutter, "And she's so crazy about dogs."

"We can't go back," she pursued, "if the sun comes out."

"It's not out yet."

"Well, but we can't be sure we'll come across the same people."

Evan sat down on a bare rock. Hunching into his jacket, he considered, then offered to return. "That is, if you go first and tell me truthfully if there's going to be any . . . anything like that."

Claudia stood beside him. "What I don't get is how you never minded the dead sheep."

"It was the way—" Evan stopped, unable to explain.

"Because you saw it being killed?" she asked gently.

"Because . . . ." He sounded close to tears.

She waited.

57

"Because I thought I was on his side. That boy. See, he's from before, when all the kids were ganging up against him. He was someone I sort of knew."

Claudia nodded. It wasn't the dog that bothered him, but the boy. She knew that even if she had seen the boy back when Evan first had, it would have been different for her. She was glad she hadn't seen the dog alive.

SEVEN

Once again holding the metal figure out in front of her, she was surprised at its heaviness, intrigued by its shape and by the face with its hint of anger in eyes that met through one long furrowing brow. And mystified by the hole, like a second mouth, like Mr. Colman's mouth in its toothless O.

Before she was aware of changing over into the Other Place, she was already there, standing on a small hill below which a track made its way toward another of those great round walls of stone. From this vantage point she could see that it was some kind of fortress, the ditch around it rising up to a secondary earth rampart. Not far from it was the playing field Evan must have seen before. And here, just below her, a man came striding, a huge man in gray to match his head. It was the powerful one she had seen standing over the little boy. He walked toward the open gate, his strides heavy but sure.

"It's all right," she whispered back to Evan. "It's very quiet."

But Evan was looking off in another direction, absorbed, and then she realized he was already there too, and watching something else.

"It's quiet, all right," Evan agreed. "But I'm not staying if that old guy looks up at me."

She followed the direction of his gaze. At some distance from the fort was a peaceful tableau within a grove of trees, several boys seated on a thick carpet of moss looking up at the tall, brittle figure of the ancient man in white. He was leaning against the trunk of a massive oak, his hands a little to the side, flat against the bark behind him. Claudia could almost see his bare feet as gnarled roots. His shaking head was like a branch swaying. One boy spoke, then another. They lolled lazily, one of them smiling in response to what the ancient was saying. And then quite suddenly there was tension in the little group. The boys were sitting straight, listening intently. The ancient spoke, his voice like the breath of a dying wind. The boys strained forward.

At that moment another figure that had been hidden among the trees also leaned out to catch the words of the white-haired man.

Evan drew back. "Look."

"Ssh."

"Eavesdropping. It's him. Let's go."

Claudia grabbed Evan. "First see what's going to happen." But Evan pulled free. "Please, Evan, he's leaving. He's going to the fort. He's not doing anything."

"Then you don't need to stay and watch him."

"But something's happening. Don't you want to find out what it is?" Following close behind, she tried to tell him about the man she had seen approaching the gate.

"Anyhow, fog's lifting," Evan pointed out.

"I know it is. That's why I don't want to miss anything. It may be days before we can come back. Or if the sun stays out—"

Evan laughed. "That would be O.K. with me."

Claudia had an idea. Thinking about what they'd just seen, it suddenly seemed to her that the boy had been different this time. "Are you sure that boy's the same one?"

Evan was sure. "He's got that monkey look."

"I think he's bigger than when he was on the shoulders of that man in purple. Maybe their time is different. Maybe the boy's older and he's outgrown his temper and doesn't kill dogs any more." She could tell from the way Evan was listening that he was drawn to the idea. "I can see what you mean about the monkey look. It's his arms. They're so thin and long."

"It's his face."

"And the way he moves. You could imagine him swinging from trees."

They were laughing now, and Claudia knew she was winning.

Evan said, "We could just see what he's up to before we quit."

To forestall disappointment as much as to prevent a hasty retreat, Claudia reminded him that they couldn't count on the times of the things they saw, but Evan pointed out that they hadn't really left yet, so they ought to be able to make it right back into the moment they had started to leave.

And they did. Still astride the turtle's back, all they had to do was turn around and retrace their steps. They exchanged a look of glee as they saw the men they recognized emerging from a round building that seemed to be made of clay and woven thatching. It looked to Claudia like a giant upturned basket with a peaked roof; she guessed it was the place they had been in at the feast. She looked at the great wall that enclosed not only the round

61

building but also, along its inside curve, a series of smaller structures made of timbers and stones and straw. They were like apartments, the line of them connecting almost all the way around the interior of the wall. She could see cattle and pigs and chickens in some of the enclosures at ground level. Looking up, she had a glimpse of women on a kind of balcony overlooking the inner court. One of them was standing and twirling a rod which seemed to be winding a thread. Another, seated, was sewing with a huge black needle.

Claudia would have continued to stare and catalogue details of dress and appearance and utensils if Evan hadn't tugged at her and pointed to the sword that hung at the side of the large gray-haired man she had seen striding toward the gate and who now stood off to one side talking with the ancient man in white. The sword seemed too small to compete with the other swords that were being carried forward by a series of warriors and presented to the boy. This small sword gleamed, its scabbard covered with a design of looping vinelike tendrils. As the man moved, leaving the ancient to join the others, the light struck his scabbard from other angles, and she could see that the pattern might be one of leaves, then of snakes or dragon bodies, then something altogether different, a flowing of circles and spirals that reminded her of old-fashioned writing.

What held her, though, was not that scabbard with its gorgeous design, its graceful line that ended in a heart-shaped terminal, but the hilt of the sword showing from the scabbard, the hilt that was golden too, but otherwise exactly like the one she still held. She looked at her own metal figure; it was dull, tinged green, but it had the same U-shaped arms and legs, the knobby feet and hands, the hole at its center.

She started to ask Evan whether he thought they were one and the same, but he was engrossed in the scene before him. The little boy was systematically breaking one sword after another and tossing them aside with such rudeness that all attention was concentrated on this incredible performance. Claudia couldn't tell whether it was the boy's superhuman strength or his insolence that held them all rapt, astonished.

Now the boy had destroyed each of the swords. He spoke to the man Claudia considered the leader. The leader turned with a look of perplexity, apparently seeking advice. He caught sight of the small golden sword and pointed to it. The huge man removed it from his belt and held it out to the leader with a gesture that bore more than reluctance. He spoke; the leader listened. And the little boy began to cast about for something to do, as if he were so full of nervous energy he could not remain still.

At this moment the ancient man in white strode into their midst and took the small weapon into his own hands. He made a speech. He looked from one to the other and finally let his gaze rest on the tallest of the men, the one in purple with the proud shaggy head.

All were silent but the dark thin-faced boy, who fidgeted as he awaited their next move. Claudia saw on the face of the proud man clad in purple the same expression she had noted at the feast; this time it was more definite, an aspect of regret and sorrow.

Now he received the sword from the old man in white. Still no one spoke or moved. He thrust aside his cloak to fix the sword at his side; Claudia was surprised to see that the tunic he wore looked spare, almost severe. The great yellow head was bowed for an instant as the sword was set in place. Then it was raised again, the cloak settling over the sword in purple folds.

With swift, easy strides the man went to the boy and placed his two strong hands on the boy's narrow shoulders, staring into his face as if searching for something. He seemed to shake the boy, though really he was only rocking him back and forth, while the boy looked back with clear, untroubled eyes. This contact lasted barely a minute. Abruptly the purple-clad warrior returned to his place beside the leader.

The leader nodded, as if in acknowledgment, and then took his own sword and handed it over to the boy.

"Will he bust that one too?" Evan whispered.

The boy tried to, but the sword would not yield to him. He seemed satisfied with the gift, and the grown men seemed satisfied that he was.

"It's getting lighter," Evan observed. "We'd better go."

Claudia knew he was right, but she longed to stay and see how the scene would end. "We have a minute."

"You'll be sorry."

"Evan, don't you want to find out how the story comes out?"

"You're a girl," he pointed out.

"So what's that got to do with it?"

"I just don't want to have to meet that kid, is all. He probably wouldn't even notice you. But I've seen him with the other boys. And now I've seen him breaking those swords in half. And the fog's thinning." He stepped

64

back into the dark shadows that merged into the gray that was the fog.

Claudia, following, could only protest because she was curious, not because she was right. She was saying, "I wonder why they didn't give him the little sword," when the air was fanned in her face and she ducked, thinking she was being dive-bombed by a bunch of angry terns. Instantly she realized that she should have known better. The terns hadn't been after her, and all that flapping was more chickenlike than those graceful, darting birds that might come plummeting from the sky. She laughed.

"Quick," Evan shouted, "catch it."

She had no intention of chasing a crow in the fog even though she could see it stepping past her along a driftwood log like a drunken tightrope walker.

Evan tore after it. The crow protested with a squawk and flapped into the air. "Stupid," Evan shouted. "Don't go over there."

Claudia started laughing again. "He can't go where we were. He hasn't got the man."

"Well, get him anyway," Evan yelled. "He'll get lost. And crow followed us because he trusts us, and if we leave him behind—"

"Oh, all right. Don't start crying. It'll mess everything up if you cry. Look, we can even get back across without getting our feet too wet. Come on, Evan, I'll help you find the damn crow."

It seemed like a magic word, for somewhere up above the back of the turtle the crow uttered a harsh, rasping croak, an unmistakable answer.

"Say it again," Evan directed on a note of relief. She

could see him wiping his nose on the sleeve of his dripping jacket. "I told you he likes swears."

"He likes us," Claudia corrected. But as she called and searched and followed the cawing farther and farther out onto the promontory, she found herself resorting to "damn" and a few other imprecations as well. The crow seemed to be laughing at them, cackling wildly at the impossible chase.

Even after she'd had enough and was trying to figure out how to convince Evan that it was no use, she kept on, urged forward by the frightened pleas he cast out toward the heartless bird and by her own sense that it was up to them to bring the crow back safe to Mr. Colman. Then she heard its cackle change to a longer, lower cry. Stupid old bird. Was it in trouble? She knew that the voracious black-backed gulls would attack anything smaller than themselves. "Stupid old house crow," she muttered. "Wild things belong to the wild."

But it wasn't wild any more, and it had lousy tail feathers and probably weak wings from not flying enough, and she could hear it squawking like a rusty hinge. Why couldn't she see it? "Damn you, which direction?" she called, feeling lost and frightened and fed up. "Damn, damn, damn," she bellowed out over the hissing surf, and stepped right off the ground.

Sliding down the cliff, she could see the edge of white curling around the rocks below her. She was falling in slow motion, not the least alarmed, already beginning to break the descent, grabbing hold of a root that broke in her hand but then holding fast to the next.

She heard Evan's voice: "Claude. Claude."

"I'm all right. Down here. I'll be up in a second."

She turned, squirming, and reached. Then she could see Evan's face. He was lying on his stomach at the edge of the cliff, reaching down to her. "O.K., give me a hand, but if you start to come, let go." She held on to him, but the earth began to crumble, giving way beneath him. "Go back," she told him, beginning to giggle, because really there was nowhere to land but the narrow stretch of beach that was exposed with the tide not yet full. It was no great drop, and really it was so funny the way everything kept collapsing under them.

Evan was laughing with her. Suddenly he cried, "Watch it, Claude. The man. Get it."

They both made a lunge for the bronze figure caught in a miniature rock slide they had started. Their hands came together over it, Evan grabbing the head, Claudia a knobby foot. They could hear the crow laughing again, or else it was a laughing gull, but the danger they had imagined seemed over. They lay there, one of them horizontal, one slanting along the cliff edge, flat out, as Tim would say, and the crow (or was it a gull?) laughed and they laughed at the joke it had played on them, and soon it seemed as if the laughter was like a song with a single voice.

Lying there gasping and laughing, they could tell that the new voice was really a part of the sound they made. Then they saw the singer of the laughing song, her head thrown back with merriment and music. Only as the fog lifted like a curtain from the cliff could they tell that she was not Rebecca after all, which was what they both first thought.

At the same time their laughter broke off, but hers went on, sounding like a bell, only dying as bells do when the clappers strike less often and less hard.

The children couldn't say a word. They had forgotten all about the crow. They had even forgotten about the fog that was parting from them and leaving them in a world of fresh, bright air, on the side not of a cliff, but a grassy hill. They were too caught up in what they saw this blonde maiden doing. She had the sword, the golden sword, and was using it to weave a fabric which seemed to hang on the air from a shaft of sunlight.

PART TWO

eight

"W<small>HY</small> do you just lie there?" Her voice still rang with mirth.

The children were sprawled as if they had been flung forward or had been crawling till they collapsed. Just behind them, gaping like a mouth in the green turf, was an opening under a gray outcropping that seemed to be supported by upright stones. Slowly they drew themselves up. Their fronts were covered with earth and twigs and pebbles. They were both a mess, but they only continued to gape at her.

"Why do you eye me like that?" she demanded.

Evan said, "We thought you were our . . . Becca."

"Maybe I am. Tell me what a becca is. I was expecting something unusual this Samain. I just didn't guess it would be the likes of you. What kind of skins do you wear?"

"They're not really skins, though some people around here call them oilskins. We call them foul-weather gear." Evan had never been more voluble. Something about her seemed to draw the words from him.

"No one I know around here calls anything oilskins. And," she added, tossing her long lock of hair, "I know a deal more than most people, at least here in Connaucht."

"You look especially like Becca," Evan murmured, "when you talk that way."

Claudia, astonished that she could understand this vision and already puzzling over the word Connaucht, finally found her tongue. "Have you seen our crow?"

The maiden shrugged. "There are many crows, ravens of war like Badb and the hooded crow of death. What crow do you seek?"

"A special crow. I mean, he's just an ordinary crow, but he's special for us."

The maiden frowned. "Let me see." She turned from them and commenced weaving again. The children watched her raise the sword and ply it on threads of red-gold. Now that she was turned aside, Claudia could see the way her hair was fastened in three braided coils with a fourth coil hanging loose and falling nearly to the ground.

The maiden sighed, muttered irritably, and then stopped to unravel a thread that had tangled. Finally she wheeled about. "I see crows and crows, and they're all mixed up with things I've never encountered before. Cathbad should have foreseen that you'd be after me with this. He should have prepared me. I keep getting the crow picture entangled with the one for the queen."

"Who's Cathbad?" Evan asked her.

"Who is Cathbad?" She was full of shocked contempt. "Everyone knows of Cathbad. You came out of the mound, didn't you? You must be at least halfway Sidh-folk. Or perhaps you are not what you seem. I don't see you clearly yet, though I can tell that Cathbad knows you. Or about you. But then he always knows more than he lets on."

71

The children shook their heads. They didn't like the way she pounced on them with her scorn.

She couldn't have been more like Rebecca than now as her tone conveyed her utter disgust at their ignorance. "He is no less than High Druid, is Cathbad, and there are in his possession more secrets than in all the Sidh-people of the mounds. Of course he comes from us Sidh-folk too, only he bestrides both worlds. Never heard of Cathbad, indeed. I'll tell you one thing, though, if he fixes you with his eye, you'll never forget him. Never."

"The man in white," Evan exclaimed.

"Well, the groundling shows some seeing power after all." She sniffed.

"Do you know all those people?" cried Claudia. "Can you tell us about them? They're in some kind of story."

"Story!" The maiden laughed. "You really are more than I bargained for."

"But I'm sure there's a story to them," Claudia persisted, "and we're really dying to know."

"You are?" The maiden looked doubtful. "I'm not sure that's possible. We Sidh-folk don't die very easily, you know. Unless, of course," she added after a moment, "you have mortal blood in you."

Claudia felt baffled. How did you tell this maiden who you were or where you were from? What did she know that would make anything you said believable to her? And just exactly what were Sidh-folk? Claudia thought she had read about them somewhere. Weren't they some kind of supernatural beings? That was what she sort of recalled.

"Are you . . . ?" she began tentatively. She didn't know how to go on.

72

"I'm Fedelm," said the maiden with a certain archness. She tilted her lovely white chin. "I am in bondage to Queen Medb and King Ailill of Connaucht. I hope it won't always be this way, but I have to go where I am sent and do my work for whatever royal master or mistress I am assigned. Of course," she added smugly, "there are compensations. Like this sword." She stroked it with long graceful fingers, then sighed. "Though I'm afraid I can't keep it for long."

"Is it gold?" Evan asked.

Fedelm laughed. "If it were, it would scarce be hard enough to weave with. No, this sword is bronze."

"That's what Mr. Colman called our man," Claudia whispered to Evan.

"What are you muttering about, groundling?"

Claudia proffered their bronze figure. "They're the same. See?"

Casting a contemptuous glance at it, Fedelm drew back with distaste. "I can't see that," she snapped. "And seeing is my profession."

"But you didn't really look at it," Claudia objected. It was almost as if the maiden had shut out the recognition. Maybe she didn't like old things.

"What's the hole for?" Evan wanted to know.

Fedelm snatched her sword away. "None of your business. That's the magic part. Only Cathbad knows its secret. Cathbad and a few other people he decides are worthy of the knowing. Like poor Fergus."

"Who's Fergus?" Evan broke in.

"Fergus is the keeper of this sword, of course. Which is why I have it for now." She stopped. "You're getting that befogged look again. I was not prepared for such igno-

73

rance. You may be from some other world than this, yet it is strange you are so unknowing."

Evan had an idea. "He must be either the man with the big arms and bristly hair or the man in the purple bathrobe."

"I can't imagine what you mean," Fedelm bridled, "but if you want to find out, I suggest you remain silent and use your ears. This sword," she went on, holding it lightly before them, "as you can see for yourselves, unless you're blind as well as dull, is not an ordinary weapon. Its power resides inside it and is hidden from all but a few. Many years ago when the Queen of Ulidia was preparing for her voyage to the Otherworld, Culann the smith, who was very young then, cast this sword for her in the ancient way that is no longer practiced or even remembered."

"Then how could he do it?" asked practical Evan.

"Cathbad told him. Culann himself had a broken mold. He fashioned the model from clay that comes from a certain well wherein lies such craft. He covered the model with so many layers of wax and clay to prepare the mold for the molten bronze that it took from Samain to Beltane before the sword was finished. Then Cathbad used the most secret sunstone which is so secret that even I cannot perform its magic. Out of that he wrought a tiny spear of iron, no bigger than a fish gorge, and Cathbad alone set it into the bead. Heart of oak is that bead with its magic spear therein, and so you have the enchantment of the sword as it was crafted."

"So how do you happen to have it?" Claudia wanted to know.

Fedelm raised a tapered hand to her mouth, yawned,

and declared it a long story. "It was an offering to us in the first place when it was laid in the queen's burial mound. Any of the Sidh-folk may take it up." She gave them a searching look. "How came you to hold that hilt if you are not one of us?"

"So you admit it's the same," Claudia declared.

Fedelm scowled at her and resumed the weaving. She muttered to herself, casting complaints from what seemed to be an endless supply of grievances. "Cathbad would go and name the boy-child after the hound he slew. And then make poor Fergus bear the consequences, when it's plain as the fringe on my sunbeam that it was the king's fault." She broke off to glare at Claudia for an instant. "Cathbad, the king, all of them. Though the king was the worst. It was he who forgot that the boy would be coming and let Culann the smith close the ramparts and set his favorite dog to guard them. It's not the first time the king's thought only of himself. And it's not the first time Fergus has had to suffer for it."

"Excuse me," Claudia ventured, "but is that the king you're in bondage to?"

"Certainly not. The king who started all that trouble over the boy they call the Hound is king of Ulidia where it all happened."

"And we're not there? In Ulidia?"

"Oh, you're hopeless." Fedelm was brandishing the sword in a rather careless manner. "Sometimes you sound almost familiar with these things; then you seem to know nothing." She let the sword hang down, and Claudia breathed more easily. "You are in the Kingdom of Connaught. Cruachu is the royal seat of Connaught, just as Emain Macha is the royal seat of Ulidia."

75

"Which means we're not where that boy is," Evan concluded. "Right?"

"That boy is no longer a boy," Fedelm told him. "A lot has happened since then."

"I don't care what's happened. I just don't want to be where he is."

Fedelm smiled. "And what if he is where you are?"

Evan glanced up. "Then I won't stay."

"Indeed. And where will you go? Back through the cave? Not for a while you won't, little groundling. And if you stray from me, you will be beyond my care. Look at you. You wouldn't reach the river in those strange garments. Someone would do away with you for an infant monster, a bull calf with a spell upon it."

Claudia contemplated Fedelm's warning. Was the maiden saying Evan couldn't return of his own volition? Did that mean they were captives?

"As a matter of fact," Fedelm went on, "I'd better do something about those oilskins before the king and queen come back from consulting that druid of theirs. Queen Medb will be in a fair fit when she returns."

"Will we see the queen?" Claudia gasped. "Here? Soon?"

"Too soon, by the looks of it. Now then, into the mouth of the cave, and quickly. Shed those ridiculous garments. You'll find some tunics about. Hurry." She snapped her fingers.

The children had to crouch to fit inside. As they groped in the darkness they discovered a heap of clothing.

"While you're there," Fedelm called to them, "be sure

76

to leave that ugly copy of my sword with your things. It's only likely to raise a lot of difficult questions."

"She's awfully bossy," Evan whispered.

"I suppose if we just ran she could catch us," Claudia replied. "Anyhow, if she's right, we need some kind of protection." She was struggling with the tunic. It was bad enough trying to figure out what to put on, but dressing all stooped over was clumsy and slow.

"Anyhow, where would we run to?" Evan wanted to know.

The darkness hid her confusion. She could only say, "Sooner or later we'll have to be getting back. Before the others start worrying."

"Hurry," Fedelm called. "I think I hear their chariots now. We must be ready for them on the path."

"How does it button?" Claudia asked her.

"Button? Oh," said Fedelm as Claudia emerged, her hands raised to the slit in the fabric at her neck, "you mean fasten." She looked Claudia over. "I suppose you do need something." She reached behind her and brought forward a small iron circlet with a bar through it. "Come here, groundling," she ordered, and pinned the material together.

The circlet was crude and as different from Fedelm's gorgeous brooch as the burlaplike fabric was from Fedelm's cloak of speckled green. "Why do I have to wear this . . . this rag?" Claudia demanded. "Why can't I have something decent like you?"

"That's decent enough for a bondsmaid. And take those things off your feet."

"What, my sneakers? Why should I?"

77

"A bondsmaid is always barefoot."

Claudia pointed to Fedelm's green sandals. "You're not."

"We are not on the same level, groundling. I am, of course, bound in service to the queen, but I am no lowly bondsmaid, I can tell you."

"Hey," Evan said with a laugh, "I need something to wear under this. It doesn't fit."

Fedelm yanked his tunic into place. She overlapped the coarse folds and fastened them with something that looked very like a safety pin, except that the catch plate was scooped and flattened like a duck's bill. "There. A fibula above your station. As for linen, that is worn only by freemen. You two groundlings certainly have strange notions. Bound to lead to trouble if you don't keep them to yourselves. And here comes the queen. Isn't it just like Cathbad to put me in this kind of position. Problems never come singly, do they? Come, this way down. And stay off the track if you don't want to be run over. I hope in the next age that Cathbad will spare me from ambitious women like Medb. And," she tossed back over her shoulder, "from visitors who do not know their places."

NINE

THE track was really a small road paved with flat, even stones. The queen's ponies were galloping hard, clattering on the paving, but the rest of the chariots were spread out on the turf. The children had to duck behind some tall furze to avoid the missiles of mud that flew up from wheels and hooves.

There was no trouble telling who was queen. She stood tall, dwarfing her charioteer, a mass of coppery hair flying out behind, held only at her brow by a golden diadem. At first her face was only a splash of white. She wore a brilliant green cloak that made even Fedelm's lovely gown seem tame.

The ponies came to a rearing halt just beyond Fedelm, but at a signal from the queen they plunged forward again, circling to the right onto the turf and coming all the way around until they were standing before Fedelm. Then the children could see that the whiteness of the queen's skin was scored by reddened lips and by eyes outlined in jet and nearly black.

"What is your business?" the queen demanded. "Speak up, girl. Why do you stand in our path weaving that garish fringe? Why, that's the sword of Fergus." The queen was suddenly silent, staring hard at Fedelm.

Claudia nudged Evan. Everyone here seemed to know something about their bronze man.

"Heed me, Queen," Fedelm was replying. "I know you are amassing the forces of Erenn to invade Ulidia, that you are determined to seize Donn Cuailgne, the great brown bull of the Ulaid."

"If you know my plans, you must understand that important affairs await my attention. We'll be off as soon as you explain your possession of that sword." Over her shoulder she bawled, "Ailill," in a voice that might have summoned pigs.

A chariot moved through the ranks and drew alongside. Its passenger seemed to be the king, his apparel fine, his looks not so much regal as poster-perfect. Like a toothpaste ad, thought Claudia, as she saw him bestowing an almost flawless smile on Fedelm. To the queen he asked a little anxiously, "What is it, my dear?"

"Look there. The sword you took from Fergus. Now it's in this girl's hands, and who knows what she's likely to do with it."

Ailill's perfect features assumed a petulant cast. "It's not my fault. I wish you had let me give it back to Fergus. I didn't want the thing. I just wanted to . . . well, embarrass him."

"All I did was point out that since you had it anyway, it might be held to make him more . . . attached to our schemes. But I warned you about its magic powers." Her voice rose dangerously. "I said, 'Keep it well, Ailill.' That's what I said. The bard himself repeated my very words to set them in his memory."

"And that is why I left it under a stone outside the rampart. How could I have known that some maid, charming though she seems to be," he added with a small

80

flourish, "would take it up and put it to this eccentric use?"

Fedelm was scowling over another tangle in her weaving and busily plying the sword they argued over.

"Tell her to give it over then," Queen Medb commanded.

"Oh, my dear," Ailill protested.

She glowered at him, and with a little sigh he stepped from the chariot and approached Fedelm. The children shrank back.

Evan whispered, "He doesn't seem all that much like a king."

Claudia nodded.

"Still," Evan pointed toward Medb, "I believe in her. Don't you, Claude?"

"Ssh," Claudia cautioned.

Fedelm was smiling beautifully at Ailill. He held out his hand.

Still smiling, Fedelm told him, "It is the queen who must ask."

Between clenched teeth, Medb spoke to Ailill. "I've had all I can stand already today without putting up with this impudent wench. It's bad enough to have an incompetent druid, but to be thwarted by a maid—"

"Tell her," said Fedelm, "that she must address me directly if she wishes to learn what that worn-out druid could not tell."

Ailill turned to Medb. "Why not ask the maid? She may have a clearer vision about these matters. She weaves a pretty fringe; it is as full of colors as the rainbow arching our river."

Fedelm began to hum a little tune. Her voice was lilting and full of laughter.

81

The queen's face seemed to darken. "Well, then," she barked, "out with it, girl. How do you see our armies?"

"I see," sang Fedelm, "red on them. I see crimson."

The queen and all her people gasped as one, the sound like a brief wind rising and flattening the grasses.

"Worthless," cried the queen, her voice ringing out and silencing her followers. "My messengers have returned from Ulidia, and all men there, including the king, are suffering from their weakness; it is as though a deep sleep had fallen upon the Ulidian warriors. So tell me, girl. How do you see our armies?"

"I see red on them," chanted Fedelm, gazing into her weaving. "I see crimson."

Silence fell on the gathering. After a moment Medb spoke with seething calm. "The men of Ulidia are under enchantment and cannot wake. We have no reason to fear the Ulaid. Now will you answer me? How do you see our armies?"

Fedelm's voice pealed like a bell. "I see red on them. I see crimson."

With a cry of rage, the queen tore the goad from her driver's hands and sent her ponies off in a lurching gallop. The charioteer was nearly thrown off his feet; the chariot itself hardly seemed to touch the track.

Medb left behind a momentary confusion. Then the others made ready to follow. Ailill's charioteer started off without him, so that he had to hail one from behind to get a ride.

The chariot that stopped carried a man both Claudia and Evan recognized from his massive head of hair, even though the yellow seemed paler, in fact mixed with white, and the cloak was shabbier than the purple one he had worn when he had carried that spoiled little boy on his shoulders.

After one keen glance at Fedelm and her weaving, this man seemed to accept what he saw. He had the air of one who is beyond surprise. Though his skin was weathered, his eyes were still clear. His voice too was just as Claudia remembered it; only this time she could understand his words.

"Now then, Ailill, in you come." He smiled. "Easy does it." He stepped down and aside to make room.

"Thank you, Fergus. So kind." Ailill allowed Fergus to hand him in. "I really am sorry about that sword. One of those awkward situations." He laughed, but it was a limp effort.

The charioteer, a portly man, viewed this exchange without expression. There was a strange grimace fixed on his face, as though he had wrenched his jaw in a permanent contortion.

"Don't fuss about it," Fedelm told the king. "It'll be there when the need is there. Fergus knows that."

Fergus inclined his head. Then with a wry smile he said, "I suppose it was more than I could have hoped, getting it off my hands."

"What?" cried Ailill. "Your enchanted sword? I must say, Fergus, that is an odd way of looking at it."

Fergus's answering smile was almost grim.

"Still," Ailill went on, "you're an odd one all around, I'd say. Lack a certain mettle, if you know what I mean."

"What metal I lack," Fergus responded more easily, "I owe to you."

The king yelped with laughter and, leaning over the wicker side of the chariot, slapped Fergus on the back.

83

"But you're a good sort, for all your foreignness. You seem to wear an invisible armor against insult and abuse. We in Connaucht are not used to such ways. You have seen how we prime our warriors with satiric songs to bring them to a proper fury before battle."

Fergus nodded. "Cathbad long ago noted my deficiency in that respect. The scourges of Ulidian bards are likewise used to bring forth the battle ardor in the Ulaid. In that way, Ailill, I was a foreigner even before I was banished from the Ulaid and came to serve you. Cathbad used to say I was outside my time."

Ailill paused, reflecting. "Yet," he muttered, perplexed, "it is you who carry the sword of Culann."

"Only the scabbard at the moment, my lord," Fergus reminded him. He drew his cloak aside to reveal the scabbard the children had already seen. Again they studied its tracery of scrolls and spirals. Looked at from their crouched position, the tip seemed not so much heart-shaped as resembling the head of a serpent, its eyes two rivets holding the tip to the delicate covering. Fergus put his hand to the hilt of the ill-fitting sword and pulled it part way out. It was made of wood, about as graceless and useless as a child's homemade plaything. He set it in again as far as it would slide.

Ailill was covered with confusion. "I don't like these things," he mumbled. "There's always trouble when one admits strangers, especially those like you and your fellow Ulidians in exile here."

"I have served you well since that time," Fergus said to him.

"Yes," answered Ailill, his tone become waspish, "and served the queen as well."

Fergus sighed. "Ailill, we have been over this so many times. My obedience to the queen and to my geise prevented my refusing her offer on that day you found us together. You know that. You are aware of how I am bound to accept such hospitality. And, you see, that is why your queen knew I could not disobey her."

"You could have told me what she was up to," Ailill charged.

"There was no chance. That day we returned from the hunt separated from the others. The morning was warm." Fergus paused, remembering. "She would swim, she said, and rest while the sun was high, and eat bread and cheese on the river bank, the black fruit from thorn bushes . . . ."

Ailill flushed. His eyes were fixed and hard. "Go on, go on."

Fergus shook his head. "It is between the queen and me, and it is finished. That's all you need to know. That, and that I carry a wooden sword to mock me." Looking up at Ailill, he remarked quietly, "It was more fitting than you can know to have stolen my sword of bronze and to have replaced it with a wooden stick, while Medb and I slumbered deep in the oakwood shade. You were right, and you were in the right. I have already said so. Now let it be."

It was Ailill's turn to shake his head. "Challenging you is like spearing a breeze that flits invisible from leaf to leaf. It is no suitable labor for a king."

With just the hint of a smile, Fergus nodded his agreement. "Especially with plans to be plotted for the hosting."

Ailill drew himself up. "Of course. Exactly what I

meant. Probably the queen grows impatient already."

Fergus stepped to his chariot, but Ailill signaled him to draw back. "I don't suppose you'd mind, Fergus, considering the state the queen is in, and how I've tarried here. I think it would look better all around if I appeared, so to speak, on my own."

The chariot disappeared down the slope and then reappeared moments later rolling along on the grassy plain below. Fedelm, gazing after it, spoke without turning her eyes on Fergus. "I suppose you know that one Ulidian does not slumber, cannot, even as all the others cannot wake."

Fergus's smile left him. He waited.

"I suppose you know that it is the dark one you hold dear as a true son. Fergus, are you listening to me?" Fedelm wheeled to him. "You know, don't you," she declared, her voice almost strident in its urgency, "that it is he who is named for the hound he slew, the great hound of Culann the smith."

"All right, all right," Fergus responded finally. "You needn't shout. I suppose I've always known that my fosterling, dark as the forest darkness from which he came, would not succumb like any Ulidian warrior to the curse of Macha. And that it is I who must guide Medb and Ailill to the land he alone defends."

"You should enjoy getting even with the King of Ulidia at last. You can have all the revenge anyone can dream of. Be glad, Fergus," she insisted harshly. "I want you to be glad."

That brought the slight smile back, but did not erase the regret that filled his eyes. "You should know better than to want what cannot be."

"I know," she snapped, more Rebecca-like again. "I

should know better than to want at all. It isn't what I'm here for. And on top of everything else, I'm saddled with the strangest pair of groundlings you ever saw. Talk about odd. Ailill should have had a look at these. I really don't know how I'm going to keep them."

"Why don't you just send us back?" Evan suggested.

"I thought I told you to stay out of sight and be still."

"We did. We were. But since you're talking about us, I thought—"

"Thought, thought. You're to do as you're told and forget about thinking."

Fergus looked on the emerging Evan with some amusement. "That's a hard task you've set him," he told Fedelm. "As hard to make a creature stop thinking as to get him to begin the process in the first place."

"Oh, stop talking like Cathbad," she retorted. "There's nothing funny about two witless—"

"Two?"

"There's another one. They seem to come in pairs. Might as well come out, girl. At least Fergus won't harm you. He's too curious about strange creatures to go about hacking them to pieces."

"Besides," Evan pointed out, "his sword's only wood."

"Still, you'd better respect him. He's one of the heroes of Erenn they sing about. He could step on you like a bug and squash you flat if he felt like it."

"Stop the nonsense, Fedelm, you're alarming them." Fergus beckoned to Claudia, who was stiff from crouching so long and therefore looked a little as though she was shrinking from him. "I'm not even in the habit of stepping on bugs," he told her with a smile. "That is, if I can avoid them."

Claudia looked into his clear eyes and heard herself

declaring, "But you mentioned hunting before when you were talking to the king. So obviously you do kill some things."

He laughed with surprise. "Many things," he corrected. "But only what I or my companions can eat. Once," he added, "I killed men as well as beasts. It is for those killings that the bards chant their lays, but I shun that glory and do not seek any killings."

"Still, you're planning to lead the queen into Ulidia," Claudia reminded him.

Fedelm said, "She doesn't understand that a bondsmaid does not address a warrior first. These two, they have no understanding."

"We do too have understanding," Evan objected, emboldened by the mildness of the man who stood before them.

Fergus knelt down so that he was Evan-high. "But you must practice care, small one." He turned to Claudia, rising again. "Yes, I will lead the queen, show her the way. A single warrior stands to defend that land, the child of one who lives in the Otherworld. I myself found him lying in a bundle of leaves and carried him to Emain Macha. I carried him in one hand, so tiny was he. When he was small, he was raised not far away, and when he was not yet big he came all by himself to Emain Macha and demanded to stay with the other boys, the sons of warriors, to learn the craft of war. It was I whom he called master."

"What will you do?" Claudia asked softly.

"What will I do?" Fergus echoed.

"You'll tell that Queen Medb all about him," Fedelm

declared. "If she takes in half of what you tell her, she'll know enough to change her mind about this foolish hosting."

"Change Medb's mind?" Fergus wore a lopsided smile.

"You'll lead the queen and lead her again. And again," Fedelm instructed.

"You mean mislead her?" Claudia wanted to know. Fergus made no answer.

Fedelm said, "It certainly is hard to keep all these little things, like whom you're serving, straight. I forgot. Of course, Fergus, we all serve Medb."

He raised his eyebrow and indicated the children. "And they? Are they her servants too?"

Fedelm gave an impatient sigh. "They are more baffling than any I have seen issue from the cave. I haven't worked out how I'm to use them yet. My weaving gets all snarled every time I try to see what part they play, and the pattern's impossible to figure out afterward. It's all Cathbad's fault."

"It's easy to blame Cathbad."

"Well, you needn't sound so lofty. I've heard you muttering the same sort of thing about the way you got that sword." She clapped. "I've got it. I know."

"Know what they're here for?"

"Of course not. But I know what to do with them." She raised her face to him, beaming.

"Oh, no." He stepped back.

"Fergus, it's only fair. After all," she wheedled, "I have your sword in safekeeping for you."

Fergus groaned. "What will I do with them?"

"Put them to work for now. Give the boy to your chari-

89

oteer. The girl should be good for something. Do you spin well?" she asked Claudia.

Common sense told Claudia that now was the time to call it quits and insist on being sent back. But there was something in Fedelm's querulous acceptance that ensnared her, and she found herself merely shaking her head.

"I should have known. Useless. Well, do you tan a soft hide? Can you grind the corn and barley fine? How about working with clay?"

"I can do some clay work," Claudia answered, adding, "But Evan is better at the decorating. Also, I'm a good berry-picker. And I know how to dig clams."

Fedelm and Fergus exchanged a full look.

"You'll give her to the cooks, and they'll find something for her. She can fetch the water and serve the meat. Come, Fergus. It's only for a while. They're not for staying. I'll take them off your hands if things really get . . . embroiled. There, I knew you wouldn't say no. And it's just for the time that I have your sword."

"I'll be traveling," he warned.

"They're used to that. I sense they've come a long way already. And look at them, Fergus. Talk about foreigners. Without someone like you who understands their position, why their lives wouldn't be worth a lump of peat. Oh, Fergus," she crooned, as he put his arms about the children's shoulders, leading them down onto the track, "you're one of the bright rays for me in this desolate land." With that, she gave a yank at her weaving frame, extinguishing the shaft of sunlight from which it hung, and disappeared from their sight.

90

TEN

As they neared the stronghold, they passed a number of low round huts with that basket look they remembered, the walls part stone and part mud and woven thatch. Evan said he thought they looked like cupcakes with coconut shreds over the frosting.

Fergus, deep in thought, seemed not to hear him. Claudia, who was somewhat reassured by Fedelm's insistence that they would not be staying for long, was losing herself in the sights and sounds and smells of her surroundings. They had to climb over several stone walls. Claudia had never seen such tiny fields. And all that stone. They passed spindly-legged sheep and stunted cattle, ponies heavy-headed and pot-bellied with hips jutting out too far. The animals huddled for warmth, eyeing the travelers without alarm, scarcely moving for them.

"How do they get out?" Evan wanted to know. He tugged at Fergus's cloak and repeated his question.

Fergus looked about as if surprised to find himself with these two ragged children in the middle of a little steading. "Why, they take down the stones," he finally answered. "How else?"

"Why aren't there gates?" Evan pursued.

"Is it all right if we ask questions?" Claudia broke in.

"Because if it is, I'd like to find out about some other kinds of things."

"Inside the rath," he told her, "it would be best to do what you are bid and to hold your tongue. I think it would be a mistake if I were singled out just now. And I shall be watched closely. I am sure of that. But," he smiled down at Claudia, "you may speak to me when we are unattended, as now. Just remember that most people are not so accepting as I. I know that other spirit-folk besides the Sidh may live among us. I have learned from Cathbad that there are things I may not understand but need not fear. I cannot fathom who you are or where you began. Perhaps you yourselves cannot tell—"

"I can. It's easy." Evan planted himself in front of Fergus. "We came here from Thrumcap Island. In Maine. That's way up near the Bay of Fundy in Canada."

"Thrumcap." Fergus shook his great head. "I have not heard of such a place, though there be many islands from the farthest shores of Erenn all the way north and then east to Pictavia."

And where is that? Claudia wondered. "What exactly is Erenn? I mean," she quickly added, seeing the look of incredulity come over Fergus, "what is it next to?"

"Why, Pictavia. I just said. Pictavia to the east, with Alba beyond in a southerly direction. To the west there is only the ocean, and, far out, the Island of Mists ruled by Donn, Lord of the Dead."

Claudia and Fergus gazed at each other, taking in their mutual strangeness. Finally, shaking his head at some unspoken thought, Fergus smiled at her. "But if you be in Fedelm's care, and Cathbad knows of you, that is enough. Still," he added, "it is best that no one else know that you have issued from the Cave of Cruachan. This is the time of Samain when things unnatural may cross over into our world. Also, there is a nervousness that passes from one to another before a great hosting. The queen herself is edgy, and all about are folk who are ready to find the evil omen in the unusual. Spears and shields are down from the walls of the feasting halls. Men, women too, go about with loosened daggers, their swords—"

"Doesn't that make you feel . . . insecure?" Claudia ventured. "I mean if everyone else has bronze swords and—"

"Iron," he corrected. "The hilts may be cast in bronze, fitted with bone or oak, but the blades will be forged of iron. And the fires are blowing hot this day with the shaping of new weapons, the repair of old. You may," he added, noting Claudia's blue-white feet and lips, "be glad of the heat they make."

"But Fedelm said yours is bronze," she blurted. "Does that mean it's no good anyway?"

"Mine is different." He gave a short laugh. "Some may consider it a prize, but they have not carried it long."

"It's very beautiful," Claudia murmured, drawing her sacklike tunic to her. When the wind whipped into it, she thought she would turn to ice, but she was in no hurry to reach the place that would silence her.

"It was dreamed of by Cathbad the druid, cast by Culann the smith, and endowed with the vision of the Sidh. Cathbad himself set it into the mound raised for a Ulidian queen who dwells with Donn in the Otherworld. The sword remained there over her grave until Culann would bury his hound. The Sidh-folk returned it to Culann in whose hands it had taken form, so that he knew it was meant for the boy who now bore the name of his hound. He left the powerful dog for them and carried the sword in its scabbard back to his smithy, where he cleaned and polished it for half a year till it shone like the king's torc. Then he saw that the Sidh-folk had made their mark in oghams. Finally he took it to Emain Macha to give it into the keeping of Cathbad until the little Hound of Culann should reach manhood and take arms."

"And that's when that little whatever-you-call-him broke everything," Evan supplied.

"You have heard the story. They sing it from Connaught to Pictavia."

"No," Evan informed him. "I saw it. I also saw that awful boy doing what he did to the dog." The memory seemed to chill him more than the bitter wind. His teeth began to chatter.

Fergus stopped short. "You were there?"

"Not exactly," Claudia hastened to explain. "Only saw it. Evan, I wish you'd let . . . ." She didn't know how to address Fergus, and time was running out.

They could see the massive wall of stone on its raised plateau. It was like a hive, buzzing with activity. The ringing of pounded metal, the clinking and hammering, the neighing of ponies, and shouted orders reached their ears. She was determined to have some gaps in the story of the sword filled in before they entered the gate.

"It was the timing," Fergus continued. "Only much more than that, as it always is, more than a simple converging of events. You see, though the little Hound was still only a child, barely a year older than when he destroyed the hound of Culann, he had not only the ambition to be a man, but, even then, the ambition of a man."

"Ambitious," muttered Evan in agreement, "and a bully."

Fergus shook his head. "How can you call him a bully when he has yet to meet in combat anyone smaller than himself? He has the strength of ten Culanns, the prowess of ten kings, the knowledge of ten druids, excepting, of course, Cathbad."

"Well, I don't like the way he acts."

"You fear him. It is well that you do. The powerful queen I now serve has not that much wisdom. Yet. Maybe she will gain it through experience."

"About the sword," Claudia prompted.

"Yes, well, the sword arrived on the scene at the exact moment that the little Hound came to ask his king to let him take arms. It is one of the rare occasions when Cathbad has slipped. He is getting older, you know, and tires. The boys he was instructing had been badgering him with questions. He told me about it later when he taught me the secret of the sword's power, how his head had been full of the drowsy whisperings of the oak, each leaf a voice to Cathbad, lulling him to sleep, since that is how the tree will speak to him through his dreams. One boy caught him unaware and demanded to know the omen for the day. Poor Cathbad. He told those boys that whoever should take arms on that day should have a short life, though his name would carry glory through many ages."

"I remember that too," Evan chattered. "The boy was sneaking around there behind a tree. And then he went and broke everything the king tried to give him."

95

"That might be a way of looking at it," Fergus admitted, "but it isn't exactly the way it is sung. And the bards will be singing of the taking of arms of the Hound of Culann as long as there are harps to play and fires to give warmth and folk who would brighten the darkness of an evening with heroes' tales."

"Then what did happen?" Claudia insisted. "Obviously he went to the king and the king didn't think he was too young. It sounds awfully irresponsible to me to give all those dangerous things to a little boy. Why, he was even smaller than Evan."

"That is true. But you mustn't blame the king. He was trapped, because that little boy you tend to deride was clever enough to tell the king that Cathbad had declared this the day for his taking of arms."

Claudia thought she understood. It was like getting provisional permission from one parent and then using that to gain permission from the other. "Why didn't Cathbad explain?"

"Because at that exact moment he was greeting Culann, and then it was too late; the little Hound was already arming himself."

"And leaving a big mess all around," Claudia supplied.

Evan added, "I bet no one made him clean it up either."

"I wonder," Fergus said with a touch of impatience, "how you can know so much and yet remain so ignorant. That boy is not only loved by me, he is praised and feared as the greatest champion of the Ulaid. Do not be fooled by his slightness; in combat he is a very monster, and when the battle fury seizes him he will be stopped by none. That is why, though the sword was meant for him, it had to be kept from his hands."

Claudia, who was dancing on her bare toes to keep warm, but still trying to hold back, said she didn't understand at all.

"You see," Fergus explained gently, "there is one great weakness in that boy: it is his terrible strength. Such strength is a curse as well as a blessing. Cathbad knew that. Give the sword to that boy and he would break it like a dry twig in half the time it took him to snap the iron blades from their hilts. Someone had to keep the sword in trust for him. When he falls, it will lead him to the Otherworld."

"So it's his," Claudia puzzled, "but he can't have it as long as he lives."

"Once he had it to lead him out of the marsh vapors when he was lost and far from home."

"It worked?"

"It worked then, as it worked for me another time, when I had to cross the water in search of three Ulidians who had fled our kingdom. Tumbled like a nutshell in rapids, I clung to the sword and hugged the bottom of my coracle and met, rearing up on a mountain of green sea, Manannan himself."

"Who's Manannan?"

"Why, God of the Sea. You know not Manannan, son of Lir?"

"We know about an island," Evan volunteered, "sounds something like that. Grand Manan, it's called."

"Let him finish," Claudia whispered to Evan, but Fergus seemed to have run down. She had to prime him. "So it worked," she repeated.

97

"Yes," he went on reluctantly, "bringing me to the place I sought and to the people I believed I was conducting to the King of Ulidia and protecting with my guidance. But I was betrayed by the king and tricked with an offer of hospitality I could not refuse, so that I led them instead to their deaths. I have not used it since. Not that way, though I carried with me into exile the secret of its enchantment. Of course it's entirely useless to Ailill. He knows what the oghams say on its blade and would prefer to keep his distance from it."

"What are oghams?"

"They are markings which speak without voice."

"What do they say?" they both asked at once.

Fergus smiled. "You will turn to ice in order to hear me out. Then I will never learn why you are here and how our destinies are to join."

They begged him to go on.

"See the man hurrying toward us? He is my charioteer. Would you work for him?" Fergus asked Evan.

"What's the matter with his face?"

"Evan," Claudia scolded.

"There are folk who believe such afflictions are wrought by bards made angry. But I know he suffered the Boardface sickness when he was young. He has not smiled since. Many will shun a man so afflicted, but I have never done so. He is good, and could use some help readying the chariot and harness and brushing the horses. And you will find a warm bed in the straw beside those willing beasts."

Claudia stopped. It was one thing to be uncertain about the length of their stay, another to be separated from Evan. She had a feeling that it was all right to follow wherever this adventure led so long as they seemed to

98

be safe. She wondered if Evan was thinking about the others, Maddie especially. Evan didn't look concerned about anything. "Will he get anything to eat?" she inquired.

Fergus laughed. "You may notice that my charioteer is well fed. This lad will not want in the care of that eater of great portions. I have to chide him now and then if the horses grow too fat to pull us well and swiftly and to remind him that he makes up the larger part of that load."

"All right, Evan will do his best, only finish telling us—"

"What do you mean, I'll do my best?" Evan countered. "I can speak for myself."

"Please," hissed Claudia. "There's so little time."

"I know," Evan argued. "And you haven't even asked him about the crow."

"The crow?" said Fergus.

"Oh, it's just a crow we're looking for. A . . . a pet."

"Avoid the crow," he warned her. "It would not look well for you to be seen with a crow. Mark my warning, both of you."

"But it knows us," Evan began.

"Yes, all right, we'll be careful. What did the sword say? I mean, the writing on it."

Fergus drew himself up. They were under the shadow of the immense fortress; here the wind was broken, and everywhere there were small fires, wheels being mended and weapons forged or straightened. Quietly he spoke: *"Gift and giver am I. Wield me who would follow. Fear me who would follow me not."*

"And you know what that means?" Claudia asked Fergus.

"Cathbad said that whoever took up that sword must both lead and follow, and only those who could do both might carry it and be carried by it."

"There must be more to it."

"You are certainly no ordinary bondsmaid," Fergus observed. "I hope you will manage to conceal the fact."

"No, but the meaning," she pressed. "Why is it such a burden for you?"

"Cathbad said that whoever carried the sword in trust for the Hound of Culann should be led across his known bounds and wander alone and distant."

"But I thought it would take you places you wanted to go," Evan argued, adding in an undertone to Claudia, "I hope it can take you home too."

"Cathbad," Fergus was explaining, "said that if I took the sword I would be a stranger ever after. It was only a matter of time, I knew, before what Cathbad declared would befall me."

"Then why did you take it?" Claudia pressed. She felt better knowing that Evan still had home on his mind. It made her feel she could afford to give herself a little more to the story Fergus told.

"It was fitting," he told her simply. "I who loved the little Hound more than any other should take the sword into my safekeeping until he was ready to follow it to the Otherworld."

"Cathbad should have kept it," Evan pronounced. "That wasn't fair."

"And then," Claudia said softly, "it happened the first time you used it to lead you to a place you wanted to reach. It ended with your banishment from Ulidia."

Fergus nodded.

"Evan's right," she exclaimed. "You never even got a chance to use it for yourself. It's not fair."

"Maybe not fair in the thinking of your people, but in the sense of things as I know them, it was fitting." He slapped the scabbard. "Not that I enjoy the consequences very much, though there is some mean satisfaction in seeing the discomfiture of others who fear it."

"And does that mean," pursued Claudia, "that you carry a secret you can never use?"

Fergus burst out laughing. "You have an empty head. Here I have crammed it with the entire story of the sword of Culann and you spill out its contents just as fast as I fill it up."

"Claude," Evan provided somewhat loftily, "the secret is like the sword."

"The secret," Fergus declared, "is the sword." He looked from one to the other. "What people fear is not what they understand about the sword or the secret, but what they do not understand. They know that if I smite with this tender weapon, it grows into the mightiest of hard-edged blades. It is lightning itself. And they know that if I should choose to use my secret knowledge, I could call upon the enchantment of the sword to lead me where I ask. But they don't know how or even why, and so they fear it. They would not cross any boundaries into the unknown."

Fergus paused, his voice dropped. "Cathbad explained the secret so that I understand how to use that power. Even if I dread it, I cannot fear it. So," he added, the laughter drained from his voice, "I took it. I have it. And I know that all too soon I must wield it again."

101

ELEVEN

IF THE area around the rath appeared to be teeming with men, women, children, and animals, inside the wall activity seemed to have reached a boiling point. It was as if the ramparts themselves were set over an unseen fire.

Claudia found herself under the command of one of the queen's handmaidens, and was immediately shunted off onto a girl not much older than herself who interspersed her comings and goings with the snatching of morsels of food, even scooping up crusts where she could from the mud-packed ground.

Claudia was too preoccupied with another problem to consider hunger. She kept darting looks at storerooms and byres, hoping to find some sign that would answer the question she could not ask. Bewildered by her predicament, she was nearly paralyzed with discomfort.

The queen's handmaiden, a tall, ebullient girl whose name was Loche, might well have understood her need if she had waited long enough to give Claudia a chance to try expressing it. But Loche was frantic with all of Medb's commands and counter-commands, and could only raise her strident voice in complaint and ridicule.

So that left Claudia with a girl more ragged than she, more animal than human, whose utterances were hardly words. How could you ask for the bathroom when it would seem that this creature must never have bathed? How could you indicate the need for a toilet when not even the queen herself might know its meaning?

In her desperation, Claudia finally sought relief in the darkest corner of a cow stall, only to discover that she was not the only one to share the cows' facilities. Squatting, she was joined by another, whose features she could not make out in the darkness. The damp straw reeked with age and use. Like an ostrich, Claudia closed her eyes to imagine privacy, then heard a voice she recognized as that of the handmaiden, Loche.

"Getting along, are you? Boardface says I must furnish you with a cloak for travel, you and the boy."

Together they ducked out of the stall and made their way toward an even ranker stench, a heap of bones and shells, rotting roots and animal dung, that made up the midden of the rath. There Claudia caught sight of the girl for whom she was supposedly working; the girl was gathering pats of dung and setting them out in rows in a square of afternoon sun.

"Fuel for the night fires," Loche explained. "In case we camp on rock or plain. They are lighter to carry than the peats."

Claudia, hoping to escape that particular work detail, wanted to say that she was weak with hunger and felt dizzy when she stooped over.

"But it's the queen we must look to now," Loche went on. "Having one of her fits because they are not all gathered about her considering their course. All the warriors are seeing to their own readiness. Look, you go back to the Great Mother over there beyond the bread-making

103

and say I have sent you to fetch milk for the queen. Then up here. Watch where I go." Loche was already climbing the steps to a balcony supported by heavy timbers with graceful carvings, the walls dressed with freshly bound rushes. This was the royal quarter. Grinning, Loche leaned over the open side of the balcony and pointed up to yet another level. She shouted down a coarse-sounding phrase that Claudia could not make out. Something about Loche made Claudia uncomfortably aware of missing Maddie, in fact even Becca, as if she'd been away from them for a long time. She turned to her errand.

Three small children chasing a squawking rooster tumbled into her, righted themselves with hilarious shrieks, and fell upon the bird. A boy of Doug's age was clambering over the side of a pigpen; Claudia could hear the snuffling, muttering commotion he caused. Moments later, squeals rent the air above all the other noises.

The Great Mother, boss of the larder, was elbow-deep in cheese-making. "Fetch me the roots over there," she told Claudia. "Ladies' bedstraw," the old woman bawled, as Claudia tried to guess which roots to choose. "It's cheese I'm doing for the great raid. And bring down a few of the nettle leaves; they will hasten the curdling."

The squealing resumed somewhere near the midden and rose into a series of shrieks, suddenly cut off. Claudia, her head held back staring at the bundled roots and stalks and leaves that hung from overhead beams, saw them blur together as the foliage of living branches may melt into a pool of green when you gaze up at them on a summer day. Then the green that was only a hint of green, with gray and lavender and red and brown all swirling together before her eyes, closed over her, and she felt herself sinking, drowning in the heavy scents.

She awoke on a heap of sweet-smelling straw. As soon as her eyes opened, a woman nearby called to the Great Mother. The big woman lumbered over and sank beside them with a wheezing groan. Her hands were huge and damp.

"I was to fetch some milk for the queen," Claudia began, adding, "Loche said."

"Let Loche come herself. A lazy, fooling, flitting maid is Loche, a maker of trouble." The woman placed her wet hands on Claudia's forehead, then on her stomach. "Are there pains, girl?"

Claudia wasn't sure whether there were pains or merely hunger pangs. "I haven't eaten," she murmured. "I've . . . been . . . a long time."

First they made her take a hot broth brewed from dark, bitter leaves. She wrinkled her nose at it, but the woman stood over her with a keen eye. Claudia gulped as fast as possible, gasping at the way it caught her throat like a pair of hands. "What is it?" she choked, handing up the wooden bowl.

"Bog myrtle," she was told, "for the sudden darkness; for falling."

Next she was handed another bowl, this one made of clay with a simple decoration at the flaring rim. She raised it in both hands and drank steadily, the milk so fresh it left a froth on her lips. "Bring one of the wheaten loaves," she heard the Great Mother telling an attendant, "one that has not quite cooled." Then the woman

105

was cutting off a huge chunk, and as the bread broke from the knife, the honey aroma Claudia had first known came to her again.

"Slowly," the woman laughed, "or you will lose it all and spoil my fresh bedding."

Claudia nodded without speaking, chewing on the sweet, grainy, rather dry crust. She would be content to sit here forever, she decided. She had had enough of swords and heroes, mysteries and dangers. She sank back, sighed, and let her eyes close on the warmth and comfort.

It was Loche who roused her with a tirade that seemed to have had no beginning and would have had no end if the Great Mother had not intervened.

"The dog takes on the nature of the master, I see," the huge woman pronounced from her long wood troughs, her dripping sacks. When Loche still continued with her ranting, the Great Mother threw off another comment. "And the bitch the nature of the mistress."

The helpers in the larder heard and laughed. Loche put on an unconvincing show of indignation. "Well, I am given a bondsmaid to help me, not to add to my numberless tasks. The queen upbraids me for this one's failure. Where's the milk I have waited for this hour and more?"

"In my stomach," Claudia answered, patting herself drowsily.

"Up, girl, and stack the dungs then. Or help with the scraping of the pig's bristles. I'll tell Fergus he can keep his bondsmaid."

"You'll not badger Fergus," the Great Mother declared, serious now, quiet.

"Oh, yes, I forgot that you Ulidians, masters and slaves alike, are as one. Then," Loche went on, seeming to have forgotten Claudia, "if you care for your champion, Fergus, give him warning. He will be tested, I think, in his loyalty to Connaught. The king has it in for him for one reason. And," she giggled, "the queen for another." She pulled Claudia to her feet. "Will you serve with us now, or go to the dung heap?" She snapped her fingers in Claudia's face. "Wake up. The feasting will start a night of much drinking. Samain is finished, the dangers past, the omens done with. Tonight they will speak of the hosting and we will need to keep their cups and horns brimming. You must earn your traveling cloak or remain at Cruachan. Or be cold."

"Soft," the Great Mother cautioned. "The girl fell down and could not rise. She will carry the dishes for me and will herself convey the queen's cup. As to Fergus, there is an old affection for our heroes, and that is all we share. Your king and queen are like the parts of the blacksmith's clamp, but they are wrong to consider Fergus a piece of iron that can be flattened and shaped to their will. Nor will I compromise him with obvious warnings. Long have I gathered and cooked and flavored the cauldron that hangs to your queen's fire. I am resigned to this service. What Fergus does I neither seek to know nor care to affect. He is yet a warrior of warriors, and I am old and live from summer to summer when my small place is filled anew with the sticky leaves drying, the bracken, broom, and agrimony, and the dank roots and barks I have known since I was a child. These I gather regardless of boundaries and the contests of kings and lords."

"You mean you care not for the traps and schemes because of your own safekeeping," Loche taunted. "You seem to be sparing Fergus questionable contacts. It is your own skin you shield with discretion."

"I do not seek to join my destiny with warriors." The woman was crumbling a curled-up leaf between her fingers and dropping the powder into a stone quern. "I am a gatherer of herbs," she said to Loche, "not of heads."

A graying servant dashed into the larder, breathless, laughter erupting and tumbling out with her words. "The queen would have you at hand, Loche. Quick. It has to do with her battle attire, which she was trying on. She is girdled round with thongs and wax and cannot get rid of them. Oh," she spluttered, "she is like a sow in a snare. I was afraid to approach and cut her free."

The queen's predicament raised their spirits and dissolved all differences in hilarity. "Keep back," warned the Great Mother, "or a tusk will slit you through the middle."

There was a fresh burst of laughter from Loche. "I risk my life and limb, but serve I must." She strode out grandly, while they all stepped back for her and bowed and flourished with their knives and rags. "Look to the milk, girl," she called back, and then went swishing importantly up the steps to take charge of the queen's tantrum.

But later it was Loche, not Medb, who received the finely shaped cup with its scrolls of inset red glass. Claudia had managed to get it all the way to the balcony without spilling by staring fixedly at the handle that looped into itself like the arch of a leaping porpoise. The cup itself, wide and shallow, spilled easily. "There," breathed Claudia with relief, handing it over, and only then noticed that Loche had on the queen's diadem and the royal brooch. "Where's the queen?" Claudia whispered.

Loche pranced and preened and declared that she, of course, was the queen. She raised the cup to her lips and drained it.

Claudia was astonished. "I thought she was waiting."

"Waiting? Medb never waits. A very eagle is Medb, swooping from prey to prey." Loche laughed. "She is just now engaged with the king. She would have us believe it a wifely gesture, but you may take my word for it, wifely or not, it has more jest than gesture. Fetch some more milk, girl. It will calm her if she returns in the mood she left on. If Ailill has increased her temper, it is the mead we will call for."

Loche picked up a mirror and held it to her face. The back of the mirror was golden with red enamel outlines of interlacing disks. Loche admired the side she was staring into; Claudia gazed with wonder at the reverse. Then the handmaiden lowered the mirror and they were face to face again. "On your way, then," cried Loche, coloring. "Be gone now."

When Claudia returned, the balcony was empty and the interior chamber, the entryway hung with cloth of gold, also unoccupied. A heap of pillows and throws of woven wool and fur were lying carelessly, strewn with fabrics, some of them recognizable as cloaks and gowns.

It looked, thought Claudia, very much like packing day. She stepped back, dislodging something hard that was wedged between cushion and floor. The object, glinting, rolled away from her bare foot. It was a bracelet in the form of a twisted dragon-dog with its tail in its mouth as if it were intent on swallowing itself. The eye was like a drop of yellow fire.

As she stood there staring, feet appeared from the ceiling, where only now she could see a hole with a ladder attached to the wall. The feet were long and bare. Bare too the legs. Finally the hem of a crimson tunic showed, the descent arrested for a moment. Then the Queen of Connaucht leaped from halfway down the ladder and landed with a thud on the floor.

She towered over Claudia, who could do nothing but stand mute with the cup of milk in her outstretched hand. The queen was wearing what seemed to be a man's tunic, for it was short, barely reaching to the knees. The belt, though elaborately decorated with bronze and perhaps real gold, was carelessly draped, loosely clasped. Medb wore a twisted neck ornament that looked like a rope of gold, and her dark copper hair hung loose and disheveled.

"Where is that Loche?" she demanded. "Always skulking about instead of bringing me my berry juice."

"I thought," Claudia ventured, "it was milk you wanted."

"Milk," roared the queen. "Would I whiten my eyebrows to terrify my foes?" She gave a short laugh. "Where is the girl with the coloring? If they cannot ready me for the battle, will they not at least ready me for the feasting?"

Claudia tried again. "The milk is fresh." She felt like a waitress trying to keep a dissatisfied customer from walking out. At that moment she heard light footsteps running along the rampart. Then Loche appeared on the

110

balcony. She was breathless, a high color to her cheeks, and the diadem awry on her tangled hair.

Claudia had the presence of mind to drop the curtain so that the queen, pacing the chamber with immense strides, caught no glimpse of the handmaiden. Then Loche was lifting the curtain and sweeping in as if busy with a hundred exacting tasks. "Leave us," she ordered grandly, taking the cup from Claudia and giving her a quick grin of thanks.

On the balcony Claudia saw the diadem Loche had been wearing carelessly tossed aside next to a dripping jug of water. Below her was that mass of seemingly chaotic humanity. The disorder and confusion were so vast, so total within this fortress that she found it hard to believe that anything like a raid on another kingdom might possibly be launched.

Leaving the queen's balcony, she felt herself caught, and was clasped in a laughing embrace, her face pressed hard against sweat-soaked leather. As quickly as she was grabbed, she was thrust out at arm's length. "You're not Loche," whispered a horrified voice, and its owner disappeared before she could even catch a glimpse of his face.

Fergus met her on the stairway and gave her a brief, careful smile before passing, leaving her shaky, uncertain, in the milling courtyard. Minutes later she saw him high on the rampart, his figure unmistakable against the violet sky, the wind whipping his heavy cloak, this one hooded, the hood itself edged with the yellow fringe of his hair.

He carried a spear, long and straight. Cloak, hood, and hair were lifted and slashed by the updrafts from

111

within the rath and the great sweep of wind that hurtled in from the coast. Only the spear and the man stood upright and still.

Claudia began to carry the boards and bowls into the great feasting hall. There was a steady stream of bondsmaids like herself, fetching and hauling and dodging each other. The warriors were gathering, their voices low with early boastings checked only by the tension felt by all. The pig on the fire hissed and burst with popping, snapping sounds, rivulets of juice and fat coursing down the brown, brittle skin.

Returning for a jug of ale, Claudia could still make out the form of the Ulidian exile until darkness fell. Ailill, on his way to the feasting hall, looked up and remarked that some fool was keeping watch so long that he looked as if he had turned into a pillar stone.

τWelve

Snow was in the air. The animals could smell it. Stomping, snorting with uneasiness, they turned rumps to wind. Even the milch cows following the armies seemed restless after the day's march.

Each night it was the custom for Medb to circle the encampment. Hers was the last chariot to be set down, the last team to be unhitched and fed.

Claudia saw Fergus go quietly from Ailill's tent. He would not be watched so closely until Medb arrived. First he went to his charioteer, Boardface. He spoke quietly, leaning over Evan for a moment with some word for him as well. Claudia waited, then met him halfway across the clearing just out of the light of the blacksmith's fire where sparks flew up from the hammering at some repair.

"Is this a time I can speak to you?"

His hand was on her shoulder. "First I will talk with some of my kinsmen." He was striding toward the tent of some of the Ulidians who had come into exile with him.

"Fergus," she heard as the tent flap was pulled aside. "You have shunned us."

"And led us a merry route," said another. "South, north, the circle nearly complete. Do you think you can continue in this way till our kinsmen awaken?"

"What does the queen say?" asked a third, while another was observing, "But it is hard to know what stand to take. The queen has made us welcome. Our own king betrayed us and drove us out. I could serve her loyally so long as she stayed from Ulidia."

"The Hound has come," Fergus whispered, stepping into the light. Claudia slipped in behind him. "I have played a stalling game, but it is over."

Voices rose in contemplation of the unexpected contest awaiting Medb. Only Fergus sounded troubled. "Already he has killed four of the queen's advance guard. She has vowed vengeance on him who slaughtered them. He will try to hold the men of Connaucht at one river ford after another. He is bound to ask for single combat."

"If she grants him single combat," one of the men spoke thoughtfully, "he may yet hold back the armies until the sleep is past." This man laughed. "I was a boy with that Hound, you know, and felt his strength the first day he did take his place in the boys' training at Emain Macha. Broke three of my ribs before I could swing my hurley stick at him."

"Fergus," said the first, "they have never seen his like. It will be a noble combat."

"It will be a bloody one," Fergus replied. "Now listen. You must go from one another after this night. The queen will think less about you, about me, if there are no little knots of Ulidians among her warriors. Especially you of royal blood. Draw no attention to yourselves, but perform your duties well, with just so much eagerness as your neighbor and never more, never less. Lose yourselves in Medb's armies."

The men considered Fergus's demands. Their sense of

brotherhood was intensified by their separation from their own people.

"What if you should need us?" asked one.

Fergus reflected. "Watch the bondsmaid." He pushed Claudia into the pool of light. One of the warriors half rose and held a stone lamp to her face; it tipped and a little of the hot fat from it dropped, blistering the back of her hand. She drew back with the pain of it, but Fergus took her hand, turned it over, and placed in it a bead which he had been wearing on a thong around his neck. The thong looped down from it casting a shadow circle. Fergus's hard grip kept the pain from spreading.

Claudia stared at the bead, which seemed to be made of wood, except that something black pierced the center, a tiny spearhead protruding from one point, the tail of that miniature spear opposite it. The bead was strung through a kind of handle made by a carved depression just below one part of the round surface.

The men were absolutely still, all of them staring at the bead. "It is Cathbad's," whispered one, "the sun-stone." The hushed name, Cathbad, echoed among them. "No," said another, "it has been worn by Fergus since that day the little Hound took arms."

"It has," Fergus agreed, "since I took the sword. It will only work for those who have been given instruction in its magic. This small bondsmaid cannot harm you with it, but she can help me by wearing it outside her cloak at any time we need to meet."

"Will she betray us?"

Fergus said, "She is known to Cathbad. Though she is not one of us, she will do my bidding. If she goes from fire to fire wearing this bead on her hair, then you will know

115

to come at once. It will only be as a last resort. Otherwise disperse and call me not brother." He drew Claudia out of the tent.

It was hard keeping up in the oversized boots she wore. They had been a parting gift from the Great Mother of the larder, who would not allow the child's feet to go bare over frost-encrusted ground. They were a poor fit, but tough and warm. Claudia slept each night with them as a pillow; it was the only way to keep such treasures.

Fergus pulled her along, only letting go quite suddenly as he came up to another hooded figure in the dark. "Is it you?" he asked. "The physician?"

"Fergus?"

"Yes."

"They were calling you just now. The queen has come. You are to share their meal."

"First," said Fergus, "may I ask for some salve. My charioteer took hold of the iron he had mended and carries a blister that may hinder his driving."

The physician had just such a salve in his bag and brought some out for Fergus. "It is steeped in healing medicines and will work as fast as you could hope."

The physician went on his way, and Fergus bent to apply the stuff to Claudia's burn.

"Why didn't you just show him my hand?"

"Go to the chariot and there, along the pole, you will find some extra cloth. It is kept for stanching blood in case of wounding. Take off a strip to bind your hand." Then he added, "Tell the boy to get under the sheepskin this night. There will be snow before morning."

Claudia protested. She had wanted to ask Fergus some questions. But Fergus put her off, saying, "Not now,

116

child. And when you serve the meat and milk, keep the hand from notice," he warned, heading for the queen's tent. "Bondsmaids of your state are not usually treated with ointments and bandages." He stopped. "And wear that trinket where it will not show. Until I say other."

Quickly she opened her cloak and set the bead inside. Against her skin it was an irritant, the bead turning now and then so that the tiny black thing jabbed her like a pinpoint. Even with her hand throbbing, she was aware of the bead like a little thorn. But she liked wearing it, for it was a mark of her service to Fergus, and that could only make her, if a little uncomfortable, enormously proud.

Loche said, "Oh, there you are. There is feasting this night, and not enough hands to bring and serve and stir the pot. Look to the cauldron. The queen's here."

Claudia made her way into the cooking area, which was crowded with people huddling beside the fires to stay warm. The cauldron hung by a chain from the temporary tripod that was dismantled each morning and erected again each night. There was no room in the queen's tent for cooking, and so it would have to be carried, still bubbling, when the stew was done. Claudia found the great wood paddle and dipped it into the mixture. Roots and huge chunks of mutton were exposed, then submerged, in the thick broth.

A boy sidled up to her and pressed a small, scooped-out tree limb into her cloak. She took it quickly, entering at once into the bargaining she had grown adept at since leaving Cruachan. "First to Boardface and the boy," she directed. She felt the answering nod. "I'll know if you fail. Last night you brought them only half a dipper."

117

"It spilled. It's hard to carry under my cloth."

"You carried it under more than your cloth," she retorted. She was learning to drive a hard bargain. Many came to her when she tended the night's stew. Two of the bondswomen, who were pregnant, gobbled whatever they could wheedle from her. She would hand out portions to all she could, but she was compelled to reserve a seemly amount for the queen's feasting or else answer for it to Loche, who was quick to strike when she was displeased.

Each day she was thinking less about home. She seldom stopped to consider whether the other kids were missing her and Evan or were worried, and not only because she recalled that Mr. Colman had said time passed differently in the Other Place. It was simply that being warm enough and full enough were suddenly, bleakly, more important than anything else, and that meant providing for Evan, whatever the risk. Next came the other children and the greedy mothers-to-be. She wondered how they could keep up with the long days' trek over rugged hills, through forests of giant oak and alder swamps, treacherous with thin, black ice.

"All right," she murmured, faced with a pair of unwavering eyes, "one more onion then. There now. It's full."

She had to go in search of Loche, because she herself did not have the authority to call on older and stronger slaves to carry the stew to the queen. Edging into the tent, she found the meal already in progress, the warriors gathered, Fergus himself with drinking horn to lips, now passing it to Ailill, and the queen gnawing on a huge joint torn from the pig that had been roasted in the pit.

The queen was gazing at three harpers, all in speckled

118

green, who seemed to have appeared from nowhere and who were making music that reminded Claudia of the aroma of the Great Mother's larder beams hung with meadowsweet and bog asphodel—a kind of musky sweetness with something else, an almost pungent scent beneath the dried honey-breath of the faded blossoms. All about her were low murmurs, the clink of metal, the clatter of earthenware, and a kind of drowsiness, many faces gone slack as if on the verge of sleep.

The scene to Claudia, fresh from the night cold and flickering darkness, was oppressively dreamlike. Standing at the entrance, the tent flap still in her hand, she looked for Loche, listened to the haunting music, listened and forgot about Loche. And then she forgot about the evening stew, forgot everything, even the queen worrying at the bone.

Medb's gnawing grew more languid; the conversation faltered; the drinking horn, a little ale dribbling from it, came to rest between Fergus and Ailill.

But now the wind whistled through the entrance gap and swirled inside the harp-drenched tent. Dust spun around the feet of the harpers and spiraled into the air. Two harpers halted to brush the dirt from their eyes. The remaining harp played thin upon the heavy torpor of the gathering.

Then the third harper was forced to clap his hands to his face, and as the music ceased, Medb rose. She swayed drunkenly, though there was no sign of mead-drinking about her. Mumbling as if just waking, she waved the joint in an arc and cast it at the harpers.

Everyone seemed too stunned to react. They stared at their swaying queen, who seemed to be heaving herself

119

free of invisible bonds. Finally she managed to rally, full-voiced with rage at being so nearly tricked into slumber.

The harpers dashed into the night. Snow swirled in behind them; in seconds Ailill, Fergus, and other warriors were ready to give chase.

Claudia was caught up and swept by the tide of pursuers. As she tore after them, she could hear their warning shouts of "Ulidians" and "The music of sleep . . . ."

Once they were beyond the fires of the encampment, the wind was so sharp and full of icy sparks that she ran blind, following the shouts, the footsteps, desperate now that she had gone this far, afraid of being left alone on the barren hill.

Then she almost ran into Fergus and the other warriors, all of whom had stopped suddenly to get their bearings in the howling desolation. One of the men pointed with his spear. He summoned a young bondservant who had followed with slingstones and shield. They all looked where the spear pointed and saw three figures racing along the spine of the hill.

They asked Fergus, "Which way will they go?"

"There is a stand of trees below this ridge," he told them. "They will seek that cover."

Claudia caught her breath. His voice sounded so businesslike in the hunting of the harpers. If they were Ulidian spies, then he would in effect be running down his own people.

The warriors separated into two bands and set off in opposite directions to cross the ridge in an attempt to encircle the harpers in the wood. Fergus struck out without a word or a look of recognition, his face set hard.

120

This was different from leading the armies into Ulidia, doubling north and south to set the march into mountain passes and rushing river fords. Claudia had heard Ailill and Medb question him sharply about these torturous trails. He had thrown up his hands, demanding that they send another to show the way if they doubted the wisdom of his leadership. There were reasons, he had insisted with quiet dignity; he had to use his judgment as he saw fit. And with many a dark and probing look, the queen had continued to follow him, not so much in trust as in the conviction that he was the most knowledgeable about the land and the people of Ulidia.

But now Fergus was after the harpers, Ulidian spies or no, and with an appearance of determination that confused Claudia. She began to follow, then realized all at once that she was too far behind to catch up any more. She crested the hill in order to see whatever she could and was able to make out the dark area that must be the stand of trees Fergus had mentioned. Three figures came streaking out from that darkness, retracing their route and making for the ridge once again. Far to the side she saw a warrior straighten and take aim; then another rose beside the first; and another.

Only then did she realize that the figures at which the men prepared to cast their slingstones were not harpers at all, but deer; and she was standing behind the quarry at which they aimed. The deer were thundering up and across the broad expanse of the hill, coming closer, their hoofs pounding. Now she could hear their straining breath, harsh, open-mouthed.

She wanted to leap into the air, higher than the fleeing animals, and signal the warriors that they were mistaken, that these were merely deer running terrified, startled out of their hiding. But there was no time. The first stone whistled over her head and fell like a shot behind her. The three deer swerved sharply and thundered straight toward the crest in a final burst of strength that might have carried them over and down the other side.

But they never made it, and instead of leaping up to stop the casting, she dropped to the ground seconds before the hoofs were upon her. She rolled aside and kept on rolling as a stone sang and hit and the harsh panting of the stricken animal was silenced. Almost at once the other two were brought down. She covered her head and lay huddled on the coarse winter heath with bracken stiff and sharp beneath the new snow. All she could hear was the moaning wind, muffled now as the snow fell harder, blotting out distances and creating a small circle of land that was part ridge and part slope, with nothing remaining of wood or, far back and sheltered, the encampment.

She only tried to peer about her when she heard some of the warriors making their way up the far side of the hill to look over the kill. The voices were loud, as they always seemed to be after a hunt, not strident, but effusive, relaxed, shouting in high spirits.

Claudia sat up. There were no deer anywhere about her. She could not believe it; she blamed the blinding snow. She felt her way in the direction of the ridge, expecting to stumble over their warm bodies. Instead she was stopped by a stone she could not remember from before. It was like a shaft, tall and narrow. She could just reach her arms around it. Then she turned and saw two more stones, each standing as high as the first, the size of men. She backed slowly away, staring at the pillars, until

122

they seemed to exist only in her mind, figments of snow blindness.

But if they were, they were part of a vision shared by those warriors who reached the hill, by the carriers and followers who clambered up beside them. She could make out Fergus standing a little to one side, his hand resting on the wooden hilt beneath his cloak. No one tried to touch the pillar stones or even approach closely, but held back in awe, though one or two of the men circled around to pick up the tracks of the deer, which stopped, simply disappeared, beside the stones.

"The snow covers footprints," said one in hopeful tones.

"At least we might have brought back deer meat," said another, "since we could not down the harps."

"Fools," spoke Ailill. "They are all one, harp and deer and stone. You could not slay them." He turned to Fergus. "Though you were right to head them off."

Fergus said, "Even so, they are returned to their land. We stand now on Ulidian ground. This ridge marks the boundary. And now these stones."

"Then tomorrow we will pass into that province we seek," Ailill answered. "At least we will have some good news to bring to Medb." He looked about him. "Where are the rest of our men?"

"But we will have to pass through the river," Fergus pointed out. "The ground is too steep and rough, and too exposed to mark a proper route. Besides, the warrior of whom I spoke awaits us at the crossing. There may we take our chariots and provisions."

"And slay him," Ailill responded eagerly.

"And meet him," Fergus replied evenly.

123

"Yes, yes, you keep telling us he is remarkable and undefeated. Well, but who would have guessed we were so close. It is cheering news on this terrible night. We will leave these stones to their cold vigil and return to our meal, to cheerful shelter."

"What about the others?" asked his arms bearer.

"They will follow us, I suppose," said the king, "or make their way along another route to camp."

They started off toward the valley from which they had come. Claudia waited while Fergus lingered. He looked as if he were taking stock of the place. She clutched her cloak and wished she had a hood, but she would not go back without him.

He stomped across the snowy turf. Pushing aside some tall furze, he stood so close to the first of the stones that he was almost part of it. A moment later, when he backed away, he appeared to leave a shadow behind, a part of himself. Yet there could be no shadows in a snowstorm at night. What she saw was a blur of white, tall, thin, not stone.

In the next second she recognized this apparition. It was clothed in the white robes of the druid Cathbad, and it blew white in the swirling whiteness, like a gust of smoke caught on the wind, or thrown snow. She started forward. As she did so, that figure and Fergus caught sight of her. Fergus, dark and real, bore down on her; the other slipped smoothly behind the next pillar, already whitened with snow.

"That was Cathbad," she cried. "I saw him."

"You should not have followed." Fergus's voice was frightening.

"You saw him too," she pressed. "He was speaking to you, wasn't he?"

Fergus dropped to his knee and felt about near her feet. Then he stood again, holding in his hand something that looked like a long strand of hillgrass. "Wear the bead on this," he commanded, twisting the strand into a coil and firmly bending the ends into hooks that would clasp one another. He stood quite still, only his fingers moving carefully until he had fashioned it to his liking.

"What is it?" she asked, taking the circlet, then knowing as she held it that it was made of a harp string, understanding that here where the deer had fallen the harps had also fallen. And not fallen. "May I look at the stones?" Without waiting for an answer, she walked from one to another as she had first done.

But there was no figure in white robes with streaming white hair. Cathbad was gone.

Much later, she shook Evan awake to check on whether he had received his full portion of the stew. He was cross and complained that it was hard enough to get to sleep without being gotten up in the middle of the night. He began scratching himself. "I'm all bitten up, Claude. Maybe that Loche has something to get rid of fleas."

"I'll find out," Claudia promised. "Are you warm enough?"

Evan yawned and nodded.

She crept out from under the skin that covered the chariot pole and made a small tent for the charioteer and Evan. She felt her way back past sleeping forms to the tent where Loche and some of the other bondsmaids

125

slept. There in the dark she removed the bead from the thong and pushed the wire through the little loop. It felt icy until her own body warmed the twisted coil.

She thought with wonder, "Now I'm wearing jewelry like the others, like Loche with her bracelet, like Medb herself with her golden diadem." But she couldn't say who these people were who wore their gold and bronze and bone and jet, their glass and wooden beads, and their great etched neckpieces. All her watching and listening had so far left her ignorant of this world she had entered. "Where are we?" she murmured wonderingly.

She heard a smothered giggle. Loche was awake, probably only just arrived from a secret meeting with one of her boyfriends. "On the hosting," was Loche's reply, "as any dimwit could tell."

Then when are we? Claudia amended, but silently this time, so that she would draw no more from the caustic Loche.

But Loche was not ready to settle down. "The queen's going to hold us up after all," she confided to Claudia. "Her monthly bleeding is on her. That is why she did not lead the chase after those harps. She will now be forced to wait, and just when she would surge through and take the great bull while all the Ulidians lie in their sick slumber." Loche gave a low laugh. "More time for us, it means."

Claudia recalled the sweaty leather tunic of the young man who had grabbed her outside the queen's chamber. She supposed there were many like that one. Loche would make full use of the time. "Will the queen mind the delay?" Claudia asked.

"She will be worse than ever. She says the harps cast a

spell over her planning and set the month askew. She says now they will have to accept the terms of the youth who waits at the ford killing all who try to cross. Have you heard about this warrior? They say that all the women find him fair, though he is a monster when the battle ardor is on him." Loche sighed. "Yet I have heard also that he is only a mean-looking youth, not formidable, and dark as a water rat."

"Loche, do you know why all Ulidian men, except for the Hound and harps, are sleeping?"

"I have heard talk of it. A curse laid on that people in an older time. Long ago a strange woman appeared in the household of a Ulidian widower; his herds and flocks flourished, his lands grew rich with fruit and grain. The woman, Macha, warned him never to speak of her, but when he went to the gathering of the Ulaid, he did boast of her great power. When the king heard him declare that Macha was swifter than any beast, he was angered and called for a race between his fleetest horses and the woman. Though she was near to childbirth and pleaded for a stay, she was forced to run the race. As she won, she fell down in her pains, bore twins, and died, but leaving this curse: that for nine times nine generations all the warriors of Ulidia in time of danger in that land would be weak as a woman in childbirth. So now they lie helpless. As for this youth, I only know he has not the look of his people; some say he is much to be feared."

Claudia fingered the bead in the darkness, then asked, "Does the queen blame Fergus? I mean, because of the harpers."

For a moment Loche didn't answer. Then, "I think it has to do with the way she feels about Fergus more than

127

what she sees in the forked branch of his loyalty. She will always blame him," Lòche added. "Until she sees him dead."

The snow hissed against the tent. Nearby, a skin, torn from its peg, whipped violently, snapping like the crack of the stone when it is cast from its leather sling. Claudia thought of Fergus's wooden sword, of how his wits alone were his weapon, his goal no encounter at all.

тbiRтEEN

Tнеy could not advance. Medb retired to her tent, where only her women and bondsmaids were admitted. Ailill and Fergus were exceptions, called in and sent forth a dozen times, each time caught in argument from which there was no ready escape.

Claudia heard Ailill defending his queen after he and Fergus had both been summarily dismissed, while Medb called for her women to come and soothe her with bathing and fresh coloring for her face. "It's being hemmed in that makes her seem . . . ," Ailill faltered, ". . . unreasonable. When she can lead her armies, she shows great sense and wisdom in the hosting."

Fergus only frowned. "Her anger will cost lives. If you wish to save your best warriors and the men of your household, it would be better to deal with the Ulidian on the terms he offers."

"Medb will not hear of it. His arrogance stings her into such a rage that all she can summon to the dealing is stubbornness. If we oppose her, we will only make it worse."

Fergus cast him a swift, appraising look. Ailill drew himself up a little, as if to show off his finery and good looks against the other's well-used cloak and shaggy appearance. But for all Ailill's kingly attire, he was the lesser of the two and must have known it.

Just then they heard cries from the outskirts of the encampment. A moment later they saw the cause of the commotion. A chariot pulled by a team of steaming ponies had galloped wildly into the clearing. The ponies, gorgeous in their battle harness with burnished bronze trappings, chest plates, and helmets, reared to a halt as men and women closed in, grabbing at the reins. The chariot had neither driver nor rider, but tied to it and dragging behind were two bodies, headless, that left long streams of blood like two precise tracks in the pathless snow.

Ailill started toward the chariot, then checked himself, his hands to his head. "You tell her," he groaned. "Fergus, I cannot face her wrath."

"Who are they?"

"Those she sent to trick the Hound after the messenger had been."

Fergus nodded. "Wrong and wasteful."

"Never mind wrong and wasteful," Ailill cried. "What will the queen do for vengeance now? She has offered him everything from a place with us to half the stock we raid and half the Ulidian bondsmen in our service."

"And he has offered you single combat, his pledge of fair and proper battle against any one of your warriors, with your right to march lasting so long as the fights shall be waged. Then must you stop till sunrise the following day when the next of your warriors are sent forth to challenge him. But one for one, Ailill. The queen was wrong to send two good warriors on a mission of treachery in the

130

shadow of her messenger. How will the Hound receive the messenger next if his safe travel was the cover for a concealed attack?"

Loche appeared, summoning them both to the queen. Word had already reached her, and she was demanding immediate retaliation. Claudia, not bidden to enter with them, could only stand by and glean what she could. Fergus's remarks were much too low to reach her, but Claudia could hear the queen's bellowings, an occasional word from Ailill in his high, placating voice, and then Medb again, with another torrent of abuse. And always there was Fergus, with the quiet murmur of his understanding, until finally Claudia heard the queen cry, "All right. Let it be. I would rather lose one or two men a day than a hundred warriors every night. Half of those who chased the harps last night never returned, their bodies found at dawn, each without a head. He shall have his terms, this Hound. Let him be told."

"Who will tell him?" came Ailill's surprisingly practical question.

"Fergus," she snapped.

Claudia strained to hear Fergus's response, but his voice was too low and level.

"Of course I will abide by the terms," Medb roared.

Fergus said something else.

"Then let him be bound in the same way," she retorted in such a tone of petulance that suddenly Claudia could not believe in these people and their deadly conflict; they had the sound of children laying the ground rules for some game of pretend. Then she recalled the headless bodies, the long streaks of blood on the snow.

131

She touched the bead inside her tunic and the sharp point told her it was real, not a dream, not a hallucination.

Minutes later she was running to Evan and the charioteer with Fergus's command to ready his chariot. She was dancing up and down with excitement when Fergus appeared; she begged and pleaded, until finally Fergus consented to let her and Evan ride at the back, ready to leap off at a word.

While the ponies were harnessed and yoked, Fergus noticed another chariot being readied, two young men of Ailill's household preparing to follow along. Many of the warriors had gone off on a boar hunt, an occupation that would keep them from chafing and would also bring in some fresh meat to the camp. But these two young men had been forced to remain with the king, and now, though Fergus tried to stop them, nothing would keep them from this brief foray to the river ford. "We only want to look at this terrible Hound," they said, laughing.

Fergus put on his long fringed mantle, closing it with the golden brooch with the intricate inlay. His shield matched the breastplates of the ponies, even to the red-gold bosses and the scallops round the edge. Evan proudly stroked the soft dark nose of his favorite pony, the dun-colored one, then guiltily patted the bay. Claudia was thrilled by the golden splendor, the color and flashing brilliance. Fergus carried his broad gray spear lightly, almost carelessly, as he stepped into his chariot behind the driver.

The children hitched up behind, their legs dangling, and clung to the wickerwork sides as the wheels began bumping and skidding. The snow clogged and lumped, then fell aside only to build up again, making the light vehicle bounce and tilt as the ponies gathered speed and headed toward the river.

Evan was telling Claudia about the pictures he had drawn on the freshly fallen snow and how they had attracted a lot of attention and then had seemed to make the people angry. "I suppose it's because they can't draw like me," he said. "They can't make real things, so they get jealous and don't want me to. And you know what, Claude? They stamped out everything. And none of them would even look at me afterward, like I was the one who'd acted bad."

"Don't forget what Fedelm said about keeping our thoughts to ourselves," Claudia reminded him. She had a sudden misgiving about the people who would not look at him. "Don't draw pictures unless they're like theirs."

"I can't do that kind," Evan began, then broke off, adding, "Though maybe I can learn."

Claudia put a hand on his arm. "Evan, I think all their pictures mean something."

He snorted and shook her off. "Of course, stupid. All pictures mean something. Every artist knows that."

It wasn't what she meant, but then she wasn't sure she could explain, even to herself. "Just . . . maybe don't draw," she told him.

"That's all right for you to say. But all I get to do is groom ponies and pick up the manure for drying and clean harness and stuff."

"I thought you were happy. Is it that you're homesick?"

"Me? I'd rather be doing this than something dumb like picking beach peas with the others."

Claudia's voice dropped. "Do you ever wonder whether they're frantic because we've been gone so long?"

Evan shrugged this off. "Our time's different. Mr. Colman said—"

"But what if he's wrong?"

Evan thought. "He's been right so far, hasn't he?"

Claudia had to admit that was true. Then she hastened to assure him that she wasn't worried either. "Only it's so queer," she added. "I mean, I keep forgetting to worry, or even think about them."

Evan said, "What's wrong with that?"

She faltered. She was thinking of what Mr. Colman had said about his father's losing his wits, but that seemed ridiculous. There was nothing wrong with her and Evan.

"Anyhow," Evan finished, "we've better things to do than worry. And I wasn't really complaining before. I love the ponies. Especially the dun. He likes me better than Boardface now. Always comes to me. It's only that I don't get to hear all the talk you do."

"But you should listen. Because you might learn something I'll never hear."

At this point Fergus signaled them to jump down. The ponies slowed for them. Then the chariot was clattering down to the river bank, and they were stamping off snow and scrambling in behind the rock pile he had indicated.

On a small plain just across the river two ponies grazed side by side, one black and one gray. The chariot was dismantled, the pole dropped, the yoke beside it. In the protected hollow next to the river two young men sat with a

134

board between them, on it ivory-colored figures that might have been chessmen.

"Looks like a picnic," said Claudia, trying to reconcile this scene of quiet repose with the headless bodies dragged into camp.

Evan clutched her. "It's him. The monkey-boy. Only grown up. See, it's him."

She focused on the dark youth and recognized him even as the other raised his head and saw the approaching chariot. Claudia caught the phrase, ". . . great proud warrior within that chariot," and saw the young man look up, then slowly rise. With care, so that the board would not be upset, he moved back and with quick buoyant steps went to meet Fergus.

The second chariot stopped just short of the rock pile, the two warriors of Ailill's household watching the scene below.

Fergus sprang from the chariot as it wheeled to the right and circled just short of the far bank. The dark young man gave a joyous shout. "Fergus. Welcome, my master." He reached out, clasping Fergus's spear hand in both of his.

The children could not see Fergus's face from where they watched, but there seemed to be a smile in his deep, low voice. "I trust your welcome."

"You may well trust it," declared the Hound, "for whatever I hunt would I share with you, be it bird or fish or only a handful of water-parsnip."

"A most unseemly greeting for our king's spokesman," commented one of the young warriors.

Claudia and Evan exchanged anxious glances.

135

Fergus must have been conscious of how this open-hearted declaration might appear. He seemed intent on getting to the point of his visit, the condition of single combat. But the Hound was too full of exuberance and joy. "If you must ever enter into battle," the Hound rushed on, "I would go to the place of combat at the ford, and watch over you while you slept."

"Surely this bears reporting," said the second of the youths in the chariot on the hillock.

Fergus did not betray any nervousness, did not allow himself so much as a glance at the two who had followed him here. Still, it was clear that he knew they listened. He pressed the Hound to accept the same terms as Medb and Ailill.

"I agree, indeed, Master Fergus," said the Hound with a laugh, extending both arms.

But Fergus withdrew, beckoning his chariot. "I cannot stay, fosterling," they heard, his tone so quiet that it barely carried. "There are some who might say I was be-traying the queen." He raised his hand in a salute, and was answered by the Hound's own upraised hand and a quick glance toward the hillock.

"What did he say?" asked the youth in the chariot to his companion.

"Couldn't hear. But see how he flies now."

Fergus's chariot swayed and creaked as the ponies charged uphill, plunging against the steepness and snow.

"He's not stopping for us," Evan whispered.

"We can walk. Or maybe hitch a ride with those."

Evan gave her a look. "Don't you know they don't carry kids like us?"

Claudia shrugged, repeating, "We can walk."

The youths drove down toward the river, then stopped. For a long time they stood in their chariot looking at the slim, dark Hound. Finally the Hound asked in a mild, unconcerned manner why the two were staring at him.

"We have heard about your numerous feats," said the first, "and thought we would see for ourselves what manner of warrior you were."

"And how do you find me?" asked the Hound, still light and easy.

"Somewhat comely," came the reply, and then, with a sneering quality, "but as for your reputation as champion sledge hammer of the smiting. . . ." Here the spokesman broke off with a laugh of disdain.

Through the laughter of the two, Claudia and Evan noted a slight shift in tone as the Hound remarked, almost more softly than before, "You know that you are safe for having left your camp under the protection of my master, Fergus."

"Your master." This brought fresh shouts of laughter.

The Hound did not smile. "I swear that but for Fergus's protection, you would return to your camp as the others have done this morning."

The laughter was over. "If it's single combat you have demanded, why then begin with me. I am not afraid of a pup like you." The speaker broke off to whisper with the other, his charioteer. Some disagreement was evident, the charioteer urging his young companion back, the youth fairly swaggering with bravado and the chance to return a hero to Ailill and Medb.

The Hound stood quiet. He watched the two as the chariot plunged away toward the camp, then swerved round again and once more charged down toward the river. He gave a shrug and reached out toward his charioteer, who was ready with sword and shield. The Hound shook his head at the shield, but took the sword belt and hitched it round his tunic, then waited ankle-deep for the rash young challenger who tore headlong into the river to meet him.

"What do you seek, lad?" asked the Hound; his right hand slowly unsheathed his sword.

"Combat, of course," shouted the youth, already flushed with triumph at having his way with his charioteer companion.

"Take my advice. Go back."

"Your concern is weakness."

"My concern is not for you, boy, but for the guarantee of Fergus." As he spoke, the Hound drew his sword and swept it down into the water; it cut away the tussock on which the young man stood.

The young man fell, floundered, struggled out of the freezing water with his breath coming in quick gasps. He struggled to free his sword.

"Go now," the Hound commanded. "I have given you warning."

"Not," gasped the youth, "until we meet in combat."

As he drew his sword, the Hound struck again, this time across the head of his challenger, shaving the hair as if the sword he wielded were the keenest razor.

"Go now," the Hound repeated. "I have given you warning. I have made a fool of you. Go."

The youth felt his head with his left hand and raised his sword with his right. "Not until we meet in combat," he cried, swinging, "and I carry off your head, or you mine."

The Hound's sword flashed so quickly that the young man was down before the children could see the sweep of the blade. Then the Hound looked up from the reddening waters that raced around his ankles and shouted to the charioteer, "Tell your queen and king that I will not suffer the insults of their striplings, nor further harassments under cover of protection. Last night there were many, this morning several. Now only will I stick to single combat if they do the same. But warn them against me. Should I see that queen or king at this place I will cast a stone like this blow I dealt their young warrior. Tell them."

The charioteer wheeled his ponies, goading them into a gallop that even outpaced Fergus's team. He must have caught up and passed Fergus, because before the Hound had returned to his side of the river Fergus's chariot was clattering down the embankment again, Fergus raging as though words were being torn from him. "What distorted demon in you caused you to violate my pledge?"

"Rail not against me," the Hound retorted. "That young fool was determined to have my head. I could not stop him any other way."

"How could you so outrage me?"

"Master Fergus, if you who gave me care cannot believe me, who then may I trust?" The Hound turned away. "Ask his charioteer whose fault it was," he added over his shoulder.

Fergus departed slowly. He let his driver hitch the body to the chariot and went himself to fetch the children from their hiding place.

"It's true," Claudia insisted, seeing his anguished look. "Isn't it?" she prompted Evan.

Evan nodded, but couldn't speak.

"It wasn't your foster-son's fault," Claudia pursued.

Fergus turned on his heel. "We will not talk about it." He walked on ahead.

Claudia felt tears stinging her eyes. She had wanted to reassure Fergus, to straighten things out.

"What's the matter?" Evan whispered, discovering that he had a voice after all.

"I wanted to make things better," she sighed, trying to keep from crying.

"Better," burst out Evan. "How can it be better for him? If that guy down there, the one he calls Hound, is killed, it will kill Fergus. And if the Hound beats everyone, then Fergus will lose and won't have any place to go."

"I know." Claudia nodded. "I just wanted him to feel better."

"Boy," laughed Evan, "you act like this is one of your stories you can put a happy ending on."

Claudia pondered this, hanging back. Evan had declined to ride on the chariot with that ghastly body so close by, which meant they had to follow another trail of blood as they tramped back toward the camp. The sun was melting the new snow, stalks and brittle husks poking through the white cover, and there were spots along the way where all that remained of the blood was the trace of that heavy, hot smell.

The walk was longer than they had supposed. Gradually they began to talk, sharing impressions of things and people they had encountered. Evan reached inside his tunic and retrieved a small brown flea. He examined it with concentration before squashing it between his nails.

When Claudia shuddered with revulsion, he said, "You didn't mind watching what that Hound did back there."

Claudia gulped. "It wasn't right next to me." How could she explain that the killing was a distant horror, that it was the drama of the encounter that stirred her? She said, "I mean, it wasn't you."

"That Hound," Evan stammered. "He could do anything."

"Not to Fergus, though. Not to someone he loves."

"How do you know?" Evan retorted. "Don't go by Fergus. He's different."

"I wonder how different, though," Claudia mused. She was remembering that Cathbad had described Fergus as outside his time. She wondered whether this small Hound of Culann was a kind of opposite, an embodiment of his time. She watched Evan scratching, then bringing forth another flea. "Loche says the leaves they use to flavor their mead will keep the bugs off. She'll give me some for you."

In gratitude, Evan crunched the insect out of her sight. She didn't hear the sound of it because of the racket made by an approaching chariot. They had to duck sideways off the track to get out of its way. Then they half-turned to gaze after it.

All at once they both knew that it carried the first of the warriors to be sent into single combat against the Hound. They fell silent again, trudging on toward the camp. They wondered how many there would be, how many headless bodies returned to Ailill and Medb, or whether one of these warriors would come back with the small dark head as his battle trophy.

141

FOURTEEN

THE snow in the encampment, trodden and ringed with fires for cooking and smithing, melted in a day and took with it the sticky ropes of red that stretched from the river all the way to the tents and bothies. The sun lasted long enough to dry out soaking skins, clearing the air of the stench of them. The warrior who had passed the children on his way to cheerful combat did not return, and another was dispatched to take his place.

On the side of the hill where the three pillar stones stood out against the sky, men and women cut turfs and built a great mound for the fallen heroes. They killed chickens and sheep and buried some of the finest cooking pots, weapons, and battle raiments.

But all that day and the next the heroes kept falling.

Loche was oblivious to the death that hovered over the armies. Tomorrow, she said, the queen would be out again. Today the sun shone and filled the air with light. "Here," called the handmaiden, tossing one of Medb's tunics at Claudia. "We are all going to the river to do a great washing. When you are away from the tents you may wear the cloth." Claudia looked doubtfully at the crimson fabric. "You don't like it?" Loche draped another across her arms. "How about this one? Cloth of gold and blue. That's the blue of the sky magic."

"Magic?" Claudia couldn't resist the lure.

"It is the painted men of Pictavia, you know, who draw magic pictures on their skin. When they die, their people put them in a fire and the smoke from their skins rises up with the color of their paint, all blue, and that is why the sky is full of that color, especially on the days when their dead are burned."

Claudia fingered the blue wool with its golden threads glinting, its border of metallic scrolls. "How do you get this . . . from the sky?"

"Put it on," Loche demanded. "We're clear away now. Wear it, and I'll tell you."

Claudia glanced back uneasily. She slipped on the gown, which fell to the ground in folds of blue and gold, looking like a sun-struck pool. Claudia waded through it, tripped, and tried to gather the material into her hand.

Loche leaned back, rocking with merriment at the sight of a short, stocky girl stumbling about in the regal cloak of the queen. Claudia began laughing too. It was the sun and the silliness of her costume and also its grandeur and the heavy scent of Medb about it and the sudden sense of freedom. She felt like running crazily through the frost-brown heather.

"The others will love to see you." Loche meant the women who had already gone ahead to begin the washing and fetch water. "Here." She pulled out from beneath her cloak the queen's diadem. "I was going to give them a show, but it's funnier on you." She thrust the golden piece at Claudia, who started to receive it, lost her hold on the fabric, and was caught again, dissolving into a blue heap.

Loche bent and set the diadem on Claudia's head,

then stood back, shaken by laughter. "Now you are swathed in the magic color." Loche bowed low. "And I am your slave."

Claudia stopped laughing and looked up. "You promised to tell me about the magic."

Carefully arranging the oversized cloak across Claudia's shoulders, Loche said, "You take the leaves of the yellow woad. The Great Mother does it. It is a special gift, the making of the blue color from the sky. If you tried it, if I did, the sky would cast out the yellow blossoms at us and we would crumble into smoke."

"I don't believe that."

"No? One of my people saw it happen to a woman who was not granted the power. She took her leaves and made a pot of them and cooked it away on the mountain, and the sky frowned, and then it bellowed like a bull going down before the ax, and it cast out the yellow woad, each blossom hotter than a hundred coals, and when it touched her, they say she simply turned to ashes."

"She must have been struck by lightning."

"She was struck down by the sky itself." Loche faced Claudia, a look of suspicion creeping into her eye. "Everyone knows about the sky. How is it that you do not? Are you of the ground then? Are you one of the Sidhfolk?" Loche drew back a step, gazing intently at Claudia. "And how came you at Samain? I have wondered off and on all this while. You have been different from the first."

Quickly Claudia returned to the question, trying to distract Loche and restore her good humor. She waved

144

her arm in mock command. "Speak, maid. Divulge the magic of this color."

Loche grinned, shaking off her doubt. "You are only stupid, after all," she said, more to herself than to Claudia, adding grudgingly, "though with passing sense on occasion." She pulled Claudia to her feet and fixed the diadem, which was so large as well as heavy that it sat low and square on Claudia's brow. "As to the magic," she finished, as she straightened here and tugged there and stepped back to assess her handiwork, "it is a wonderful thing to see when the Great Mother makes it happen. She steeps the ground leaves in the pot and places the woolen with it, just as you do with all the ordinary colors, and then when she removes the material, she places it beneath a sky like this, on such a day as this. Then the color comes down on the shafts of the sun. You can see when it happens, just as they say you can see the color rising to the sky when the Painted People are cast to the flames."

Sensing how close she had come to danger, Claudia choked back her argument. With Loche helping to pick up the long skirt, they started along the track again. Soon they were giggling, and Loche began to run. Claudia, trying to follow, felt the diadem slip, reached for it, and then stumbled again in her voluminous costume.

"Wait," gasped Loche, "I'm going back to get some others. They must all see you. Keep on, slow as you are, and we'll catch up. We intend to have a glimpse of that champion across the river too."

Claudia drew up. "I'm not going there."

"Upstream, of course. All the women who have seen

him say he is dark but most comely, and wonderfully strong. I shall wear the red," she declared, "in case he may see me from afar." Loche gave Claudia a push that almost sent her toppling. "Tell them you are the queen. Go." She ran back to bring the others.

Claudia continued on as carefully as she could, the weight of her cloak in her arms, the weight of the diadem on her forehead. "I am the queen," she murmured, trying out the phrase on a pair of curious rabbits who sat tall to watch. At her words they turned tail and raced upland.

The sun prickled her face; it felt good. She started running, first cautiously, then with skips and bounds. She would get there ahead of Loche and throw the women at the riverside into an uproar. Loche would arrive in time to save her from a beating. All eyes would behold her in the royal blue, the gold upon her head, and, yes, even the dark young warrior might take note, so that she would be forever part of his life's images, just as he would always be in her memory.

She held the folds higher with one hand, and with the other clasped the diadem to her head. And still she could run, even leap. Off to the side of the track stood clumps of weeds, steeple-high, the stalks still bearing the hulls of blossoms from the summer past. She scaled the heather, then the gorse, and would try this straight weed, impossibly tall, that beckoned and challenged her. She leaped, felt it drag at her trailing cloak, the hulls like burrs, like sticky fingers clutching at the blue folds of the queen's garment, and she was sprawling, face down, in a heap of fabric and weed, her own still small and somewhat clumsy self.

She sat up as best she could and reached out to free the material. But what she found in her hand was not stalks or empty hulls, not a single plant, but the speckled gown of Fedelm, the green more muted than before, more the color of the winter heath.

"I knew I shouldn't try that one," gasped Claudia, "wherever it is. Whatever it is," she added breathlessly.

"You had to try it," Fedelm retorted. "That's what it was there for, to be irresistible to you. To stop you." She reached down and pulled a single stalk from under a blue fold. "Agrimony is what it is called. Though," she added sharply, "you in your ignorance may know it only as sticklewort. Now, off with those outrageous garments."

"It's only a joke," Claudia protested. "Loche told me—"

"I cannot take on all the fools of this land. Loche seeks trouble, and she will find it soon enough. Why Fergus has to put you in the hands of such a one—"

"Fergus did the best he could. He has plenty on his mind right now without worrying about us."

"Indeed. As if I didn't know it. Why then must you be a further trial to him? To rescue you from this sport, he would only incur the queen's greater irritation."

"I wasn't asking . . . expecting. . . ."

"And if he failed to keep you from this folly," Fedelm continued, "he would blame himself for what befell you. Either way is bad for him. You are careless, thoughtless, and burdensome. I have half a mind to end your visit at once."

Claudia tried to speak, but Fedelm cut her off. "Oh, I know that Cathbad sees a part for you somehow, even if he can't lend me the sight of it. You are under his protection, but that doesn't mean that you are the only one to keep track of. If I have to come to your aid again, it will be over for you, I promise you. And," she added, "that goes for your brother groundling too. They will not suffer those images he draws. They know that spirits lurk in the shadow-pictures. One more of those drawings. . . ." She let the unfinished threat hang on the air.

"But I thought I . . . we couldn't go home yet," Claudia stammered. "Do you mean you could put me back any time?"

"Not all the way," Fedelm admitted. "But I can send you into the ground until the season splits the year apart to let you all the way through."

"But we can't go until we see what happens to Fergus. I mean, to the sword."

"Can you not?" snapped Fedelm, shaking her gown free from the heap of Medb's cloak. "Just stick to your washing and serving and obey Fergus, and stray not from your appointed place." She kicked at the blue fabric. "Wash it well. It smells."

"Also," Claudia ventured, "there's the crow. We haven't found him yet. We mustn't go back without the crow."

Fedelm shrugged. "It can only bring you trouble. Keep clear of it."

"But it isn't ours," Claudia tried to explain.

Fedelm laughed. "A good thing too. Else even I might shun you groundlings. Badb is everywhere, dropping from the sky most every day."

"But that's not our crow. Ours eats out of our hand and—"

"What difference? They do share their carrion, the

men of Erenn and the hooded crow of battle. The one
draws blood, the other lives upon it. Avoid the crow. Put
off the queen's array. Learn to stand aloof, as I do."

"But I can't," Claudia objected. "I get involved. I'm
not like you. I want to see everything and be there
and—"

Fedelm lifted the diadem. "You could not see this
while you wore it. Stand back. Watch, but let not others
see you."

"I'm not invisible," Claudia grumbled.

"There are ways of seeing without being seen."

Claudia sulked. "Loche won't understand. She'll be
angry. She hits me, you know, when she's angry."

"Loche flouts all the rules of her people when she puts
on her queen's attire. She will be caught."

"By the queen?" Claudia's eyes widened. "Can you
look in your fringe and tell me exactly?"

Fedelm trilled, "I see red. I see crimson."

Claudia reached out to grasp her sleeve. "Please, can
you tell me—"

Fedelm laughed lightly. "I tell you, but you hear not. I
show you, but you are sightless. Surely you are a joke that
Cathbad plays on me to set off the gloom of my crimson
vision. You are like a moth blown from across the western
sea; you come fluttering to earth at my feet; I pick you
up and set you flying into the alien air, and so must I
keep watch over you till the year is out and your wings
shred and drop and you are no more." She smiled
bleakly. "Why could he not have sent me a pretty one
with all the pinks and lavenders of spring-topped hills? A
poor joke, I say. But then, Cathbad is getting on, and
maybe his powers are waning."

149

Voices came to them just then, and the instant Claudia turned to greet Loche and explain why she had removed the queen's garments, Fedelm slipped softly behind the stand of agrimony which once more edged the track. Claudia peered between the stalks; she passed her hand through them so that the brittle husks fell to the ground. There was no sign of Fedelm within or around the dead weed.

Loche was more than disappointed when she saw Claudia in her coarse tunic. First she dealt Claudia a stinging blow; then she snatched the diadem and started prancing off toward the river, the others carrying their shrieks and raucous laughter after her.

Claudia, stunned for a moment, shouted, "Don't. It's dangerous." She caught up with them and passed Loche, turning to face her. "Don't wear it any more, Loche. You'll be caught. I know."

But Loche pushed by her. "Back to the camp, girl, or you'll have to crawl back. I mean it. And if you tell any of the queen's special women—"

"I won't. I promise." Claudia tried to make her stop, but this time Loche called on the others to get rid of her, and in another moment Claudia lay winded on the track.

She returned to the camp in a daze and was soon set to work grinding nuts. The tedious, rhythmic task was a relief after the hilarity of Loche, the strain of her meeting with Fedelm, and the brooding sense of foreboding that had followed. Besides, she felt somewhat battered and bruised.

The stone she worked with was smooth and just the right size for her hands. She would lose herself in the

150

comfort of this rolling, pressing motion that produced the fine aromatic powder that began to peak like a sand castle in the wooden trough beside her.

She paid no attention to the clamor of the women returning with their wash until a flash of something golden caught the sun, mirroring its blinding brightness for a minute, making her avert her head. One who had walked with Loche held out a shard of metal before Claudia. "Look, girl."

Not till then did Claudia glance up. The woman was holding a part of what had been Medb's diadem.

Astonished, Claudia could only wait for the woman to go on.

"A single cast," the woman intoned with deadly fury. "Split the diadem in three parts. The head of Loche as well."

Claudia gasped.

The woman stepped nearer. "You knew." The others closed in around Claudia. "What are you, girl? It is said you came at Samain last. Out of the darkness between the dead season and the season reborn—"

"It was daytime," Claudia stammered. "Not darkness. Afternoon."

"That is when you came to us at the rath. But we know that you issued from the Cave of Cruachan, and it was the Feast of Samain, for Medb had gone to her druid as she does every year for auguries and sureties. The boy makes shadow scenes, and you, girl, you have the sight and are not one of us and with Loche you knew—"

"What did she know? What are you doing with my—" Medb's voice broke off. She strode through the little band

151

of glowering women, took in Claudia at a glance, dismissed her as trivial, and reached for the broken diadem. "Explain," she commanded.

A babble arose from the throng, each woman trying to speak her own tale of horror observed first hand. The account came through in fragments like the broken diadem itself.

Medb was cold with rage, angry at the foolish women who could not resist showing themselves to the monster at the ford. Of Loche she merely said, "It was what she deserved for taking that which was mine," and when the women renewed their outcry against Claudia, Medb silenced them. "Have you not wasted enough time on wanton pranks? This bondsmaid wields no special powers. If I must have my forces reduced by the prowess of one Ulidian champion, I will have no more spoilage of my personal possessions." She indicated the diadem and Claudia in the same gesture.

"This one belongs to Fergus," said the spokeswoman in an insinuating tone.

Medb hesitated, then snapped, "No matter. What is Fergus's is mine. I'll have an end to waste within the household. Let no one stand idle. You have your work. And," she muttered, "I am less one worker now." As the women dispersed, Medb nudged Claudia with her knee. "Where is your master, girl?"

Claudia swallowed hard. "I have been grinding the nuts—" she began, stalling.

"Find him, then. Bring him at once. I have kept to my tent too long, I see. I will have a look at this Ulidian marvel myself."

"But he has sworn to kill you," Claudia blurted.

"And has done so, he thinks, though it was my hand-maiden whose head he split. Bring Fergus. We will get away for a while. To the river ford."

"Are you going to the river, my dear?" asked Ailill, coming up to her. "To watch the combat? Surely you would not try the waters; they are freezing with the runoff from the melted snow, and this day will end chill when the sun goes to earth."

"Your concern is all very well, Ailill, but spare me your suspicion." She wheeled about. "I seek Fergus's protection. That is all." She was off to her tent, the golden shard still in her hand.

FIFTEEN

CLAUDIA came upon Fergus seated on a heap of skins burnishing his scabbard. For a minute or two she stood quietly watching as the huge hand wrapped in kidskin coursed over the beautiful tracery. He was not looking at his work; his eyes held distance, depth, solitude.

"May I touch it?" she asked finally, her voice so low she was surprised to see that he heard. She pointed to the heart-shaped serpent head at the tip.

"Is it the chape that attracts you?" He held the tip toward her.

"Is the man who made this . . . is Culann the smith someone . . . special?"

"All smiths are special. They have a gift of making that is godlike."

She stroked the heavy chape. "I suppose it's stuck on to make the thin sides strong at the bottom, where the blade sits."

He nodded. "That is its purpose."

"Only it becomes part of the whole design. And all the circles, they . . . balance, only. . . ." She faltered, gazing at the leaf pattern twining with adornments that were extensions, like curling tendrils. "Still they're not symmetrical. They don't really match."

"Symmetry is an idea, like valor, like fair play, a perfection that has no living pattern. Though," he added thoughtfully, "some may come close. As this scabbard does."

Suddenly she remembered one of the questions she had meant to ask him. "What is a geise? Why must you obey it?"

"Have you not laws to guide folk where you come from?"

"Oh, yes, there are lots of laws." She thought. "Thousands. Probably millions."

He smiled, returned the scabbard to his knee, and resumed the rubbing. "It must take a long time to learn them all."

Claudia couldn't think how to explain about those laws. She said, "They keep changing."

Fergus puzzled over this. "Are there no rules of conduct that are constant?"

"In a way. They're called . . . ," she tried to think, ". . . principles." She tried again. "It's what they call moral laws which all the thousands of laws come from, like, 'Thou shalt not kill.' "

"Is that a law for everyone?"

She nodded.

"I should like to dwell in such a place. It sounds not unlike our Otherworld."

Claudia saw her error. "Only," she hastened to add, "it isn't the way things work out. I mean . . . ." She was floundering.

Fergus looked at her searchingly. "They kill? They break the law?"

"It's like . . . ." She tried again. "It's an idea," she finished lamely.

155

"Like symmetry," he supplied gently.

Helplessly she nodded again. Then she remembered about the geise. Again she questioned him.

"It's the opposite of your moral principle for everyone, which is only, after all, an idea," Fergus told her. "It is a special rule for each person, and it is as real as a man's taste, his sight, his hearing, his sense of touch. When a druid sets a geise, he is declaring the highest truth. Some geises are revealed at birth; others are attached to a person through events or acts. When my fosterling killed the hound of Culann, Cathbad set on him not just a name, but a geise that he should never eat the flesh of dog. A man who is trapped into breaking one of his geises will die, but death is nothing compared with that breaking. It is like dividing a man from himself. No worse thing can happen."

Claudia considered this. She might have said that there was a similar force in her own world called conscience, but Fergus had spoken of the geise as a palpable reality, and she didn't know how to reconcile what he had defined with whatever she had picked up about conscience from family and friends, school and reading, even TV and the movies. "And yours?" she asked.

"You have heard me tell of it."

She recalled that first meeting when Ailill had justified taking the sword because of Fergus's attentions to the queen. "Never to refuse an invitation to share another's hospitality," she murmured.

Fergus smiled wryly. "And much trouble has it led to."

"Yes," she agreed, thinking now of his betrayal and banishment from Ulidia, then once more of Medb's advantage over him. "The queen," she cried. "I forgot I was sent to bring you to her." She finished telling him about Loche and the queen while he attached the scabbard and sheathed the wooden sword. She was humiliated for him that he must put so crude and mocking a thing into his beautiful scabbard.

Later, trudging behind the men and women accompanying the queen, she suddenly found herself wondering whether Fergus had some presentiment about his sword, whether that was why he had worked on the scabbard.

As they approached the rocky mound behind which she and Evan had hidden, all the warriors surrounded Medb with their shields so that she would be sheltered from the cast of a slingstone. Fergus stood to one side.

Medb's voice issued from within the shelter. "What are you doing in here? You're crowding me. There is breathing space for only one."

"But my dear," came the plaintive reply, "the threat was made against me as well. In fact," wailed the voice, "I'm in even graver danger, since he thinks he has killed you already."

"Out. This is my excursion. Besides, he has been informed by now of his mistake. He will be all the more eager to strike me down for having been tricked by that foolish maiden."

"Poor thing," murmured Ailill's voice.

"Fool," responded Medb. "Now will you remove yourself from my shelter of shields? You can stand behind the whole of it. There. The terrible Hound will not see you if you stay low."

Ailill crept out, found himself on the river side, and hastened to remove himself from the sight of the warrior across the river.

Medb parted two of the shields just enough to see. She drew in her breath. "Is that the famous Hound of whom you speak, Fergus?" Her voice was thick with derision. "He is no more than a boy."

Fergus answered mildly, "He fears no one, nothing."

"Tell him we march tomorrow while the fighting goes on. He will be left behind, worried to death like a fox run to ground."

"Speak to him yourself, lady. I believe," Fergus added with a touch of irony, "he will hear you."

"Hound," roared the queen, "even now you will be challenged, for we are after the great bull of your herd and cannot spend another day in idleness."

"As long as I live," came the answer, "I shall not yield to you."

"You may boast after slaughtering so many, but now I am abroad again and will go forward to our errand." Her voice dropping, she demanded that one of the shield-bearers go to the place of combat at the ford. They must not delay another second.

"But my dear," Ailill protested, "we are not ready to march. The camp is not broken. No preparations—"

"Follow me who will be in the vanguard of this hosting," cried the queen. "Ailill may return to pack our things and see to the provisions. Who is with me?"

Several voices, more chiming in, joined to announce their support.

"Which will to the ford?"

No one spoke.

"You." She pushed out blindly, and one of the shield-bearers standing guard on the farther side was shoved back. "You will give him battle while we make our way at the river bend. Send the chariots back to the place where the washing was done, for stones abound in the shallows, and we can cross this day while our good and loyal warrior wages his combat."

The good and loyal warrior was complaining that he had left his best sword at camp. Three other shield-bearers instantly offered him theirs. The Hound, overhearing the problem through all the tumult, offered to meet the warrior with fresh-cut staves instead. Meanwhile the queen bade her champion fair fortune and withdrew under her shelter, leaping to her chariot as soon as she was out of casting range.

Claudia never got to see the combat. Nor did she wish to. It was enough to keep up with the chariots making for the river bend, knowing that at least she would not be separated from Evan.

Medb's chariot went first. When the horses reared back at the river's edge, she took the goad from her driver and forced them to go splashing in. Fergus caught Claudia up before descending to the bank. She clung, half to Evan, half to the side of the chariot, and only the steep pitch downward kept her from losing her grip and being flung from the vehicle.

The river was far deeper than Medb had supposed. As they struggled to cross, the waters, swollen by the sudden melting of the snow, seemed to rise swiftly. On reaching the opposite shore, the ponies were so exhausted that Fergus and his charioteer and the children had to leap from the chariot and lead them up to the higher land. Others who followed did the same. Only Medb, standing with flailing goad, beat her ponies into a plunging gallop that strained every muscle and brought foam to their flanks and blood to their mouths.

Not until they had cleared the lowland and could rest did Claudia and the others turn to look back at the river. Chariots, warriors, men and women, ponies still yoked to floating debris, all were being swept away by the surging flood.

There were screams from animals and humans alike as fresh torrents coursed along the river bed. The water was rising and seizing even some of those who had managed to reach the farther bank. In a matter of seconds each victim was sucked under the swirling water or carried out of sight round the bend.

"How many will perish?" asked Medb, grim-voiced, for once subdued.

Fergus stood with his arms around the shivering children, for at a moment like this no one would notice or care. Claudia clung to him, her whole body shaking, her eyes pressed into his dripping cloak. Fergus shook his head. He could not tell. Some had not yet entered the river and were safe on the other side.

"We are too small a hosting," Medb considered. "Let one of the men test the river farther upstream so that the others may join us." She looked about and made her choice. The valiant warrior went off at once, still breathless, struggling to find a footing along the crumbling bank. Moments later the river returned him to his queen, then carried him away beyond her to the ford.

"What of the Hound then?" she wanted to know. And when Fergus remained silent, she burst out, "Blame me not for that one's death. It is the hosting you must think of, not of the man. Fergus, you are too soft."

"And where," asked Fergus, "will you find men to follow you if you dispose of them with such recklessness?"

She eyed him steadily. "Are you saying that I may not count on you?"

He returned her gaze. "I am dependable, as you know. But . . . ." He clapped his hand to the wooden hilt, and her eyes followed the gesture. There was a brief silence between them.

"You will guide us as before," she told him finally.

"The Hound?"

"We will not wait to know the end of that combat. They may both have been swept away."

Fergus inclined his head, but said nothing.

"Oh," she roared, "I despise your lack of words. Your silence is more boastful than all the taunts I have ever heard."

"I serve you, Medb, and will do so now. But if I must sing praises to the truest warrior, I will chant my lay for the little Hound before whom even this river did swell in wonder and support."

"So you don't think he has been drowned," she responded, her voice lower and nearly under control.

Fergus said, "He will be turning his back on all this wreckage before we have gathered our meager forces."

"Underway already?" she gasped.

"At play, I imagine." Fergus looked at the reddening sun. "I suppose not at the game of wooden wisdom. Probably something active for the warming of his blood. You would find him with his hurley stick, he and his charioteer. Unless, of course, you choose to send him another warrior before the sun is down."

161

Medb smiled. "Fergus, you better me at words when you do speak. I wonder why I mind your silence. Well," she added, giving his face an intimate pat before turning away to issue more orders, "I should be thankful it is only a black-haired Hound for whom you would chant your lay. There should be room between us for such a one. And when he is vanquished . . . ." She left the sentence hanging.

Fergus stood holding the children until their shivering subsided. Cold dusk lay over them like a sodden coverlet. But Fergus was there with his body warm beneath his dripping cloak, his arms full and hard against them. All the time he stood there listening to Medb shouting orders across the river and receiving answers and shouting yet again, he spoke not a word.

SIXTEEN

THEY marched in fits and starts, again and again halted by the prowess of the Hound of Culann. Sometimes the children would catch a glimpse of him. He was always just ahead, always ready to meet the next warrior in single combat.

Some days were hard, one night deep in snow drifts on a mountain pass, several straight days of rain after that. Sometimes they were without shelter, without food.

It was a long time before all of the warriors rejoined Medb's little vanguard. But on they pressed, spurred by the raging queen, herself driven by the knowledge of her dwindling heroes, as one by one they fell to the dark defender of Ulidia.

She laid waste the land she drove through, cutting a swath of death and destruction, sparing none. Daily the children heard cries, animal and human, as a handful of Connaucht warriors overran a Ulidian farmstead or stronghold. Boys were killed; women and girls were driven back to Cruachu along with the sheep and cattle that were not slaughtered on the spot. And always the dwellings were left in ruin or burned to the ground.

"Why all this for a cow?" wondered Evan as he pulled off soaking leather boots and tucked his wrinkled feet under him. It was his turn to ride in the chariot.

Fergus, at the side of the chariot, heard him. "A bull it is, not a cow. And no ordinary bull is Donn Cuailgne. He is endowed with human reason and divine strength."

"Still," Claudia joined in, "all these people dying, just to take him."

"He stands for all our ancestors," Fergus told her, then corrected himself, "I mean, Ulidian. He is the protector of the herd, of the land, of the yet unborn. For Medb to subdue Donn Cuailgne would be to destroy the power of the Ulaid."

Claudia wondered whether they would ever see the remarkable beast they sought. She was beginning to feel that it too was an idea, like symmetry, a kind of perfection that may be spoken of but never perceived.

As they came out of the mountains they encountered less snow and more wild animals. Red deer were hunted, some of them does heavy with fawn. This killing sickened Claudia, but when the pit was dug, she herself called upon to scoop the clay for it, she would eventually find herself drawn to the cooking place.

Evan never minded this part. He even carried the stones past the carcass during the skinning, when steam rose from the still-warm flesh. Claudia would wait until the first layer of clay was spread, then make up for her squeamishness by gathering twice her share of the wood to be strewn evenly over the clay. After that, as layer of clay followed wood and wood followed clay, she would overcome her revulsion. By the time the fire was lit and the roasting underway, she would crouch at the edge of the pit whenever there was room for her, breathing in the smell of the meat that escaped through the air vents in the final covering of clay.

164

After weeks of struggle through a deep, sunless forest, Medb's armies finally met on a grassy plain. There winds blew almost constantly, but the weather, though wet, grew milder. The days of interminable drizzle reminded Claudia of a Fundy fog. Then drenching storms came, but the tents held and the cows gave milk and the provisions of corn and barley and mead and ale caught up with them at last. There was even talk about the Feast of Beltane being near at hand. Soon the fires would be lit to celebrate the return of the sun.

Everyone felt relief but Medb, who brooded over her losses. She sent a messenger to the nearest river to assess the condition of the invincible Hound. When the messenger returned, Claudia, bringing the board of steaming bread, waited to hear his report.

The queen broke off a piece of the loaf, stared at it as if surprised to see it in her hand, and then gobbled all of it hungrily, forgetting to pass on what remained. There was a passion to her devouring which spoke more of preoccupation than greed. Never had she appeared more beautiful, her pale skin taut and glowing, her hair, finally tended by handmaidens again, plaited into thick copper coils that gleamed with a metallic shine.

"Does he play?" she demanded. "At what was he occupied?"

"The charioteer was dressing his wounds. They talked of seeking help. He will send the charioteer to bring the Ulidians to defend their cattle. He rested then."

"No wooden wisdom? No hurley? He must be weakening. Now will we find a mighty adversary for tomorrow."

Ailill looked as if he would prefer to be elsewhere.

"Who is left?" she asked him.

165

"Our champions are slain."

She turned on him, swinging her hand so that the mead in the cup she held sloshed out, spattering them both. "Clumsy," she hissed. "See what you've done. Move back. Make room. How can a person make plans without space for thinking?"

In the silence that ensued, Claudia became aware of the growing tension.

Then Medb spoke. "All the most valorous of our household gone. And you who remain are cowards. Go then in numbers. I will have that dog's head for a trophy. Before Beltane. Then we will take the bull."

Her followers were speechless. It was Ailill who managed to utter the words, "Fair play. You are bound to the single combat."

"And who shall keep me to that pledge?" she demanded, rising slowly, upsetting a bowl of nuts which scattered everywhere, at the feet of men and bondsmaids, some rolling all the way to the fire.

Fergus stood up, faced her, a look of deep weariness on his face, and something else, resignation perhaps. "I am the guarantor of that pledge, yours and the Hound's."

"No one will go to the ford for me. Numbers remain, but they are lesser men. They are not of your worthiness, Fergus. And so I must let them approach as an army. Unless," she added, smiling coldly, "you would stand and do battle on my behalf."

A nut popped and went up in tiny flames, scorching the hem of her gown. She did not move. Her smile was fixed.

Claudia watched with fascination as the brown edge crept along the golden border of her gown. A thin, rank smoke issued from the smoldering wool. Fergus stepped briskly past Ailill and took the cup from Medb's hand. He tipped it, so that the remaining mead doused the scorched and burning cloth, and gave it back into her hand again. Then he strode from the tent.

Claudia ran after him. "Am I to take out the bead? Do you want your men?"

"Only my charioteer." Fergus did not slow his pace, so she had to keep on running. "The bead must still be hidden, for the need will be greater after tomorrow."

There was talk of spring in the air. Claudia wandered from fire to fire to hear the gossip, and it was all of Fergus and how he would meet the Hound at the ford, how the queen had forced him, how he had yielded and yielded not. Some said he would slay the terrible Ulidian; others declared that Fergus lived his last night. At one fire Claudia became aware of a searching look and recognized one of the Ulidian exiles. She shook her head at him and moved away.

But she would not go to the place where the bondsmaids slept. She had to keep an eye on Fergus, who sat with his charioteer, sometimes in conversation, sometimes in deep repose.

Much later she saw Medb slip from her tent and make her way to Fergus. Claudia, afraid to come close, hoped that Evan was awake and listening. But she watched in the dim pre-dawn light. She saw Medb stop beside Fergus. The queen stretched out her arms, enclosing his head, and tried to draw him to her.

Fergus got to his feet, not exactly shaking her off, but simply disencumbering himself of her. His speech was directed toward his charioteer, who sprang up from dozing

167

and proceeded to draw off Fergus's cloak and dress him in strange garments, winding him in thongs and covering him with a tunic that seemed to be stiffened with some kind of coating. Medb stood back, watching in silence, but Fergus attended to his battle dress. He spoke only of his ox-hide girdle, his ponies' chestplates, his covering tunic that was as silky and pliable as the one beneath it was rigid and hard. Before sunrise he was fully attired, fastening his gleaming scabbard and loosening the wooden sword.

But Medb did not see this gesture. She was already stepping from one cover to the next, and as the first in the camp began to stir, she reached her tent unobserved by any save Claudia.

Fergus seemed not to notice the children. They simply stood by while he and Boardface mounted the chariot; then they hitched on behind.

They held on with all their might as the light chariot sped through the dawn mists that rose from the rain-drenched sod. They came to a depression where the wheels began to sink and skid, but then they gained the elevation of a causeway formed of planks set on a bedding of brush. It seemed that the causeway itself must sink into the bog that stretched away on either side of them. But on the ponies went, and the chariot followed with a muffled, ghostly clattering.

Claudia stared wide-eyed, fascinated and repelled by the immense flatness that was neither earth nor water, but something between the two. Glistening wetly, quivering with a life of its own, the bog seemed to her like something poisonous and thick bubbling in a giant cauldron. Vapors like steam issued from it, smelling of things long dead or, worse still, of the dying.

When finally they left the bog behind, the air cleared. They saw that the sun had already risen. The charioteer slowed the ponies to pass through a wooded glen that glistened with bracken and silver lichens. And then they heard the river.

The charioteer, at a gesture from Fergus, stayed back. There were trees to keep the children out of sight. They lay on their stomachs, hugging the mossy turf, inching forward until they could hear the clink of shield and scabbard from across the river.

From where they lay they could see the Hound. They could make out some of the wounds he bore, a stiffness in his limbs beneath his jaunty stance. Without his charioteer, he had to attend to his battle dress alone. When he heard a warrior approaching, he finished fastening his tunic and turned to the ford.

The new challenger had entered the water first, a fact that brought a scowl of displeasure to the face of the dark youth. He plunged in, then saw who it was and came to a standstill. The spring-swollen waters swirled between him and Fergus as they stood facing one another, each with level eye and with a stillness of countenance that was like a final summing up.

The Hound was the first to speak. "Welcome . . . Master. . . ."

"I trust that welcome."

"You may—" The Hound broke off, then burst out, "But you come as a warrior to the ford." He hesitated in confusion, taking in the battle attire, the time, the occasion. His tone grew bitter. He gestured toward the wooden sword. "My master Fergus must bear some hidden strength to approach this ford of combat with that."

"Nothing hidden," came the soft-toned answer.

"But your scabbard . . . I cannot . . . . It is as good as empty."

"It matters not, my fosterling," said Fergus in his quiet way. "Even if that sword of Culann were in it, I would not draw it against you." He smiled. "Besides, I doubt that sword would smite you."

"Then what . . . ?"

"Yield to me, little Hound."

There was a choked exclamation. "I have stood till this day."

"Yield. For the sake of all the care and honor I have given you, for the fosterage that let me call you son, yield before me now. And I will yield to you in my turn."

"When will that be?" the Hound demanded hoarsely.

"When you are covered with wounds. When still more blood is shed. When all the forces of Ulidia oppose Medb, then I will flee from you and all her armies will follow. That is my promise."

The Hound stepped up to Fergus. He said something the children could not hear and his hand rested briefly on the taller man's shoulder. Fergus's hand covered the slim, dark-skinned hand, then drew it off with great gentleness, and the Hound of Culann tore himself away and fled across the river, disappearing into a wood on the opposite side.

Fergus waded out; he took his time returning to the chariot. By then followers from the camp were arriving, eager to watch the combat. They gazed in amazement at

the unscathed hero, marveled at the routing of the Ulidian warrior. There were shouts of praise, and then more
people from the encampment appeared and had to have
this marvel recounted.

Fergus stood tall and quiet against the assault of their
adulation.

Only Medb, who appeared suddenly, looking drawn
and harried, reviled him with a heat that astounded everyone. "Pursue him," she rasped. Had she not been
shouting from her chariot, she might have flung herself
against Fergus or torn at him with her fingers. "He has
fled from you. Pursue him, Fergus."

But Fergus firmly declined. "I have done what no man
of yours could accomplish. I will do no more until all who
remain in your camp, singly according to the terms that
bind you, take their stand against the boy."

Evan clapped his hands together; Claudia had to
pounce on him to keep them from being discovered. But
she was elated too, and ran to Fergus when it was time to
return, her face uplifted to him as if he were the sun itself.

She could hardly believe he had spoken when she
heard him say, his voice so low that it barely carried,
"Tonight. Take out the bead. It is time."

SEVENTEEN

It was Medb's brooding anger that transformed the mood of the camp. The softening air had brought a dreaminess, even indolence, to the hard-pressed warriors and their followers. They wanted to enjoy the easy victory that Fergus had brought them this day; they wanted to spread out in the sun and laugh at nothing and watch the lambs on the hillside springing joyously on stiltlike legs.

Claudia went with a group to gather the early asphodel that bloomed patchily yellow in the mirror of the bog. Then word came that they were to break camp and push on. The shimmering blossoms were left strewn along the causeway, sun-splinters dropped as women and girls hurried back, anxious to collect their belongings, fearful of being left behind.

Many chariots had left by the time Claudia had returned. She was swept up in the scurrying, in rising tempers, in the resentments of all those who preferred the gathering of dye plants to the gathering of armies.

This time Claudia was with the rear guard. She saw the last of the tents brought down, the vessels of barley loaded, the skins rolled on poles for dragging. The refuse was neither burned nor buried, and birds were circling, hawks and crows together, even some gulls blown in from the sea. The sun-filled sky became crowded with shadows and beating wings, the gentle air harsh with the rapacious cries of scavengers and the high-pitched whistling of winged hunters.

It was only by chance that Claudia, looking up from fastening bundles with rawhide ropes, saw the crow that hovered close by without lighting anywhere. She had to squint against the brightness, then against the recognition. The voice of Fedelm was in her ear telling her to turn away, but the voice of her family and teachers spoke to her of responsibility. They told her to always put back what she had borrowed, to look after those who could not look after themselves, and to be kind to animals. And there was the crow, stranded, uncertain, as alien as she to this world. It was up to her to rescue it.

She wondered whether she was just imagining the glint of recognition in its beady eye. Perhaps it hovered near her because it expected some morsel to be left in her wake. Maybe it was merely clever, not beseeching.

All at once she knew how to test it. She would not have to risk whatever it was that Fedelm threatened, at least not without first making certain this was really their crow. Kneeling on the bundled roll, she called the crow in Evan's manner. "Son of a bitch," she crooned up at it.

It dropped to her like a stone. "Son of a bitch," she repeated with a grin, the utterance coming easily this time. She put out her hand, and the crow stepped on it and waddled sideways up her arm, coming to rest on her shoulder where it pecked at something in her hair and hunched down to make itself comfortable.

Only then, as she returned to her task, did she become

aware of her audience. It was not like that other time after Loche had been killed. The women who surveyed her kept their distance, ringing her but standing several paces back. Their eyes reflected a kind of horror she had never seen before.

She tried to speak to one, but that one turned quickly, averting her eyes. She addressed another, and this one too looked away. She said helplessly, "This is only a pet bird," and then, "He is my friend." She reached up and took the crow on her hand to show them it was a mere bird, and a rather scraggly one at that. But when she stroked it, their only response was to back away. Several of them ran from her.

After that she was at a loss. She had no idea how to get rid of the crow even if she wanted to. Once they were underway, she found herself following the women at some distance. If she increased her pace, they moved on faster still. And when, confused and breathless, they all finally arrived at the next encampment, Claudia was denied admittance to the cooking place, to the queen's tent; in fact she seemed to be regarded by all as a total outcast.

The transformation was so complete and so rapid that she went about in a daze, astonished at the way men and women stumbled to avoid her, dashed from her path, covered their eyes when she looked at them. Meanwhile the crow had flapped off to pick up a meal. Once it returned to check on her, and then disappeared again for a while. Its coming caused cries of alarm, fingers pointed, and some of the boys were yanked from its shadow.

It seemed as if the sun would never sink behind the lumpy hills. But finally the shadows grew long enough to hide in, the crow settled down to roost on a nearby shaft

174

of stone, and Claudia was able to creep over to Evan and squirm under the chariot pole. Though it was not cold, she was shivering. She had eaten nothing, but was too tense to feel empty.

"They say you're the child of the war goddess, Badb."

"It's the crow. I found it. I mean, it found me."

"Also," Evan continued, "that it has come as a crow but is really the Hound of Culann."

"Oh, for God's sake. Can't you tell them? Straighten them out?"

"Me?"

"Well, someone. Fergus." Suddenly she remembered that tonight she must take out the bead and wear it on her braid. And walk boldly from fire to fire, so that all who were supposed to know would see, would come to Fergus. She had to clamp her mouth shut to keep her teeth from chattering.

"Fergus told Boardface he felt ready to use his sword. Claude, I can't tell whether he's very angry or very sad." He paused. "Why do they think that old crow is the Hound? Because of his black feathers?"

"I don't know." But even as she said this, she did know. "I swore at it. Called it a son of a bitch."

Evan giggled. "Anyone could tell you were swearing."

"They don't have the same swears. And their swears always . . . mean something. And my tone . . . I sounded, you know, as if I was luring it. Oh," she moaned, "I've loused everything up." She pressed down into the turf and felt the bead against her like a pebble, hard, a stab of reality.

"Why don't you just act like normal, and maybe they'll forget."

175

It was an encouraging idea. Everyone was still so busy settling in that maybe she could just slip back into acceptance by going about her tasks and minding her own business.

Two major projects were going on, one the gathering of brush and cutting of peats, the other the construction of a mound out of turfs cut in an enormous circle on the crown of the hill. If she could lose herself in all this activity, maybe by the time the warriors settled down before their fires she might be able to pass without causing a commotion.

She crawled out from under the chariot and moved off in the direction from which the brush haulers appeared. But as soon as they saw her they dropped their bundles of dried gorse and bramble, turned, circling to the right, and fled.

Picking up their scattered brush and carrying it for them, she was able to proceed all the way to the heap on which the brush was being deposited. There she was noticed again, only this time the reaction was different. They let her place the dried stuff on the pile, all of them standing as if at attention. It was like taking part in a ritual known to all but herself.

Something more seemed to be expected of her, but she could not guess what it was. Probably the best move would be to return for more brush. But when she started out, the men and women closed ranks, forming a ring that was open only in the direction of the enormous brush heap. Yet none would set eyes on her.

She had no idea how to break the impasse, and then it was broken for her by an old woman, not huge and generous of proportion like the Great Mother, but wizened and small, with eyes that glittered without expression.

The woman carried food in a bowl and held it out toward the pile of brush. Then she was prodded a bit, until she swiveled and the bowl was extended toward Claudia. Suddenly Claudia was hungry. It was the aroma of crushed grains, dusty, perhaps even a bit moldy, but with a rich, nutlike flavor that went straight to her empty stomach.

She took the bowl, and though no eye seemed to fall on her, a sigh escaped from the throng as she dipped her fingers into the cereal and began to eat. Maybe it was a peace offering. At any event, she had accepted this gift, and surely that would mean improved relations.

Only she was not allowed to work. Apparently her new status was one of honor. They made it clear that she was to follow the old crone, and she was led to an area already cleared and laid with skins. There she was made to sit while vessels of mead were carried to her. She felt obliged to drink, though the liquid, falsely sweet, burned all the way down. After the mead, ale and more grains were brought.

Still no one spoke to her, no one looked upon her but the little old woman through whose hands each bowl or cup was passed. Then she realized that the woman was blind, which must have been why she was allowed to deal with Claudia directly. Once she understood this, Claudia decided to bide her time. If she seemed reconciled to being a well-fed prisoner, then after a while she would be able to elude her sightless guard.

Meanwhile the mound-building continued in the dusk, and a second pile of brush was begun, a miniature mountain of tangled hair against the pale gray sky. The brush piles puzzled Claudia more than the mound, which might simply be raised at Medb's command in anticipation of imminent victory. But when even after sundown the atmosphere remained gently warm, it was hard to imagine a purpose for such huge fires.

It was easier than she had supposed to slink away. No one dared to look at her on her bed of skins, and so no one noticed when the bed was empty. The old woman nodded in the gray light.

Claudia had managed to spill a good amount of mead and almost all of the ale, but even so she was dizzy and clumsy from what she'd drunk. She made her way slowly, stopping wherever she found darkness, until she was close enough to hear the sounds of revelry from the queen's tent. Perhaps Fergus was in there. She wished there were some way to signal him. But he was probably eating and drinking until it was time to meet the other exiles, and trusting her to see that they appeared on schedule. Even as she decided this, she saw him draw back the tent flap and step out into the night.

Was she late? She had no way of judging, except that until minutes ago the sky had contained enough light to indicate that it was still early for her to begin her errand, especially now when it would be so hard to go about unnoticed.

Fergus was looking toward her place of captivity.

"Here," she whispered, not daring to reveal herself, still crouching into the darkness.

He turned questioningly, then waited.

"Over here."

He was beside her, drawing her back with him so that before she knew it, they were with the feeding ponies, their whispers lost in the munching and blowing sounds of the weary beasts. The animal smells were reassuring to Claudia, who was beginning to feel sick.

"It is almost too late," Fergus murmured. "She has one young Ulidian inside and fills him with mead from her own cup. She would send him to the ford at sunrise so that his older brother will be forced to avenge his death. It is that older brother I would warn, for he is also foster-brother to the Hound. Still, you cannot begin before the other exiles are there to see you. For you will be taken."

Claudia tried to shake her head free of the sweet, dizzying confusion. "Taken where? Why? What are they doing to me?"

"The raid is almost finished. They took the bull in this morning's hosting, driving it west with the herd while we were yet at the ford. The Ulidians are rising from their long sleep and soon will meet us on the great plain ahead. If they rout Medb's warriors, they will pursue the bull."

"But what about me?" Claudia cried.

She felt him turn to regard her. "Why, it is almost over." He sounded surprised that she did not know this. "But before you go, you will alert my kinsmen here, especially the brother of the one who is feasted inside. That young one will be served with mead all this night so that he goes foolishly where he is bid. We must also get word to the Hound not to kill the young fool, to wound him just enough to send him back. Then the older brother will not be trapped into avenging that death and getting himself killed."

"But the Hound wouldn't kill his foster-brother, would he?"

179

"He would not want to, but he would consider it a weakness to flee again. The bards are singing satires to-night. To hone the pride of warriors. If that young fool is killed, either the older one will have to kill the Hound, with whom he has sworn the blood brotherhood, or be killed by him. And all the others, my fellow Ulidians, would follow."

"But we'll warn them." Claudia spoke with urgency to rouse Fergus from this note of defeat. "I'll get to every one of the exiles, so that they'll know in time to resist. I'll go as soon as you tell me." She began to braid her hair, dividing it unevenly, leaving out strands, but getting enough going for a proper braid. At the end she found herself unable to detach the bead and tie it in place. She felt Fergus's hand on her head, then meeting hers at the end of the braid. As soon as her hands were free, she reached for the bead.

"Will you wear the harp string still?"

"I'll always keep it."

"They will give it to the goddess when they put you in the bog."

"What?"

"When they return you to your mother goddess. Badb threatens their spring planting with her war furies. The queen thought the raid would be completed a long time ago. Well before the men of Ulidia awakened from their debility. But the Hound still holds her forces off, and the Ulidians are just now readying to battle. All Medb's people are far from the spring planting in Connaucht; they are still serving the war goddess, who is angry because her daughter is yet in bondage here."

Claudia, uneasy, almost irritated at having to

180

straighten out such a silly mistake, fingered the bead. "But I'm not her daughter. You know that."

Fergus was still holding the end of her braid for her. "I know not who you are. Only that you are no ordinary bondsmaid and are known to Cathbad. And come from the ground, to which you will be returned."

"But not that way," she burst out, then checked herself. She'd never convince him if she lost control of herself. "I mean," she explained a little shakily but without shouting, "I don't want to be put in the bog."

"I don't want you put there, or even led through the fires, till the message is delivered."

"Don't you care about me?" She was stung by his remoteness, his matter-of-fact tone.

He spoke quietly. "I am not afraid of you."

"That's not what I mean." She knew she was on the edge of panic. She had thought it would be a simple matter to set him straight. But he was out of reach, beyond her. "I'm just a child. A girl." Looking at his troubled eyes, she could tell that what he saw before him was not her at all, but blood and loss, his foster-son and kinsmen. "I come from another place and another time," she pleaded, "but I'm not anyone's daughter that matters. I mean, my mother is not a goddess. She doesn't even believe in war." She knew she was growing hysterical, but she was gripped with a terror that stemmed more from the way Fergus spoke and looked than from the danger he described. "Anyhow," she babbled, "what will happen to my brother?"

"I suppose he will return to the Otherworld too."

"But—" She stopped. She was beginning to realize that Fergus thought the sacrifice would enable her to return to the place from which she had come. Since she was from the mounds, she was simply to be dispatched in an appropriate manner. He thought she would not die, because she was timeless. Very slowly she tried to explain. "Fedelm said I can only go back at the end of the year, between the end of one and the beginning of the next."

He nodded. "That is why it will be done with the Beltane fires." Still with the end of her braid in one hand, Fergus took the bead with the other and held it up between them. "The seasons are continuous, like the surface of this bead. You cannot divide a circle with only one break." His finger traced a circle around the bead. "The year is like the circle my finger has drawn. If you break it on one side, it will not separate unless you break it on the other as well. Then it becomes two halves. Do you see?"

Claudia sighed. It was like the lecture on symmetry; only this time her life hung in the balance. She wanted to remind him, but knew it was pointless. He was dealing with what was fitting and with what was urgent to him. Those other lives mattered more than hers. And she would have to hear him out, because somewhere in his telling must be signs and meanings that might save her. If she reached him at all, it would be with her understanding.

"The year is split into two parts," he was telling her. She nodded soberly and waited. "You came at Samain, the end of the sun time and the beginning of the darkness when all the spirits and mound folk and the gods themselves may pass into our world—and we into theirs. Now we are at Beltane, which is sometimes also called Cetsamain, when the darkness and cold are finished and the

182

sun stands high and things that grow replenish themselves. We make our offerings of seed, of ewes and heifers fed the grain we harvested. When winter has been hard and the planting delayed, we sometimes offer other creatures, all with bellies full of what the earth yielded up the summer past. I think Medb hopes that your mother war goddess will share you with the gods of our grains and fruits, because from what I learned you are the only person to go with the animals. Usually there is someone set aside for the Feast of Beltane."

"It's called killing two birds with one stone," Claudia managed, and to her amazement knew that she was smiling.

"It is a good description."

The smile left her. "You said you weren't afraid of me, as if I had some special power. I don't. Not any." At last he was looking at her. She forced herself to slow down as she added, almost inaudibly, "And I'm afraid."

He frowned with puzzlement. "You don't want to go back?"

"If I'm killed, I'll never get back."

Fergus drew away from her. He seemed to be scrutinizing her. "I have wondered since the first how you could seem so like a mortal child and yet be not human. And of course why Fedelm put you two groundlings in my care. Somehow . . . ." He paused, thinking some more to himself.

She felt tears welling. It was as though he were returning to her after an interminable absence.

"Somehow I came to think of you as in my care only because you were for my . . . use." He smiled at her.

"Well, we have helped each other. And will do so one more time."

She felt giddy with relief. "Will you get Fedelm?"

"I can't summon her. No, I will have to rescue you when they are all turned to the fires." He pointed. "That way lies Cruachan, but it is a long distance, and we will not be able to undertake such a journey. Still, it is the direction that matters. Get the boy."

She started off, but he called her again. "I didn't think. Of course you cannot risk being seen." He pushed her back against the ponies and disappeared.

She waited anxiously, remembering what still lay ahead if she was to help Fergus keep the Hound from battle with his foster-brother and kinsmen. She used a loose thread from her tunic to attach the bead to her braid. Her fingers felt the hard edge of the diminutive spear that was lodged within it. Would she never learn of its magic and how it was used with the sword?

There was a soft snort of welcome from one of the ponies. Fergus and Evan appeared, Evan dwarfed by the bulk of the man beside him.

"I don't get it," Evan was already protesting. "Why do we have to go now, just before all the action begins?"

"Your sister is unwilling to be led between the fires and given to the bog."

"Evan, they're going to sacrifice me."

"You mean kill you?" Evan listened to their silence. "But they think you're really special, Claude. I've heard them talking. You're important to them. So you see, you're . . . you've just got to be wrong."

"Before they light the great fires in the circle, your sister will carry out her last task for me. If she is caught, then even Fedelm may not save her from the bog. And if she is caught, my kinsmen and my fosterling will be lost as well, and that is many more lives than hers."

Evan was impressed with the solemnity of his tone. "What can I do?"

"Follow her wherever she goes, and if anyone sounds an alarm, do what you can to distract the people around her."

"Not anyone who just sees me and gets up and quietly goes away," Claudia warned. "That will be one of the exiles."

"You mean only if they grab you." Evan seemed to relish saying this.

"No one will touch her. Not until after she has been led between the fires. But they would surround her."

"And then what?" Evan wanted to know.

"And then I will meet with my kinsmen, and one of them will go to warn the Hound of Culann of the trap that is being set. And we will work out a plan for delaying as best we can. Soon . . . soon the armies will come, the Ulaid."

"And we won't be here?" Evan exclaimed.

"Only if we fail. And then it will be you alone. Your sister will not be here." Fergus let that sink in a moment and felt for Claudia's braid. His fingers answered his question. All he said was, "Go now."

Evan hesitated. "I'll never see you with the sword?"

"You told me that you had seen . . . things before we met first at the Cave of Cruachan. Maybe you will see things that are later. I am not sure," Fergus added, "that

I hope that I will see you again, though I will miss you two groundlings with your curiosity and loyalty and faraway notions."

"Yes," Evan told him, "I saw you with that Hound on your shoulders."

Fergus had his half-smile. "I used to carry him like that when he was still a squirming pup. It helped to keep him from trouble." He roused himself from that memory. "You saw that?" He gazed thoughtfully at Evan. "It was many years back. Long before you could have been born."

Claudia wanted to say, But all of this is before we were born, but she couldn't figure out what that meant or what it might do to Fergus. Instead she said in a choked whisper, "I want to know how things turn out." She couldn't add, for you. All she could say was, "I want to know."

"You already know all you need to know."

She shook her head, but he would not let her interrupt. "Knowing what happens matters less than knowing what manner of folk you have dealt with. You know me, and I you, and no events can change that. If you fail or I fail tonight, it will not alter what you now know." He touched her braid lightly, then gave her a small shove. "On your way, daughter, or we will talk this night away, and with it many lives."

EIGHTEEN

THE night was charged with excitement. The whole camp thrummed with voices. Bondsmen and women had completed the tumulus at the summit and laid the enormous piles of brush, but only the flames from the many lesser fires sputtered and splashed the soot-dark air with bright, convulsive dabs of yellow and orange.

Claudia had made her first contact, had seen the eye meet hers in the flickering firelight, the dark shape of a man rising as if idly, ambling out of the shivering circle of light.

It was not easy to get herself noticed and yet go unrecognized. She found that once she had edged up to a group, the best approach was to turn so that the braid hanging down her back was prominent and lighted, her face in darkness.

Passing Medb's tent, she had to duck behind the squat water tub as a bondsmaid appeared carrying cakes for the king and queen and the hapless young man who was being coaxed with endearments and mead into stupefaction.

The queen herself sounded more than ordinarily exuberant. Perhaps it was the custom to drink a great deal of beer and ale at Beltane. "So will we bring this loitering to its conclusion," Medb was chortling.

There was the usual mumbled response, some underling vying for a favored position with his prompt agreement. Then Ailill's voice: "It will take the Ulaid some days to make ready for battle. We have succeeded in laying waste much of Ulidia. Besides taking the great bull, our armies have carried off womenfolk, horses, flocks, and herds; we have leveled their hills. Surely we might do well to let our people celebrate Beltane with resting as well as rejoicing."

An exclamation of disgust followed. "What, cease now when the Hound is exhausted? He will be brought to bay with his own pack. The scent is already laid. See?" Her laughter broke off, and Claudia imagined her gesturing toward the drunken young Ulidian. "Where is that druid?" Medb was snapping her fingers. "Find him."

A bondsmaid dashed from the tent in search of the druid, and Medb's voice resumed. "At Samain he said that I would return from this raid. The information was meager, though welcome, since it was about the one person whose survival most concerned me. So I will not berate him. Though, Ailill, when we have brought the captured bull all the way to Connaucht, then maybe we will be in a position to attract one of the younger, brighter druids."

"They say," ventured Ailill, "that in druidic circles, the older are the wiser. Cathbad—"

"Not that name," roared the queen. "I will not hear it."

The bondsmaid was returning at a run. Dashing into the tent, she declared breathlessly that the druid would attend the queen as soon as he had checked on the maid who was to be sacrificed, and was it true what they said about her being a shape-shifter, because there might be some problem if she was, and could Fergus vouch for her.

Claudia and Evan exchanged looks, then ran.

Evan stopped in his tracks. "Wait. This is crazy. Keep away from that druid."

"If I'm not there ahead of him," Claudia gasped, "I'm finished."

"Sounds to me like you're finished if you are there."

"No, Evan, really. He'll sound the alarm. Hurry." She started off again.

They reached the place just ahead of the white-clad figure whose form stood out in the firelight. A retinue of attendants followed him, keeping his progress slow with conversation.

"Stay near," Claudia whispered. "If I'm stuck here, you'll have to tell Fergus. There are still more men to be alerted."

But as she dropped to her hands and knees to crawl under cover of darkness to the pallet of skins, she was arrested by the sight of something there in her place. She let out a small gasp, and the something rearranged itself into the body of a maid draped in a rough cloak and hood but unmistakably bearing the features of Fedelm.

"Well, make haste," hissed the apparition. She beckoned Claudia. "The old man may recognize me." She tucked a fold of her speckled green gown under the cloak.

Claudia was too stunned to move. The low murmurs of the druid and his attendants could be heard approaching. The old woman, her face a mask of blindness, was apparently deaf as well, for she heard neither those voices nor Fedelm's ungentle urgings.

"Haste, groundling. Else we will both be found out.

Besides, my gown is going to be full of hairs and animal smells from this foul bed. Why Fergus could not handle things any better than this . . . ." She never finished her diatribe, but hunched back into her cloak in an attitude of sleep just as the druid appeared before her.

Claudia, still hidden in the darkness, saw in this druid a caricature of Cathbad. He too had long white hair, but it was groomed and fine where Cathbad's was shredded and wisped like old moss hanging from the great oak trees they had seen in the forest. This druid was thin without the transparent look of the frail Cathbad.

"Raise your arms," he commanded.

Yawning and clutching the hood so that her face barely showed, Fedelm hunched still farther into her cloak before obeying.

"They are not wings," the druid observed. "Girl, do you fly?"

"I serve," she responded sullenly.

"She has a raven head," one of his attendants whispered. "It was seen. She is a shape-shifter."

"I will go and kill the crow and see what I can learn from its entrails."

"We cannot find it," the attendant answered. "Will a rooster do?"

The druid sighed, already moving off. "At least she has been fed according to the laws, and is ready." His tone was dull and querulous. "If she is not the daughter of Badb, still the goddess of the earth will be glad for this offering."

"And the rooster?"

"Save it. They like to see these things, and with a

190

makeshift ceremony like this there will be little enough to sacrifice . . . ." His voice faded away.

The children remained motionless until the old crone began nodding again. Then Fedelm shrugged off the cloak and joined them.

She cast Claudia one of her contemptuous glances with the sparkle of glee that always seemed to lurk beneath. "I suppose I should be glad of you for livening these dreary months. Foolish, tedious warfare. Still, I am lazy by nature, and I find your interference in our world unsettling. It is one thing to welcome diversion, another to come up against a pair of willful groundlings who insist on ignoring all the rules. Even Fergus appreciates some limits. But you—"

Claudia paid no attention to this tirade. "Will you get us out?"

"I don't suppose you would be willing to go the other way? It would save a deal of effort. I really cannot promise you a safe return if you are unwilling to go into the bog."

"Really," Claudia assured her, "I think it would be horrible." She shuddered. "Sucked into the muddy ground like that. It would be drowning and suffocation all together."

"No, it would not. They choke you first. Probably using your own torc on your neck. That is, if you make it through the Beltane fires. I have seen it done, and let me tell you no maid has ever made such a fuss about it before. Most consider it an honor."

"Well, I'm not most."

Fedelm nodded. "I was not certain about that. The

threads kept pulling and snagging, and I could not read your future in my fringe." Fedelm gave a short, impatient sigh. "I suppose that means I must spirit you away before you are slain."

"That's what she's getting at," Evan put in, adding, "But if we're going to miss the best part, seeing the sword and all, I hope you'll at least tell us what happens."

"Then you don't know?" Fedelm seemed genuinely surprised.

"Oh, Evan, not now. I've lost enough time. I've got to get going and signal the rest of the Ulidian exiles."

"You will do no such thing. All you would get for your trouble is capture, and this time they would guard you so carefully I might not be able to accomplish anything. No, we will make our way at once."

Claudia pulled back. "I promised Fergus. I have to finish what I've begun for him. He . . . he's counting on me."

"You have stayed too long with Fergus already. I can tell that. You are just as full of folly as he is with his hopeless quest. He will not save his kinsmen. These are futile gestures."

"We have to try," Claudia burst out. "I can't desert him."

"Stay," ordered Fedelm. "You tax my patience."

"Stay," echoed Evan. "She'll tell us what's going to happen. We'll hear about the sword, Claude. About Fergus."

"I don't care," Claudia shot back at them. "I'm not interested in prophesies. I'm going to change what happens." She dashed toward one of the fires she had not yet visited.

192

Her determination was rewarded, another signal given and received. On she moved, emboldened by the ease with which she had carried out this task in defiance of Fedelm. More than ever she felt herself impelled by a devotion to Fergus and his cause, the more so since Fedelm pronounced it lost. She knew that what swept her along was an alien current, the river of a life different from her own. Medb was caught in it with her single-minded pursuit of the divine bull; the Hound was no less trapped in his proud, lonely stand against her armies; and Fergus staggered between, drawn into cross-eddies, heedless of ruin.

Exultant with the fervor of her commitment, she stepped more boldly, then more blindly, and at the next fire it was not one of the Ulidians who rose from a patch of straw, but a woman of Connaucht.

Within seconds Claudia was surrounded by a gathering wall of shields that loomed toward her out of the night. The action was so quick, Claudia so immersed in her task, that she was unable to utter a single cry.

She could not look away from those shields, which seemed to stare at her like disembodied faces, each one different from the next. Some had single bosses of red-gold, others bore figures, one a leaping salmon, the next two serpentine creatures devouring one another, after that the head of a boar, and then a three-winged figure that was half beast and half blossom. On some shields colors glowed warm amber and blood red, while others had the look of ice, white bronze with ornaments, curved shields with cutting edges or rounded rims, silver-hard.

None of the bearers of those shields looked into the circle they made, but kept their heads turned away from her. Yet they managed a halting but relentless progress that forced her to keep moving, sometimes even backward or sideways as she turned within the circle, now toward a shield with rings of gold crossing each other, now a shield of iron gray embossed with black.

Several times she stumbled against them and the circle came to a standstill while she recovered her balance. When she fell, the shields were always unyielding, and she would come away bruised or scraped.

No matter where she looked or how she turned, she was propelled onward and was helpless. And then her eyes moved from a shield of white with red-gold animal designs to a shield she recognized. It was scalloped, with bosses of red-gold, the ornament like a phrase from the music of the scabbard she had fingered, the circles and spirals entwined like tendrils from a growing vine, all in-looped and curling back upon themselves.

Here she had wasted precious minutes under the spell of the shields, while this was the one she was meant to see. She reached out, pressing against it, half afraid that it would offer up the same resistance as the others.

It gave almost imperceptibly, a slight in-pulling, and then it resumed its place as a part of the wall of bronze and iron, of wood and hide and of gold and precious stones that encircled her.

She could not judge how close they were to their destination, could only guess that time was running out. Again she pushed, and this time the shield dipped down and sideways. She guessed that she was to fall in that direction.

She let out a cry as she went down so that they would think that she had injured herself. She could see Fergus

194

stepping sideways, the shield-bearer next to him falling right across his foot. It happened so quickly that it was over before the shields could close ranks. Even now they had to avoid her, these warriors, lest her magic taint them with her touch.

Meanwhile, Fergus's shield was guarding her, its scalloped edge cutting at those who would close in, though to all appearances he was simply protecting the tripped-up warrior from fatal contact.

As she ducked and ran, she heard one of the warriors utter a sharp cry of recognition. "The bead," he exclaimed, and then, "Fergus." She could not tell what followed, for she was already out of earshot, and running hard.

Once she got her bearings, she headed in the direction Fergus had indicated, grateful for the open heath which made it possible to run full tilt, though it meant that she was exposed and vulnerable. She knew she was pursued, but she didn't dare to look back.

Minutes passed. Then the thudding and panting seemed to bear down on her, and a voice gasped, "Blundering to the end. You are going the wrong way." She was sobbing with exhaustion as Fedelm pushed her and Evan toward a clump of furze. "Scratchy, but we have nothing better." They rolled down a gentle slope and crawled into the spiny bushes, which tore at their hair and faces and snagged on their garments.

Evan, his voice tinged with surprise and something like admiration, said, "You were really going, Claude. We had trouble catching up."

Just as he spoke, a throng of men and women swept up beyond them along the plain to the west. "And none too

195

soon," Fedelm said softly. "We will have to wait for their return before we can be on our way." She turned toward Claudia. "You would make your noble gesture. And where do you think Fergus is now? With his kinsmen? Or leaving that sorry lot of Ulidians while he goes chasing after his little lost groundling?"

"But doesn't he know you'll care for me?"

"Small good I can do when you are so obstinate. He forms attachments that are costly. Besides," she added on a note of smugness, "I suppose he will want his bead back. It was not a gift, you know."

Claudia's hands flew to her braid and found the bead still in place. "Gift and giver am I," she murmured.

"What? Oh, that sword. I will be glad to see it sheathed again. It is not an easy gift."

"That's what Fergus said."

"He should know."

Claudia, her heart still pounding, asked, "Did I really make it worse for him?"

"You have grandiose notions of yourself, groundling. In the end you make little difference, save what goes on inside him. As for events . . . ." She shrugged off the thought.

The runners were returning, for the Beltane fires had been lighted. The three lying in the furze could see the mantle of night being lifted by the great blaze. All the space between land and sky seemed to hang in a queer atmosphere that was both luminous and thin.

Voices reached them, breathless, frightened, questioning the meaning of Claudia's disappearance. The chasers sounded anxious to return, to offer special favors of their own so that the war furies, cheated of the daughter of Badb, would not spread the slaughter to their households. Somewhere, running silent, was Fergus, for of course he would have had to give chase, as would the warrior who had recognized her at the moment of her escape and cried out so rashly.

Claudia decided to leave the bead with Fedelm, trusting that it would be returned to Fergus. Her fingers sought it and for an instant closed over it. Here she held magic, though for her it could only be a bead with a secret. But before she had time to remove it, Fedelm was on her feet again, drawing them after her.

"But that's the wrong way," Claudia protested as they began to retrace their steps, heading off slightly to keep a greater distance from the encampment.

"You will not go back through the Cave of Cruachan. I keep telling you, it is far from here."

"Where will we go?" Claudia asked.

"Where are we?" Evan demanded.

"Ahead is the Plain of Meath. There where the land swells and the sods were raised is Clathra, and its very summit, burning now, is the center of all Erenn. The flames will lift the sky from its place above the land and make a space through which we may pass. It is almost as dangerous a time as at the Feast of Samain. And see, there to the north stands a great pillar stone. That is where we head now, though we must cross the light from the Hill of Clathra." She eyed Claudia. "No objections, please. It is that, or the fire itself, and you are not yet free of the flames."

Claudia answered meekly, "I wasn't going to object."

197

"If they were planning to lead her through the fire," Evan pointed out in his practical, insistent way, "how could they have pushed her into the bog? She'd just be ashes."

They were trotting three abreast, heading uphill, but the slope was so gradual that it wasn't a difficult climb. Now the fires seemed to be below them. It was a trick of the light, because Fedelm and the children were not higher, but merely coursing across the next hill and leaving Clathra to the south.

Fedelm answered Evan. "They would not burn her up. But the fires are hot, and it is not pleasant to go through them." She paused a moment, gazing back. "There are youths who will leap some of the flames, and maids of their choice will run with them hand in hand between the fires." Even as she said this, they could look back and see the figures, like dancers leaping and racing, arching against the flames, twisting, dropping.

"Don't they get burned? I wouldn't do that for anything."

"They may get a little burned, but they will have strong babies for their reaping. And," she continued, turning to Evan, "they are bold who leap the flames. Not children."

"I bet they drink a lot of that ale to make them bold. And," he added in an undertone, "stupid."

Fedelm laughed. "It pleases the gods as well as the men that they drink and eat of the grains which the earth has delivered." She shook her head, her yellow braids tossing. "Anyway, it is the liking of the maids that emboldens them. There are other fires besides the ones that

198

blaze at Beltane. As any who serve this queen may quickly learn."

After that, they traveled in silence.

As usual, it was Claudia who tired before Evan. "Will there be a place to . . . go into at the pillar stone?"

"Between the stone and the great dun beyond you will find an earthen circle. Inside the circle is a mound; it is the barrow raised by a people not known to us and long disappeared, but their queen lies there still with all her goods—slaves and hounds, her gold and precious stones, her vessels yet full—"

"A grave?" squeaked Claudia. "You mean we have to go into a grave?"

"You may choose the well, if you prefer." Fedelm gathered her long, grass-green folds about her. "I prefer the barrow, which is dry and a deal cleaner than any well. Though they say there are marvelous things in the well, offerings from olden times at the bottom of it. Still, if you don't like the idea of the fires and the bog, I should think you would welcome this grave passage instead." She regarded Claudia, then cast a glance southward. "Can you not run faster? I believe some have caught sight of us and are following." She fixed Claudia with her eye. "They are no doubt determined to bring you back before the fires die."

Claudia was gasping and floundering like a fish. She would have reminded Fedelm that she had been doing far more strenuous things than they, but it took wind to speak and she had none to spare.

"Look," cried Evan, pointing skyward.

They looked up and saw, high above them, a single

199

black bird circling in a downward spiral.

"Badb," murmured Fedelm. "She will lead them to us."

"It's our crow," Evan shouted, full of delight. "We'll get it back after all."

"We cannot escape Badb's eye," Fedelm muttered. She seemed to be considering another course. "If the hunters close the gap, I may have to go ahead with the boy to ensure the opening."

"What, and leave Claudia behind?"

"She has more to fear if we fail to reach the barrow before sunrise. If we are too late, it will be closed to us."

"I was thinking that it's Claudia that needs to get out. I could take her place, and they wouldn't know until it was too late, and then she'd be safe out of this and I'd be able to stay and see the end."

"The end?" Fedelm laughed. "You comprehend so little, groundling. Still, it is a relief to know your offer is not steeped in the sticky nobility that Fergus brewed so enticingly for your sister."

Claudia was beginning to see the dancing figures before her eyes. Flames leaped up and black outline-creatures shot in and out of them as if charged with electricity.

Taking in her condition, Fedelm glanced again at the sky, then frowned. "Here we must leave you," she decided, drawing the bronze sword from under a green fold. "Carry it, but heed this warning: if you fail to leave it in the passage of the barrow, you will not come out again, neither here nor there."

Evan, beside himself with excitement, reached out and was cuffed aside by the quicker Fedelm. "Touch it not."

200

She thrust the man-hilt into Claudia's trembling hand.

Claudia tried to give it back. "I'm too tired. I'll never remember to let it go. That is, if I make it. You carry the thing." Breathless and weak, she pressed it toward Fedelm, who stepped quickly back as the tip of the blade pushed into her middle.

"Now must you draw blood? Smite not the giver, groundling. It is sharp." With that she turned, picking up speed and hauling the reluctant Evan after her. "Follow," she called back over her shoulder. "Gain the pillar stone before Badb, and there you may briefly rest. Then follow again. We will put our foot in the entrance lest the sunrise close the mound to you."

For a while after she had been left, Claudia slowed down. Then, cresting a small rise, she caught sight of those who had taken up the chase again, a small enough band but determined-looking and either fresher than she or oblivious to fatigue because of the mead-soaked festivities. The sword was a hindrance, just so much weight and awkwardness to carry as she struggled forward, trying to widen the distance between the hunters and herself.

She wondered whether Fedelm had given her the sword to fight them off. But she knew nothing about smiting things, let alone people. The men were gaining on her. In a moment she would have to turn, sword in hand, and face them.

And now that time was upon her. She wheeled about. Without knowing why she did it, she shifted the sword and took the blade in her hands, disregarding the razor edge that cut her palms. She was trembling and her breath came in tiny, hoarse gasps.

They were coming abreast and spreading to encircle

her when she stretched out toward them, holding the hilt at arm's length so that the head of the bronze man nearly touched one of her pursuers. Slowly she turned with it, as if offering it to each of them politely, the blade cold and cutting in her terrified grip.

They fell back as if she were cutting them down. In an instant they lay prostrate, face down in the turf, like grasses fallen to the scythe.

Hearing others approach, she wasted no time, but returned the hilt to her bleeding hand and tore up the slope. She no longer thought of the barrow within the earthen circle that lay beyond. If only she could reach the stone, she would drop to the turf like the warriors she had left, and there she would stay until she had gained her breath and her sight and her mind.

She sensed rather than perceived a beating darkness that swooped over her as she ran. It was like a concentration of night in one small part of the gray sky. She didn't dare stop or raise her tearing eyes to the creature flying above her. She didn't believe in the goddess Badb, but she knew that the powerful wings that stroked the air into immense black waves could not belong to any scraggly crow that had sat on her shoulders, pecked at her hair, eaten from her hand.

Nearing the stone, her eyes blurred and she thought she saw something like a reverse shadow, white against the gray stone. As she was about to fling herself to the ground, the white shadow spread like a film of mist. There were ghostly folds undulating above the grass like a flowing robe.

Her first thought was that this was Medb's druid and that she had been trapped. But this figure was too insubstantial to be the well-groomed man she had seen. It had a transparent presence, the long wisps of hair and beard as flimsy as a harbor fog shredded by fir trees before it is blown away.

On the eastern horizon the sky was breaking into color as if stained by the Beltane flames. She would never make the barrow now. Already the new pursuers were drawing near. She felt her knees give way, but just as she was sinking to the turf, a voice more terrible than any she had heard arrested her. "Follow," it commanded. "Follow." It might have been the sword itself that spoke, for the voice was everywhere, ringing, and at the same time before her.

Crying, protesting, she stumbled to her feet. "I'm too tired. I've had enough. I don't want this any more," she whimpered, and knew that she was obeying, going forward, clinging to the hilt as though it were pulling her.

Through her tears she saw that she was leaving the stone, the sanctuary, and heading off toward her final destination. She looked longingly at the place where she might have rested; now the white shadow was in front of the stone shaft so that it seemed to be merging with it. Only the face remained for an instant, the eyes like deep blue ice in the whiteness of a magic snow. And then the snow was melting, the ice sinking into the depth of the stone, and in another second all that remained was a film of mossy lichen, white-silver in the waning night.

All about her the grasses stirred. A great sigh swept across the plain, a hollow whisper. "Follow," it told her, an echo of the terrible voice. "Follow, follow." The darkness lifted, winging upward into the paling sky.

A clamor broke through the freshening wind, voices

bearing down on her once more. She put on one last burst of speed, and there was the raised earthen circle. Half rolling, half tumbling, she cast herself over its crown just as she felt a hand grabbing at her tunic. There were cries of triumph mingled with fear and rage.

But where was the grave entrance? She was staggering around the barrow, certain it had already closed, leaving no trace of the passage.

A sudden tugging of the sword jolted her and pitched her forward. She was aware of the mottled green of a bush in new leaf. One of her pursuers had her foot; she could feel the leather boot slipping from it. Her face was pressed into the leaves, but the leaves were soft and flat; they were the speckled fabric of Fedelm's gown. She could hear Evan declaring his unreadiness to enter the dark chamber beyond.

"Besides," he was yelling, "we haven't got the crow. We can't go back without the crow."

"Daughter of Badb," a man behind her shouted.

Fedelm's voice was everywhere at once, snapping at Evan and exhorting Claudia to cleave yet to the sword, which seemed to be what connected them. Then she could hear Fedelm muttering, "I will never again complain about sitting around all day weaving threads of future. Help me, boy. Else she will be cut in half, broken as this sword will one day be."

"Her hand's all slippery," Evan grunted, but his irrepressible curiosity kept him going. "If the sword's broken, what'll happen to the hilt? Oh, you're so lucky. I wish I could see things that haven't happened yet."

Claudia could feel herself being pulled. She swiveled around to face the darkness, her arms at full length

204

ahead of her. Just as she thought she might be safe, she felt something at her back, a hand grasping at her braid with such strength that for an instant she thought her hair might be torn from its roots. Twisting, she tried to clutch at her head, but her hands still gripped the sword, her fingers locked around the bronze man, so that she merely glimpsed the face behind her. It seemed contorted, as though ringed with flames that were consuming it. Then it was gone, only the wild locks coiling in a tangled circle of fire.

"You have the sight too," Fedelm was saying to Evan. "Don't let up; keep pulling. Only," she added, "your sight's in another direction."

"I see just like everyone else," Evan retorted, gasping. "I'm getting tired. I think she's stuck."

"It's the sunstone drawing her back. And Fergus after the bead." Fedelm yanked at the sword. "She'll come now. And as for seeing, there's few have seen as much as you, let alone come."

The ordinary voices ahead of Claudia were like those of two fishermen hauling in their catch and chattering while she, at their casual mercy, was delivered into killing darkness. She found herself fighting them, confused and panic-stricken, longing to stay with the burning face of Fergus, forgetting that it had disappeared, blazing.

"You mean others . . . others like us have come here?"

"Others," Fedelm grunted, hauling on the sword to which Claudia still clung. "We have fearsome visitations in the open seam of the year, as well as those who take the shape of mortals. But be assured that those monsters may be no more outlandish than a pair of small-sized

205

groundlings clad in oilskin. Such is the staying power of the barnacle beside the mighty whale. Now then, girl," Fedelm snapped, prying Claudia's rigid fingers from the hilt, "follow your brother groundling."

Claudia heard only the word "follow," and it was like an enchantment releasing her from that grip on her braid that had all the power of an immense magnet. Instantly she was propelled after Evan into the ancient burial place where darkness was eternal.

PART THREE

NINETEEN

SHE came out of one darkness into another. She could hear Evan still protesting about the crow and Fedelm's voice snapping at him. It was minutes before the voice became Rebecca's, the hand that hauled at her own Rebecca's. Claudia heard, "She's here at the bottom of the cliff. I've got her. She must've fallen."

"Leave her alone." Evan was protecting her. "She's tired. She's had a hard run is all."

Then it was Fedelm again, just for an instant, as Claudia felt her arm yanked, then dropped, an exclamation of disgust.

"She's all sticky. The idiot's gone and cut her hand."

Claudia sat up slowly, stiffly. "It was the blade."

Rebecca dropped to her knees. "So you're all right. I thought you might be unconscious. What blade?"

Tim and Maddie were running up. Claudia heard: "Evan! Didn't you hear us calling?" And then: "They both O.K.? What've you been doing? Sleeping?" Laughter from Tim. "You mean to tell me while you girls were swearing and wringing your hands our little sister and brother were comfortably snoozing away till low tide?"

Rebecca said, "Claudia's done something to her hands."

208

Maddie reached for the hands. Claudia drew them back.

"They're all right. It isn't anything. It was just from holding the sword wrong way around."

"God," bellowed Rebecca. "This kid's too much for me." She turned to Evan. "What happened?"

Evan grinned up at her. "Where do you want me to begin?"

There was a long silence while three frantic-looking older ones looked down on the two who seemed drowsy, not quite awake.

Then Claudia turned her hands over to examine the palms. Maddie peered at them, declared them only superficially cut, probably from Claudia's grabbing onto things as she slipped and fell.

Claudia's face took on a distant expression they had all seen before. It finished their concern. Now they were merely scolding and complaining about the ruined day on account of two thoughtless, careless kids who were too wrapped up in their games of make-believe to consider that their disappearance might have caused some really bad moments for the others.

"We didn't mean to," Evan began. "It was the crow. We lost him."

"And that old Colman what's-his-name," Tim was snorting, "telling us we couldn't get to where you were. A big help."

"Well, we couldn't," Maddie put in. "At least not till the tide dropped."

"A crummy way to spend our first afternoon of sunshine," Rebecca brought out.

That made them look up at the night bright with stars

209

and gauzy strips of cloud like transparent ribbons. While they were staring, the stars seemed to dim and the ribbons to thicken and deepen until they were undulating like seaweed under blue-green waves.

"Northern lights," Maddie breathed. "Oh, look."

The display seemed endless, great sheets of light spreading, shimmering, casting themselves higher and higher, until all the sky was aflame with the cold pale brilliance, pushing back the boundaries of night, filling the universe with a spectral light.

They stayed for a long time before the sky began to shrink to its ordinary proportions again, the lights to pale and dissolve. It was Tim who spoke first, his voice low and even: "It makes you forget . . . everything else."

Claudia told herself she would never forget his saying that, but she could only answer him with a smile. Then she got to her feet, and all of a sudden she was just plain Claudia, stiff and achy and quite cold, with a hollow feeling in her middle that was more than hunger and yet seemed ready to be assuaged by whatever food they had left.

They went back to their camp in silence. It wasn't until much later when Claudia was subsiding into sleep that she remembered they had left the bronze hilt on the islet. What if the tide came in extra high before morning? She sat straight up. She would have to wait until the others were asleep. She doubted that they would stand for any more trips out there, especially in the dark.

It didn't take long. Everyone was exhausted. Less than half an hour later Claudia put on her sneakers and made her way in the cloud-filmed light back to the islet. The tide was still well down. With relief she made the crossing, sensing that she was following a course she had not traveled in a long time. Yet it was familiar, easy. In no time she was up on the turtle's back, slowing as she started on the downward slope, pausing at the cliff, then edging over with care.

Casting about, she had a moment's panic, then recalled that she would not find the hilt glowing and burnished, glinting in the pale moonlight. So she retraced her steps, feeling with her hands, which she cupped to spare the palms, and came across it quite suddenly.

Scrambling back up the embankment, she decided to return the hilt in the morning when she had Evan along to help explain about the crow. He might even prefer to take it to Colman alone. That would be fine with her. At the top of the cliff, she squatted creakily and looked at the bronze man. She tried to think of the places it had led her, but they seemed too distant to believe in. Thousands of gentle tongues lapped at the very solid earth on which she crouched; otherwise the bay was still, tranquil. "Gift and giver am I," she whispered to the bronze man, but the only voice to reach her ears was her own.

She started the next day with a determination to keep all of the Other Place alive and real, but her efforts to give it form and substance through descriptions she could share never got off the ground. Her first reference to warriors and Queen Medb stirred resentment in Rebecca, amusement in Tim, a kind of worry in Maddie. There was a long argument at breakfast with a few moments of rancor, but mostly humor prevailed. The day was gorgeous, the fish ample, and no one in much of a hurry for hard work after all the exertions of yesterday.

"If Susan and Dad turned up now, though," Rebecca

drawled, scraping the pink seeds from a rose hip, "I'd turn you two in. I'd tell all."

"I wouldn't," came Maddie's prompt reply. "It would spoil the group dynamics to lose them. Besides, they're going to turn over a new leaf. Aren't you, kids?"

Evan turned over a page of his pad. "Like this," he agreed, and began sketching anew.

Maddie smiled and leaned over to approve of his pictures.

He looked up. "They wouldn't let me draw in the Other Place."

Maddie pulled back.

Tim laughed. "Some new leaf."

Claudia took the opportunity to nudge Evan. "You going to take it back?"

He nodded. "Just a sec."

"What are you two up to now?" Rebecca demanded.

Evan said, "You sound just like Fedelm."

Rebecca began to swear, and to placate her, Claudia suggested a hairdo she had seen. Braids and one long lock. Rebecca unbent a little and told Claudia to go ahead, try.

So Claudia set to work on Rebecca's golden hair, parting and reparting, laboriously combing out the one long lock. The effect was stunning, and everyone said so.

"Where did you dream it up?" Maddie wanted to know.

"Oh, that's the way Fedelm—" Evan started to tell them, but Claudia cut him short.

"I just sort of saw it."

"What's Evan talking about?"

"You don't believe us, so there's no point telling you."

Evan lifted up the pad to Claudia and turned back a page. "How's this?" Claudia smiled at the picture of Fedelm. The others had to see it too.

"Hey," said Tim, turning to Evan. "How'd you know what Claudia was going to do to Becca's hair before she'd finished?"

Evan opened his mouth, caught a look from Claudia, and then just shrugged.

The older ones exchanged a series of glances. Finally Maddie spoke. "O.K. Out with it."

Claudia shifted uncomfortably.

"What's she after?" Evan wanted to know.

"She wants," Claudia told him, "to know exactly where we were. Only they're not altogether sure of themselves, though of course they must be right because they're older and reality-oriented."

"What I want to know," Maddie amended, "what we all want to know is where you *think* you've been."

So that was the way they were going to find out without having to believe what they were told. Claudia would not play that game.

After a pause, Maddie tried again. "All right. It's a real place to you. Where is it? Sable Island? Some Viking thing?"

Evan shook his head.

"Look, we just want to know what you think you've been up to."

"Oh," said Evan, "that's different. I took care of the ponies and helped clean the leather and polish the war stuff."

"And Claudia?"

Claudia hung her head.

213

"What did Claudia do, Evan?"

"Lots of different things. Cooked and ground meal and brought things to the queen . . . ."

Rebecca laughed. "I'm glad she was at least realistic enough not to cast herself in the role of the queen."

Evan gave her a look. "She had more to do than me. Also she helped . . . someone. Only we don't know whether it really helped or not. We have to go back and—"

"No one's going back to that damn islet," Tim burst out.

"Well they can while the visibility's good. It's just in the fog, Tim." Maddie smiled at Evan. "Was it fun?"

Just like Mother, Claudia thought.

Evan said, "Except my feet got cold. And I had fleas. There was some stuff that helped, but you couldn't always get it." He pulled up his shirt, and they all stared at the tiny red bites.

"Something bit him," Maddie admitted. "Probably black flies."

Claudia sighed. Then she thought of the bead. She pulled her shirt down to the spot over the collar bone where the bead had hung against her skin.

"You get bitten too?" Tim asked.

"It's from the magic bead," Evan informed him.

But when they found this was the only red spot on her, they decided the kids had gotten into something they were allergic to, Evan more than Claudia.

Evan ignored their diagnosis and pointed out the torc. "That's what she wore the bead on."

"Let's see," Maddie said. "Can you take it off?"

Claudia unhitched the ends that Fergus had bent into

214

hooks. She handed the necklet to Maddie, who examined it and gave it to Tim.

"Where'd you get this?" Tim asked Claudia.

"From . . . ." She hesitated. Fergus had given it to her, but he had picked it up beside the pillar stones. "From the ground," she finished.

"From out there?"

She nodded.

"Beats me. I don't know what it is," he said to Maddie.

"Claudia," Evan declared, erasing something vigorously and blowing at his paper, "says it's a harp string."

"And you don't agree?" Tim prodded.

"Didn't say that. Only I wasn't there." He was drawing all the time he spoke. Now he looked up thoughtfully, squinting into the sun. "I guess I'm not sorry about missing that hunt. Half the guys never came back. They were killed."

"Evan, really." Maddie laughed.

Tim joined her. "I like the way you kids make up people and then do them in. Like building with blocks and knocking everything down."

"It's sick, if you ask me," Rebecca commented. "Can't she use him in her games without making up all that violence?"

"It's a side of Claudia none of us ever dreamed of," Tim observed.

"Don't blame her," Evan rallied. "She didn't like it any more than I did. Especially at the end."

"Anyway," Maddie said brightly, "you've come to the end, right? So that's that, and now you don't have to go back any more. Not into that story."

"Oh, but we do have to," Evan burst out.

Claudia thought, Shut up; oh, shut up. She said, "How about taking that hilt back now?" Let them think whatever they like.

Evan went to get it while they looked after him with unconcern. They had seen the bronze figure already, had remarked on its curious appearance, and laughed when told that it was the hilt of a sword.

Maddie suggested that they take advantage of the sun and go for a swim. "The cove's pretty protected; it shouldn't be too freezing. And you never know how long we have before the fog closes in again."

"If the fog comes back," Rebecca said with a laugh, "I'm going to swim home."

Tim looked out to sea. "We may be in for a stretch of clear weather."

"Wouldn't that be great?" Maddie beamed, and at the same time Claudia cried out, "Don't say that. It has to fog in again before our time's up. It has to."

All three stared at her. She felt herself flushing under their gaze. Then Tim laughed, tossing the torc into her lap. "The artistic temperament. Has to be endured by us ordinary types."

Claudia grabbed at the necklet and started to put it on. Maddie stooped to gather up some of the debris. Without intending to, Claudia said, "The people in olden times didn't clean up very well. I mean, they littered."

Tim laughed again. "Of course, stupid. What do you think middens are all about, anyway?"

Claudia picked up a load of bones and carried them down to the rocks, where she was instantly surrounded by a cloud of wailing gulls. When she returned, they were

216

talking about her. They broke off as she appeared. She pretended she didn't know and reached down to gather up Evan's pad and pencils. She saw that he had begun to draw the scabbard, had even lightly sketched in the wooden hilt. She would save all these scribblings; they comprised a record that could be precious to them and perhaps to others someday. Again her hand went to the wire around her neck.

"You going to keep wearing that thing?" Rebecca asked with a condescending smile. She was beautifully, painfully like Fedelm.

"You look so great that way," Claudia mumbled.

Rebecca, caught off guard, could only growl something awkward and turn away.

Then Claudia noticed that Tim was gazing at her in a queer sort of way. He pointed to her torc. "Where did you say you got that?"

"What's the matter?" Maddie laughed. "They getting to you?"

Tim rubbed his chin thoughtfully. "It's just," he began, pausing, considering, "that I've never heard of wire . . . copper, I guess it is, or some kind of bronze . . . ." Again he paused. All three girls were watching him now. "I mean, that metal stuff sinks. It would never wash ashore."

Slowly their eyes turned on Claudia. There was no sound but the muttering of the gulls that had long since cleaned the last of the breakfast debris and were settling down to wait for the next sign of action.

Then Rebecca kicked a bunch of stringy seaweed into the embers. Hissing steam shot up. "You're all soft in the head," she informed them, breaking the spell of their si-

217

lence. "So it came on a piece of driftwood or something. There are so many obvious explanations it isn't funny."

Each of them turned away, Tim and Maddie a little embarrassed, Claudia strangely relieved. Suddenly she knew it didn't matter whether they believed her or not. Anything would be better than exposing herself and Fergus and all the others to their picky little questions. She would have to find a way to make Evan more careful, and she would have to watch herself too.

Inside the cove the water was almost bearable. "Great," Claudia pronounced it. "Bracing," chattered Maddie. "For those," gasped Tim, "with a protective layer of—" He had to duck before he could finish, all three girls after him at once.

They were laughing at nothing, at the sun, at the way their clothes, presumably being washed, clung and came away from beach and turf covered with sand and pebbles and fir needles and compost. They had huge appetites and nothing more to eat, but they agreed to postpone food collecting till they had worked themselves hot and dry gathering stones for the shelter they were trying to build on the other side of the island.

It was well into the afternoon before Claudia managed to get away to the hut. Evan was cleaning out the crow's roosting place. "Thinks it'll be back in a day or so."

"Unless the blackbacks got him," Mr. Colman qualified. "He's been off before, though not this long."

"Anyway, I'm getting it ready. Mr. Colman's going out to check his traps. Taking lobsters to the mainland. I said I'd keep watch."

"If you go . . . ." She faltered. Would the magic work without Mr. Colman?

"He's leaving the hilt," Evan supplied.

She sighed and plumped down in front of the leaky stove. "Anyway, there isn't a sign of fog. We're stuck."

"Catch the early morning smoke," the old man told her. "Tricky, though. Burns right off soon as the sun gets up. Mark it."

"Do you know what happens?" she asked him. "I mean, to Fergus?"

"He doesn't even know their names," Evan broke in. "Listen, Claude, I've already asked all those questions."

It had been the wrong question anyway. She needed to understand so much more than that. If all they had seen and done was from an earlier time, did that time go on independent of the time they were in? She said, "If it's still going on, then we can change it. And if it's not, then . . . why, then it's ended." Groping with these words, she went to the hearth and lifted the stone. There lay the hilt, encrusted, discolored, the details blurred and nearly erased. She did not touch it, but stood for a long time gazing at it, while Evan made several trips to the door with filth scooped up between two shingles.

That night she worked on her private log while the older ones sat around talking. When they got to considering the inequality of the draft and whether girls who were in sympathy with antiwar guys should go into voluntary exile with them, Claudia couldn't keep from commenting, "Exile's no joke, though. It puts you in a terrible position."

It stopped them cold. Rebecca looked smugly amused and murmured: "Out of the mouths of babes . . . ."

"What do you know about it?" Tim said in an astonished, slightly indignant voice.

219

Maddie the peacemaker quickly suggested that Claudia had probably learned about some romantic exile in history, since she was the kind of reader who would even take up a biography if you left it in her way. She said this on a fond note that somehow rankled more than what the other two had said.

Claudia returned to her writing, but Evan spoke up: "Knows more than you guys."

Claudia didn't know whether she felt like hugging him or kicking him. She bent over her pad.

"Tell us about it," Rebecca offered with a smile; Claudia thought her evil.

"It's this man we know," Evan began haltingly, a little suspicious of Rebecca's interest but clearly trapped by the lure. "Fergus." He paused, but they were all waiting for him to continue, so he plodded on. "See, he's working for the King and Queen of Connaught because—"

"What's Connaught?"

Claudia hoped one of the older two could supply the answer, but apparently they'd never heard of it either.

"It's this place. I don't know where exactly. It's awfully hard to explain. It's even hard to tell who the good guys are. I mean, with the warriors. The king's different."

Maddie sighed. "It's always so nice and straightforward in fairy tales. All those clear moral choices."

Evan looked at her as though he wasn't sure she was worth wasting any more explaining on.

But Rebecca was still at him. "What about the king?"

"Bad. They're all bad," he said abruptly, his voice suddenly on the edge of tears. "Playing games, like that wooden wisdom, with everyone else's lives. Only it's real lives, not wooden men. It's people like . . . like Mr. Col-

220

man, that smell and . . . and bleed . . . ." He stumbled to his feet.

"Evan." Maddie reached out to him.

"I'm going to bed."

"Well," Rebecca declared cheeringly, "maybe the queen made up for the king."

Evan wheeled around. "The queen," he shouted into their midst. "The queen's the worst of all. She's a pig. I hate her." Then he dove for his sleeping bag.

Rebecca turned on Claudia. "You see where all your story-making leads him?"

Maddie wondered whether someone ought to go talk to him. Claudia told them to leave him alone. There was a long silence.

"His supplies holding out?" Tim finally asked, sounding friendly and almost equal.

She nodded. She knew Tim was trying to turn the conversation onto a neutral subject.

As they relaxed, the atmosphere seemed to soften. There was something about sharing a fire that made separate people seem connected. Claudia was feeling very much connected just now and reluctant to leave. She looked down at the page and dimly made out what she had written. It was like a story. Cathbad. Fergus and the Hound. Fedelm. Loche. The Great Mother. Medb and Ailill. Boardface. It was a story.

She heard her own voice joining in with theirs now and then, a word of gossip, a point about the hut they were trying to build. She found herself thinking of the way the stone walls looked at Cruachu.

"Claudia," she heard, "you're falling asleep."

She nodded in agreement, murmured drowsily, made

221

no move to leave the fire. She felt Maddie prodding her, then Tim pulling her up.

"Sweet dreams," Maddie called.

"For God's sake," laughed Rebecca, "don't encourage that one to dream."

TWENTY

THE dawn was filmy, not thick as in a proper fog. But from what Mr. Colman had suggested about the early morning smoke, it would probably do. The trouble was that Evan's sleeping bag was empty.

Claudia registered this fact, rubbing her eyes, pushing back her hair. She wasn't alarmed. Mostly she was just taken aback.

She dressed quickly and ran to check in the hut, where she found what she had guessed and now dreaded she would find—the hearth slab pulled back, the bronze hilt gone. She rocked back on her heels, aghast.

Then, as she stumbled down the slope and splashed along the half-submerged bar, she realized that she felt betrayed. Evan was doing something unpardonable and greedy, consuming a slice of time without a thought for sharing. Probably wouldn't even understand what he saw. It would be wasted on him. And all she would get would be a bunch of secondhand pictures. Gone the bodies and faces, the sound of the cloak rustling, the voices warm, alive; gone the recognition she craved, Fergus, Fedelm . . . . She had been counting on it so, a look, a single moment in which their eyes met across time and told her they knew she was there.

But the fog was lifting. Light cut through the vapors,

making rents that curled back instead of filling. The early sun was flaying the delicate tissue of gray that hung ragged on the horizon.

When she first caught sight of Evan, he seemed to be tearing through the clinging fog patches. He was swinging both hands, each clutching something, and struggling as if to break free. Now he was racing blindly along the turtle's back. His face was small and very white. He was coming toward her at a dead run.

When he showed no signs of stopping at her call, she set herself in his path. The impact toppled them both, and for some reason this made her even more furious with him. She was kneeling and shaking him, screaming at him while his head snapped back and forth and he made no move to help himself.

Then she noticed the hilt lying off to the side and suddenly let go, slid over to retrieve it, and held it in both her hands as if she would never let it go. She glared at him.

"Everyone's dead," he finally whispered.

"Fergus?"

He shook his head. "No. But . . . oh, hundreds and hundreds."

"You saw the battle?"

"Hundreds."

"Evan." She was about to shake him again, but his stunned expression brought her up short. "It was . . . ghastly?"

He nodded, dazed, "Where's my . . . . I had something." He looked around. Not far from where the hilt had fallen there was another object, a piece of wood broken off from something. It was gracefully arched, round-ing in a familiar curved line around a well-worn hole. He reached for it. "The yoke. I don't know, but I think it's from the Hound's chariot. Only it's different now. It's so . . . gray." He frowned. "Still, he was breaking, breaking everything. Like before. Like when he was a kid with those swords and everything. He didn't have any weapons. He looked awful, a mess, covered with bandages. Only he was breaking up the chariot and using pieces of it like spears, like hammers, and the piece I got hold of was, well, smooth, you know, not gray . . . ."

"But where were you, Evan? How could you have been right in the midst of it?"

"On Fergus's chariot. Boardface was funny; he never knew I was there. Only—you know what, Claude?—the dun pony gave that sort of snorting, blowing hello he always did for me—"

"And Fergus?"

"Well, Fergus, he was with the king and queen at first." Evan sounded as if he was beginning to recover. "Boy, were those two nervous. More and more bunches of warriors kept coming from the other side. The messenger would report one band on its way, and by the time Ailill had asked Fergus whose band it was, another would be announced, and then another. And Fergus so quiet and sort of proud when he told about them. He knew them all. The Ulidians made one of those big mounds for their king right off, so that he sat higher than anyone else. And all these companies of warriors kept coming. And Ailill and Medb got more sort of close and . . . and . . . ."

"Uptight?"

"Yes, and Fergus looking like he couldn't care less. And—"

225

"Did he see you?"

"What?"

"Fergus. Did he see you?"

"What do you mean, Claude? He can't see us unless we're really there."

"Well, he might've . . . sensed . . . ."

"Are you kidding? This was the great battle. Do you think he had time to think about us?"

"If I'd been—"

"All you think about is you."

"Well, I didn't go off and leave you behind."

"I'm sorry, Claude. I really am. I tried to wake you, but you were so sound asleep I was afraid you'd just be mad. And then I thought of waiting, only what if this was the last chance, and then I just, well . . . ."

They sat under the last vestiges of misty shreds that clung to the tip of the headland. Claudia plucked a stem of the low-lying bunchberry they hadn't trampled. She began to pick off one scarlet berry after another. Absently she popped them into her mouth and made a face at the dry seediness. When she was finished, she stared at the circle of pointed leaves with their slightly arched surfaces ribbed as if to outline their perfect shape. Without its brilliant center, the sprig looked hollow.

Evan was staring at it too. "You took its head off." It wasn't an accusation, but an observation. "I never thought there could be so many people slicing off other people's heads. Or cutting them into pieces. I don't ever want to go back there. Not ever."

"It can't be worse than bombs, than napalm, all that." She was still gazing at the decapitated bunchberry. "Nothing could be."

226

"I've never seen those things. I mean, on the TV the war's all blurred and jerky, and you can't . . . ."

She said softly, "I want to go back. To see Fergus and—"

"Fergus was different."

She raised her eyes. "How?"

"I don't know. More like the others. Like the Hound."

"I don't believe you."

"He looked like he could do . . . anything."

"I don't believe he would. He's different. He's what Cathbad said, not of his time."

"How do you know? You don't even know what that time is. Anyhow, you didn't see him with his sword."

"His sword. Did it change him?"

"Well, he seemed changed. Not just sad." Evan paused, considering. "Like he'd made up his mind about something bad. He got quieter and quieter. And when the messenger described the last band of warriors that didn't have a leader, something seemed to happen to Fergus. You see, Ailill wanted him to say who these were too. So Fergus told him these warriors belonged with the Hound, who lay too wounded to be with them. Only Fergus seemed to know that Ailill really had figured it out for himself and just wanted to rub it in. And Medb couldn't keep from crowing either. You could just see her, you know . . . ."

"Gloating?" supplied Claudia.

"Yes, and more, because of Fergus, because of what it did to him. 'They have good cause to be downcast,' she said, 'because there is not any evil we have not done them.' That was what she told Fergus. She said, 'We have plundered them and we have ravaged them from

227

Samain until the beginning of spring. We have carried off their women and boys, their horses, their herds, their flocks, and their cattle. We have leveled their hills.' I think she would have just kept on like that, but Fergus couldn't take it. You should've heard him, Claude. His voice was shaking. He told her, 'You have no reason to boast, Medb, for you did no injury to them that the leader of that good band has not avenged on you, since every mound and every grave, every tombstone and every tomb from here to the western part of Erenn is a mound and a grave, a tombstone and a tomb for some warrior who fell by the valiant leader of that band.' Then he said some more that I can't remember and told her how they had had to tie the Hound down to keep him on his sickbed. Also he warned her about the strength of those men who would be defending their lord in the battle."

Claudia sat back. "And I missed that."

"Well, you'd have hated to hear the ponies screaming when they got hurt and fell down. Even with all the yelling and howling from the warriors, you could tell every time that happened. I was so scared for my team, my dun—"

"But what happened to Fergus?"

"Well, it was all mixed up, and it really looked bad, so Medb told Fergus it would be fitting if he led her men in the fighting. She went through all that business about how he had been given land and wealth and respect in Connaucht, and especially she mentioned kindness. So he pulled out his wooden sword. His face looked, not lop-sided like Boardface's, but frozen that way. Then Ailill sent for the real sword. You could tell he was worried."

228

"Fedelm must have brought the sword. Did you see her?"

Evan shook his head. "But it was just the way we'd seen it with her. And with you. Shining."

Claudia remembered it in her own hands. "Like a torch." She tried to visualize the scene. "And did they . . . fall back when he took it?"

"They made room for him." Evan laughed. His laughter broke off. "Fergus, though . . . . He just held it. His hands up like this." Evan balanced the broken yoke piece on upturned palms. "He spoke to the sword, welcoming it, only he didn't sound glad at all."

Claudia clutched at him. "Don't leave out a single thing."

Evan shook her off. "You should be glad I got this much. Listen, these were his exact words. 'Weary are the champions of the war goddess.' That's what he said, and then he asked Medb, 'On whom should I ply this sword?' Just like he had no idea what they wanted him to do with it. So of course she told him to use it everywhere on everyone. You know Medb. I hate her."

"Go on, Evan, just tell what happened."

"It was awful. They all went into the battle. I was holding onto the pole between the ponies and couldn't see much, which was all right with me, but I could hear all the screams and howling on both sides, everywhere, and I guess Fergus stayed in the chariot till just before he came up against the King of Ulidia. By then he was down on the ground, but we were all hemmed in and couldn't get away."

"Did that king look the same as the time we saw him at the feast?"

229

"I couldn't even recognize him, everything was such a mess. Neither could Fergus, because they were all jammed up against each other, shield to shield. I could hear Fergus shouting because he wanted to know whose shield was blocking him. I lifted up my head and held onto the harness so I could see. I kept forgetting I wasn't all the way there. I guess I wasn't really in danger, but when you're in the middle—"

"Just go on," Claudia cried.

"Well, this guy behind the shield yelled back to Fergus, 'There is a man here younger and mightier than you, one who tricked you and killed those under your safeguard, one who banished you from your land and people, one who drove you into the wild realm to live among the foxes and deer, one who made you dependent on a powerful woman, and one who will drive you off in the presence of all the men of Erenn,' and of course by then you could tell that Fergus knew it was the king. That's when he was like the Hound and would do anything. He took the sword in both his hands. I don't know how to explain this, Claude, because at first I thought he was going to break it. Only then it was clear it was that king he was going to break. But when he swung the sword back over his head, it touched all the way to the ground behind him. It was enormous."

"You mean it grew?"

"Well, I didn't see it grow. I saw it bigger. But all sorts of other things were going on, all the fighting, and this big black thunderhead came down, and everything got dark with queer lights under it. There was a terrific wind. I had to duck because it was so sudden and fierce."

"Like wings."

"Yes, giant wings. How did you know? You couldn't help ducking. Only first I saw this man, one of the exiles who'd gone to live in Connaucht with Fergus, force his way to Fergus and grasp his arms so he couldn't kill the king. This guy called him 'Master,' just like the Hound, and begged him not to strike the blow. Fergus looked awful, ugly. He roared that he wouldn't live if he didn't destroy the Ulidian king. And it was getting darker all the time. I was afraid to watch, only I did a little, and the man was still holding Fergus and telling him he must strike a different blow to make his anger go away." Evan stopped.

"What is it? Go on."

"Fergus . . . his voice . . . . Like crying, really. 'Then how am I to wield it?' is what he said. I thought he'd been wounded." And the guy holding onto him told him to turn his hand sideways and strike down the hills themselves if he had to, but not to betray himself and the honor of all the Ulaid. You know how they talk, Claude. Except that this guy sounded so full of . . . I guess it was pity."

Claudia thought this over for a bit. "And that was all then?"

"I wish it had been. That guy let go of Fergus, Fergus swung the sword over the heads of the king and his men, only sideways, and then I lost track of it. It wasn't there any more. It seemed to be a lightning bolt. It flashed right there where we were. There was this tremendous explosion, and we all just dropped, both sides, everyone, and the ground shook and boomed. I had my arms around the neck of my dun-colored pony, and he was shaking. I don't know if he knew it was me or not. And

231

then just as we were beginning to be all right again, in came the Hound, breaking everything in his way, throwing pieces of broken chariots and conking people with . . . ." He held up the piece of yoke.

"How did you get it?" She looked at him to see if there were any bruises. But Evan hadn't been seen, so how could he have been hit?

"There was a way out through the path he left. I just waited till the Hound got to Fergus. All the time he was slashing his way in, he was calling, 'Turn to me, Master Fergus.' But Fergus seemed sort of deaf, I guess from all the racket and the storm or whatever it was, and the Hound got madder and madder and started yelling all these things about how he'd grind Fergus like a stone or swoop down on him like a hawk if Fergus wouldn't stop, till finally he got through to him, and the Hound told him it was his own foster-son, covered with wounds, come to claim his due."

"What did he look like?"

"Who, the Hound? A mess."

"No. Fergus. When he discovered it was the Hound."

"Listen, Claude, he took off in one direction, masses of warriors after him, and I took off in the other. And then I bumped into you. I didn't even know I was holding onto this." He looked at the wooden piece. "Do you think I hit with it? I wonder if I hit anyone."

"Then I'll never know what he was thinking, what he was feeling."

"You can't tell that anyway."

"You can tell a lot." Claudia dug into the green turf with a leg of the bronze man. She felt cheated. "It might be the last time." She could hear herself sounding like a sore loser.

"I said I was sorry. There'll be other times, and I'll never go without you again. I promise."

"I know. I'm not mad any more." She really wasn't. Only empty.

"Anyway," he tried to cheer her up, "you didn't miss Fedelm. Maybe next time we'll see her. And listen, Claude, I haven't told you about what that king looked like. You wanted to know. He was really something, with curled hair. Even his beard was curled and separated into two forks. And he had on this bright purple cloak I would've sworn was the one Fergus used to wear, the one with the pleats— What's the matter?"

Claudia was getting up. "I just don't want to hear any more now." She started down the turtle's tail.

Evan came trotting after her. "Are you going to stay sore?"

She didn't answer. She looked at Evan. He was feeling guilty and sorry and anxious to please her, and she was feeling nasty and ungenerous. "You can draw how it looked," she told him, but even that came out sounding grudging. She tried again. "You want to put the man back? You're so much faster than I am." She managed a half smile.

She didn't know whether it worked or whether he was just glad to get away from her, but he took the hilt and passed her, turning off to climb the embankment, his shortcut to the hut.

TWENTY-ONE

Bᴿᴏᴛʜᴇʀ and sisters seemed to have arrived at some kind of agreement, for they studiously ignored all further allusions to the Other Place. But Claudia and Evan could feel surreptitious glances in the direction of the piece of carved wood that Evan dragged over to dry beside the fire. Their only lapse from this detachment was Tim's seemingly absent-minded reaching for the yoke section to feed to the fire.

Claudia and Evan seized it just in time.

"Sorry. Something special?"

"Sure is."

And no more was said, though it was a labored absence of inquiry.

The whole day was like that, full of things half started, projects abandoned when nothing seemed to be going right. Long dispirited silences.

Once Rebecca muttered something to the effect that she'd thought nothing could be worse than the fog. She left the statement hanging.

Maddie, trying to lighten their mood, reminded them that their time was nearly up. They talked about how they could end their island stay in good spirits. They considered the phoniness of sunny dispositions put on for

234

show, for effect. They went off on separate quests, one for sorrel, two for clams, one for drawing, and one for none of anybody else's business.

Claudia kept trying to sort out how she really felt about leaving. She wasn't sure whether the sullen dread that stalked her thoughts was a reaction to the general atmosphere or a sense of something painful, of sorrow and loss, that was connected with the Other Place. Still she knew that if she could be sure of seeing Fergus once more, she would risk almost anything to get there.

By bedtime she had come to the conclusion that she was ready to leave the island, that what she really wanted was to be prevented from seeing and hearing any more. It was a relief to sink into the darkness, to listen to the night sounds of land and sea, the fitful wind that seemed to have sprung up from nowhere, aimless but with a cutting edge that made her feel like ducking down deep inside her sleeping bag.

She fought against waking. She would bury herself in the darkness, in the creaking of the trees, the moaning of the wind itself. But something kept on slapping until finally she gave in. She would find what was making that irritating noise and fix it, if she could, without ever quite opening her eyes.

She hauled herself out of the sleeping bag. Creeping toward the sound, she groped with one hand, cultivating a deliberate blindness that would permit her to sink right back into sleep. Someone's foul-weather jacket was flapping on a rock, whipping and smacking the metal fastenings. She grabbed the jacket and rolled it up.

A weird wind. Not a hint of rain, yet somehow driving.

235

She could hear the sea making up against the shore. Something distant—a bell buoy?—clanged through a tunnel of emptiness, and then the wind took over again, wailing. It sounded mournful, human.

Claudia forgot about her sleeping bag, forgot about sleep. Her eyes were wide. She could make out the night dance of the trees, tall and black, sometimes disappearing into a dark void, sometimes arched and springing into view. She thought of the figures against the Beltane fires. There was a kind of frenzy to this dance.

She was walking now and hugging her sweater tight around her though she wasn't really cold. Her feet were antennae recording her progress: now they padded along the cushion of moss, the fringes of needles at the base of the firs; now they gripped a granite surface that seemed to hold some remnant of warmth from yesterday's sun; now they stepped onto rocks that had been awash already and were cold as the sea. She sucked in her breath, but nothing could keep her back.

She hardly recognized the islet. She was thinking only of the terrible lament that was carried to her on the wind.

All about her, low-growing branches bent down, prostrate. Above, sweeping over the trees, swirling and torn as if pierced by the tallest limbs, the crying wind led her forward over the ridge to the bare turf that sloped to the cliff.

Here the spume leapt up from the waves and cast a film over the darkness. She could see rocks turned soft and mossy by clinging vapors. Water and air merged, so that it was impossible to tell where one left off and the other started. She peered down at a rounded boulder half-submerged; it was like a human figure kneeling at the edge of the sea.

A wave struck. When the spray landed, it fell every which way, some foam sliding backward and then clinging to the soft gray surface, some flung forward like strands of hair hanging from a bowed head. Then the wind seemed to catch its breath. Even the sea hesitated. And when, a moment later, the wailing commenced once more, it was from that spray-laden rock that it issued.

Quaking, Claudia hunched down, then leaned over. It wasn't the recognition so much as the weeping that struck her as strange and ominous. Fedelm of the laughing song had been transformed into this grief-stricken maiden who scrubbed at something in her hands, wringing it and wringing it in anguish, while uttering a wailing cry that rose and fell like a wind that had lost its direction.

Maybe it wasn't Fedelm after all, but someone with her likeness. In the spectral light surrounding her, this maiden's hair was loose, a pale gossamer covering her shoulders and back and altogether hiding her face.

"Fedelm?" Claudia whispered. The wind whipped the name from her lips and sent it flying. Claudia called again, this time with some voice.

The maiden below broke off her wailing, though her body continued to sway with the rhythm of her lament and her hands continued to dip and scrub and wring at the garment she held. "Who calls?"

Claudia answered softly, "The groundling."

"Which groundling calls Fedelm from her keening?"

"The one you gave to Fergus."

"Oh, Fergus, Fergus." The lament resumed.

Claudia waited a long time. "Are you crying about Fergus?"

"Oh, Fergus," Fedelm wept, "if you were but in this place now . . . ."

"If Fergus were here, what?" Claudia demanded. "Why don't you tell me what this is all about? If you need Fergus, why don't you get him?"

"Too late. Medb has Fergus in Connaucht; he is hidden from all these events that surround the Hound. All is over." She raised the garment. "I wash and I wash." She wrung it, and water the color of blood ran from her hands. "So groundling, wherever you are, stay back."

"You mean you can't see me?" All at once Claudia was aware of how the night still contained her. It didn't begin to pale till the cliff dropped away, the darkness thinning into the faintly gray atmosphere below.

"It is only because this is Samain that I can hear you. As for seeing, no. I can travel some, but you are yet distant. Besides, there is too much redness before me. All I see is the Hound making ready for his last combat. His people have failed to keep him from it. Even his charioteer could not prevail. Nor the horse, the Gray of Macha, which for the first time ran from the harness. The Hound himself had to command it to stand. It knows. All the animals know. The birds have ceased their singing; the hares and martens have gone deep into the woods where no light ever enters; the wolves and deer are huddled together in the deepest hollows of the glens." She paused. "I suppose that is why your voice can reach me at all. Because of the silence."

Together they listened to that silence. Then Fedelm

238

bent to her washing and wailing, and a moment later Claudia could hear hoofs pounding, creaking wheels bearing down on them.

The chariot passing between them hesitated briefly as the Hound and his charioteer caught sight of Fedelm. Not a word was spoken, but Fedelm half turned and lifted the garment up before the men. They saw what Claudia saw: the tunic Fedelm held up to the Hound was the tunic he wore; it was yellow as Fedelm's hair, its threads just as fine; the border, in-turned scrolls of gold on pine-dark green, was patterned at the throat and hemline, except that the one Fedelm held up to show was rent by a terrible gash across the front and was bloodied.

"Dear brother," whispered the charioteer, "let us return."

"On," rasped the Hound. "Never have I turned from combat save once, and that I did with trust, with life and honor guaranteed."

"The Gray refused the bit. It was the first time ever he would not come. Master, the day is evil. Let us go."

"It has been set since Cathbad spoke and I took arms. There is but one man with persuasion enough to turn me from a battle." The Hound paused. "And I know not where he stays, my master Fergus." His tone hardened. "No, I would not live another day were I to flee from those awaiting me."

"Stupid," hissed Claudia.

Fedelm wept and plunged the tunic into the water. Swirls of red clouded her hands and covered the cloth. She was stooped, her back to them, when the chariot surged forward, the reluctant gray and black ponies forced by the goad to a gallop.

"Why didn't you say something?" Claudia charged. "You could have stopped them."

Fedelm shook her head. "I have seen," she moaned. "I have already seen."

"Seen what?"

"Look for yourself. Across the plain."

Claudia rose to her feet and scanned the distance. There was something strange about her position. She was still on the islet cliff; yet below, in every direction, were plains and hills and a river. From her islet darkness she was peering into a dim daylight world beyond. "But I can't see anything," she began. "Yes, I can. It's the chariot. At the curve."

"And beyond? What see you beyond, there where the wood comes down to the vale?"

"A fire."

"A fire surely. Who tends that fire? Medb has sent them. Look, girl."

Claudia saw three grotesque figures huddled around the fire. As the chariot approached, one of the figures arose and flung itself in the path of the horses, which came to a rearing halt. It was an old woman. She reached up, as if to take the gray pony by the bridle. At this he flung his head high and struck out with his forefeet.

"What's she saying to them?" Claudia wanted to know.

"Wheedling. Begging them not to refuse her poor offering."

"Oh, is that all." Claudia shrugged.

But Fedelm was keening again. Red flowed from the tunic. And all at once Claudia knew. It wasn't that she could see so clearly or that she could hear what those distant figures said. It was Fedelm's wailing that spoke to her without words. It must be a dog they were roasting on the spit over their fire, and it was the meat of the dog they were offering to the Hound. "He can't," Claudia burst out. "He knows he mustn't. It's his geise not to."

"And so it is his geise to refuse no food from the hearth of the lowly." The little fire was flickering, lighting the tiny figures as in a dream.

"He couldn't even hear us now," Claudia reflected as she saw the Hound reach for the meat with his left hand, then—a sudden, puzzling sight—saw the hand drop to his side. "But he's not. He didn't take it. I don't think . . . ." She was all mixed up. There, distant, and tiny as doll food, was the dog leg after all, held low beside his thigh.

Fedelm was swaying and shaking her head. "Never will he hold a shield again. Now will he go into combat defenseless."

Concentrating on the faraway figures, Claudia tried to make out what Fedelm was saying. She had to check back, comparing the Hound's left arm with his right. "It's . . . smaller," she remarked wonderingly.

Fedelm only nodded as she swayed over her bloody garment. "Withered. As it took the flesh of dog." She sighed. "It is almost over."

Claudia sank back. She listened to the keening and told herself that nothing could be done. Even the Hound knew he was going to his death.

"What will happen . . . ?" she asked finally. She sensed that if Fergus were witness to these events, they would become at once more real and more terrible to

241

her. Afraid, she couldn't even bring herself to speak his name. "What will happen to . . . to the others?"

Fedelm didn't answer.

"Fedelm," Claudia insisted.

"It has begun," cried Fedelm, ignoring Claudia's question. "Not a band, but an entire host to meet him. His spear is raised."

"But how can he fight so many?" Suddenly, urgently, Claudia longed for Fergus to appear, though whether to stem the tide of doom or to force her to confront its reality, she could not tell.

"He stays his spear, for a bard has stepped forward, and all bards are above attack. The bard is asking for the Hound's spear."

"That's crazy," Claudia blurted. "What right—"

"The Hound must comply, for the bard threatens to revile him and destroy his name." Fedelm paused. "It is done. But the spear, of its own, has killed the bard. And now the foe takes up that spear and hurls it at the Hound."

"And kills him?" gasped Claudia.

"It is the charioteer who falls. The Hound kneels, draws out the spear and holds it high, dripping with the blood of his dear companion."

"And kills the one that did it," Claudia supplied.

"And once again is stopped by a bard who demands that spear."

"I hope this time he has enough sense to refuse."

"He protests, but must yield it, or his kinsmen be mocked."

"No, it's just a trick. Fedelm, doesn't he know it's a trick?"

Fedelm's voice sounded a single low note of anguish. "And this bard falls as well, and the spear is hurled back." She sighed. "This time the Hound must draw the spear from the Gray of Macha. He releases the beast from the chariot pole. Oh, there is blood running down the shining breastplate. The horse plunges like a wounded seal, the smoothness gone, the grace and speed all gone, and nearly tramples one more bard who steps out now from the enemy host."

"Another?" gasped Claudia.

"His threat is satire against all of Ulidia."

"What does it matter?" Claudia cried. "Why is the Hound so stupid? Tell him, Fedelm. Let me tell him."

Fedelm nearly laughed through her weeping. "And what would you say to the Hound of Culann at this moment?"

"I'd tell him never mind what the bards compose. They're only words, those satires. Nothing but words."

"Oh, groundling, your notions are so out of place and out of time. Words are more powerful than any weapons. They will not flake and peel like iron, nor dull as the burnished bronze to the look of a stagnant mire. They can destroy the name of a man, mock his memory and the honor of his people. Worse, they can reduce him to nothing, cast him into oblivion, so that none will recall his name in generations to come or praise his deeds or valor." Fedelm gazed into the reddened tunic.

"What else do you see?"

Fedelm dropped the ragged mess into the water. "Look for yourself. I have seen enough."

"How can I? I don't have your sight." But as she spoke, she knew that her sight was not as it had been.

243

Even without Fergus, she was seeing the Hound with a different eye. He was not hunter alone, but hunted; not just feared, but hated. He was more and at the same time less than this fierce restless energy at bay; he was a boy she recognized, haughty and quick, cut off from every living thing.

Wordlessly Fedelm pointed, this time along the shoreline. Claudia leaned out over the cliff. "I still can't see enough," she protested. "I'll have to get closer." She rolled over on her stomach and let her legs down, swinging with her feet for a toe hold.

"Stay back," hissed Fedelm. "I am powerless this day. You would be lost."

Claudia scrambled back. "It's so hard to see," she complained. Still, she was beginning to make out tiny figures. It was like looking through the wrong end of the field glasses. "Anyhow, how did you know I was coming through? I thought you couldn't see me."

"I see danger, groundling." Fedelm's voice was like a plaintive song now as she added, "I see him go to drink the water and bathe his wound; they allow this, for he is finished." She stirred the water with the ragged tunic. All was blood red.

Claudia looked back to the distant figures. Now she could make them out, the hosts of warriors everywhere coming up behind the wounded Hound, who was turning to face them, his back at a pillar stone standing at the water's edge. He seemed preoccupied with something. "What's he doing?" Claudia wondered out loud.

"Binding himself to the stone. To keep from falling."

The warriors kept coming, hundreds of them, weapons glinting, forming a living crescent that nearly surrounded

244

the dying Hound. Then the crescent separated as if it were suddenly ripped apart. The Gray of Macha was galloping into the throng, lashing out all about him. At last he broke through into the space between the gathering enemy and the Hound. He halted before his master, the gray muzzle to the gray-white face.

The host inched forward. The pony whirled and charged, striking down warriors and tearing with his teeth. Again he approached the Ulidian hero, whose body was beginning to sag against the pillar stone. Once more the host spread like a shadow at the sinking of the sun, and once more the Gray of Macha wheeled and struck. When he turned back to the Hound, his head was lower; he merely nuzzled the limp, withered hand. It was all he could do to face the warriors for the last time. Yet the armies of Medb held back as if he were still powerful enough to cut them down. Blood dripped from the flaring nostrils and flowed from countless wounds, but his eyes kept watch and at the slightest movement from a single warrior the pony's ears twitched. The Hound was quite still, but he too held his eyes to his waiting enemy.

Fedelm stopped wailing. Even the wind had abated, as if the sky itself had ceased to breathe. Then, out of that empty sky, something small and black came plummeting. It might have been a stone cast from a thunderous sling, for it hurtled toward the pillar in a streak. At the last instant, with spreading wings, it broke its fall, circling above the Hound. Suddenly real and ungainly, talons splayed, wings beating for balance, it fell to his shoulder. The moment the crow landed, a roar issued from the armed crescent; all the warriors surged forward as one; horse and Hound were obliterated.

245

Claudia started forward.

"Stay back," came Fedelm's voice.

"But what are they doing?" Claudia cried out.

Fedelm lifted up the tunic. It was torn in many places now; even the scrollwork was ripped and blood-soaked. The keening resumed.

Claudia blinked. She had to fasten on something bearable, practical. "Does . . . Fergus know?" Wrong question. Whatever the answer, it would be unbearable.

"The sword will be broken. Fergus will be given the lands of his fosterling."

"Then he'll be home," Claudia exclaimed. Something salvaged after all. It was like a reprieve. "Fergus will be where he belongs."

Fedelm was shaking her head.

"Fergus won't return?"

Fedelm held up the cloth. It wasn't recognizable anymore. It might have been a tunic once, or perhaps a cloth for scrubbing the great bronze cauldron of the queen.

"I don't want it to end sadly," Claudia whispered. "Why can't Fergus be happy?" Maybe after all she really could make a difference. "Fedelm," she began, "help me to come through."

"The time is past."

"Isn't this still Samain Day?"

"Look up, you headstrong creature. Whoever you are, wherever you come from, you must have enough wit to see that you cannot go where the Hound will travel, where Fergus—"

"Will Fergus die too?"

"Groundling, understand that only mortals die. By your own word, you are mortal enough to fear the bog.

Step not upon this blood-soaked beach. See what awaits you." Fedelm was pointing to a fir branch jutting out down the coastline at some distance from the islet. On it perched the crow, its scrawny wings drawn up about its head. It didn't have the look of the death bird that had dropped to the shoulder of the Hound. It looked smaller and merely bedraggled.

"It's our crow," Claudia shouted. "Wait till I tell Evan." She turned excitedly to Fedelm, but all that remained was the blood-stained water which gradually thinned out into millions of ripples under a dying wind.

Claudia was still on the edge of the cliff. On the horizon a faint redness was oozing its color into the depth of the bay. Clouds reflected the fiery glow and were drained white.

Claudia glanced again at the fir down on the main part of the island. The crow had moved to another branch. Below her the stone that looked like a stooping figure was turning gray in the sunrise.

It was a dream, she decided on her way back. I only dreamed it. She found everyone still asleep. Her feet were freezing, so she snuggled back down inside her sleeping bag to get them warm.

It wasn't hard, when she was the last to wake, to believe that she had dreamed every bit of it.

TWENTY-TWO

SHE couldn't shrug off her uneasiness. Even after Evan pointed out that it could only have been a dream because she hadn't had the bronze hilt with her and the crow had, in fact, not turned up, she still couldn't rid herself of the feeling of exhaustion and emptiness that followed that night.

Maddie asked her if she felt all right. Evan spoke for her: she'd had a nightmare, a whole bunch of nightmares; she was just tired. They were not impressed, so he embellished the theme; she had been sleepwalking, he told them. They didn't believe him, but they didn't like the sound of that anyway.

"It was such a queer night," Maddie offered. "That sudden wind. Did you hear it? I thought we were in for one of those bad northeasters. Then it just . . . just suddenly died."

Tim scanned the eastern horizon. The wind had veered from the north. "Light's still queer," he observed. The water had turned steely gray; a small chop was making up.

"Well, cheer up." Maddie smiled at Claudia. "Only one more day to go."

248

Claudia wandered off to be alone. Did she look forward to having her mother and Phil come to take them off the island? Maybe this curiously leaden feeling was merely boredom. But it had been Samain Day, she reminded herself; maybe you didn't need the bronze man on the Feast of Samain. Why were the figures so distant then, so different from the beginning when she could smell the breads and broth? Why had Fedelm wept and wept, Fedelm who could do anything?

She was still pondering these questions when Evan bellowed from halfway down the sheep track that he could see the parents coming. Reacting slowly, she was the last to make it to the cove where they were all gathered to meet Phil and Susan rowing in from the anchored boat.

Everyone was talking at once, laughing, demanding gifts from the mainland, juice and milk, mail and messages. Phil and Susan wanted to know all about their week, and accounts of food-gathering and cooking, beachcombing and hut-building, all ran together, a jumble of exploits.

It was after they had reached the campsite and the parents were explaining about coming early because of uncertain weather conditions that Susan first noticed Claudia's listlessness. Evan, his tone a little defensive, promptly mentioned sleepwalking and hinted at other mysterious occupations.

Claudia recognized the searching look that came over her mother when she was "reading between the lines," as she called it. To her surprise, it was Tim who came to her rescue by inviting everyone to laugh it off. She didn't even resent it when he told their mother that the little kids were in possession of an old sword hilt which had a mind of its own and took them back to the time when it had its blade.

"It's that crazy old man," Rebecca supplied. "A worse influence on Evan than even Claudia."

Phil remarked that Evan looked all right to him, so Rebecca pointed out the yoke. "Ask about that. Go ahead. Ask what he thinks it is."

Evan went to stand protectively beside his yoke. Claudia could see that he was dying to tell Phil all about it. And Phil was curious. He reached out, taking the piece of carved wood from Evan. "Must belong to that fellow over at Head Harbor," he mused. "The guy who does all that carving on his boat. Probably one of those bilge pump handles he's rigged up." He gazed at it, frowned. "I'd say it's been in the water a good long time."

Evan flushed. "It's a yoke," he pronounced tightly.

"A what?"

Rebecca gave a triumphant laugh.

Evan sent Claudia an imploring look. She knew he wanted to show Phil the hilt. She shook her head at him.

Phil intercepted the gesture. "What is this?" He smiled.

"I told you," Rebecca responded. "It's Claudia making up all those half-assed stories."

"They're not half-assed," said Evan.

"They're not stories," said Claudia. "Evan, draw them a picture of the yoke. The whole thing."

Evan seemed glad to have an excuse to duck out, but that left Claudia standing alone against Rebecca's tirade.

"She fills him full of all that crap about swords and this Fergus—"

"Who's Fergus?" Phil interrupted. "The island recluse?"

"He's one of those characters of theirs," Tim put in.

"He's not a character," Claudia corrected. "He lived—"

"See what I mean?" hooted Rebecca.

"Let Claudia finish," Phil told her.

Susan questioned whether he should be encouraging Claudia like this, and Claudia shouted for Evan to hurry up with the drawing.

"Yeah," Rebecca intoned, "what that kid needs isn't encouragement, but a shrink."

"What's a shrink?" asked Evan, returning with a sheet of paper.

"A headhunter," came Phil's prompt reply.

"Phil," Susan warned. She turned to Evan. "A psychiatrist, dear. A doctor."

"Claudia doesn't need a doctor."

"It's a special kind of doctor who helps you see things—"

"Like Fedelm?"

"Like what?"

"No, Evan," Claudia tried to explain. "More like Cathbad, I think."

"Who's Cathbad?" Phil demanded.

"Phil, don't start shouting."

"He's a druid we know," Evan said in passing. It was Claudia he was trying to talk to. "How's this?" He was showing her the picture he had quickly sketched.

"A druid?" yelped Phil. "A DRUID?" He began to laugh, and the more he laughed, the more Susan bit her lip and looked disapproving.

Evan's sketch was rough, but it showed the pony team

251

with the oval yoke pads fitting across their withers, the reins leading through the holes at the curved ends.

"But look," Tim pointed out, peering over Claudia's shoulder, "the piece you have is flat here."

"Busted." Evan was unfazed. He showed Tim what was left of the curve. "Sometimes they put sheepskin underneath to make it easier. Our ponies," he finished proudly, "never got sores. You've got to keep their hair from matting. They sweat, see, and then you have to rub them down or even wash them with snow."

Phil, who had managed to stop laughing, looked it over and pronounced it an interesting picture.

"Except he forgot the breastplates and helmets," Claudia murmured.

The others pretended they hadn't heard, but Evan said, "I'll put them in, and then I'll take it up to Mr. Colman for a good-by present."

The talk turned to other matters, such as who would eat the clams that had been dug and who would eat the steak that had been brought. And who would sleep on the boat for this last night. Claudia, maybe, in case of more nightmares.

Suddenly Claudia was choked with panic. Now that the decision was being made for her, she knew it was wrong. She would have to get a chance to talk to Evan alone. Except for the picture of the ponies yoked to the chariot, he seemed to be reconciled to moving aboard and leaving the Other Place behind.

She tagged along when he asked Phil to come meet Mr. Colman and see the way he'd cleaned up the shack. Father and son were chatting amiably until Evan was sure the others were out of earshot. "You know any druids?" He sounded eager, but wary too.

Phil looked down at him before answering carefully, "Not personally." Claudia thought Phil was struggling to contain his laughter.

She heard the others catching up with them. They had decided to show up for the presentation of Evan's picture. Besides, Rebecca thought Susan ought to see where Evan had been spending so much time and just what sort of old fool Mr. Colman really was.

It was when they discovered he wasn't back yet that Claudia found her way out of the dilemma about sleeping on the boat. "Sometimes he comes in late and leaves again early in the morning. Evan and I will have to stay on the island just to be sure to get to see him."

Evan started to contradict her, but she glared at him. He got the unspoken message; only as soon as Phil seemed preoccupied with the peat, Evan edged over to her and whispered, "He'll be back soon. You know that."

Phil, fingering the peat, looked up at them. "Where'd he dig this up?"

Casually Claudia indicated the islet. "They all burn peat over there, except when they're in the forests."

"Don't forget the dung," Evan added. He started to explain to his open-mouthed father about the drying of manure.

Phil was murmuring, "I'll be damned. Where in God's name is there any peat around here?"

"Want me to show you how to light them, Dad?" Evan opened the cast-iron stove and poked the cold ash.

"No, don't," Rebecca said. "It makes you all weepy."

253

"Does it?" Phil remarked, his voice sounding queer, dry. "You're all familiar with this?"

Everyone started filling in at once, layers of accounts smothering Evan's simple explanation. Claudia remained silent; she couldn't understand why Mr. Colman had let the fire die.

Later, she tried to explain to Evan how his gift for Mr. Colman was their only excuse for staying ashore. He had never seemed more dense and stubborn; he even suggested that the parents spend the night on the island too, which would have ruined their last chance to visit the Other Place. Fortunately there was the weather problem; the Coast Guard had issued two conflicting forecasts for the Gulf of Maine and the Bay of Fundy. Something was up, some disturbance or pressure system, and Phil decided to stay with the boat and wait it out, whatever it was. To Claudia's relief, her mother went with him.

But even after the parents had left, Evan seemed restive and reluctant. "Everything's different now," he told her.

Knowing he was right only made her lash out at him. She felt mean and a little frightened.

"It's too late," he maintained. "Probably it'll be something altogether different there, the way Mr. Colman says it sometimes is. Nothing you'd recognize."

"But why?" she insisted. "Why should it be?" She craved any reassurance she could get, a wavering on his part, a faulty argument.

"Anyhow, maybe you can't go there when you've got, you know, grownups around."

"Mr. Colman's a grownup," she shot back.

Evan sighed. He wasn't equal to her intensity. He was

254

full of real food and he felt good and sleepy. "I should go say good-by right now," he remarked, but without much conviction.

She didn't know whether it would be better for him to see Mr. Colman, who might spark his interest again, or get right to sleep. If they were going to take turns keeping watch for the night fog, he should get what rest he could. Oh, she didn't know. Besides, she had her own doubts to deal with. Not exactly doubts, she decided; just the knowledge she had been trying to deny by pushing Evan around.

She had secreted some of their marvelous feast into her pockets against the long vigil ahead. Now, as Evan slept, she fished out a mashed cupcake, extracting it from the waxed paper. She ate every crumb and every flake of icing and then licked thoughtfully at the wrapping. "Fergus," she whispered. "Fedelm. Medb." She stopped. The Hound was dead, Fedelm utterly changed, and all of them so far from her that they had no reality at all. What was real was a piece of limp, crumby wax paper with a sweetness that remained long after it had lost its shape.

She put her head down on her hands, shifted her weight once, then again, so that the coil on her neck would not bite into her skin. Her torc, her harp string. She rested that way, her fingers closed around it as if it were a talisman promising her safe travel through ages of fog as deep as the centuries.

When she tried to wake Evan for his turn, he was curled into a tight knot. She could roll him like a puppy, but that was all. She gave up. If she had to, she would stay awake all night by herself.

Twice she crawled out of her sleeping bag and went to

255

stand by the shore. She studied the overcast sky. She would settle for anything, even a little of the ground mist that sometimes rose from the warmer land mass and hovered over the water until the sun burned it off.

The third time she went out to check the weather she met Rebecca.

"Did you hear something?" Rebecca whispered.

Claudia shook her head.

"Funny. I thought I heard . . . . It sounded like someone swearing."

"Maybe they were talking out on the boat." What if Rebecca followed her? She made herself stay quiet for a long time.

At last her patient wakefulness was rewarded. Wisps like smoke from smoldering ashes seeped up through the fingers of the firs. She prodded Evan, shook him, sat him up.

His head lolled; he pushed her away. "I don't care," he mumbled. "It's all over anyway. Leave me alone."

She was in the grip of a desperate determination. "What if it's your dun pony? What if he's in trouble, and you could save him?"

Evan rubbed his eyes. "If it happened all that time ago, how can you change anything?" After a moment he added, "You can't, can you?"

She was stumped. Then meanness took over. "He's there and he can sense when you're there too. You said so. Evan, you'll never know whether he makes it . . . out of the bog. The mud sucking him in, Evan. He's struggling."

Evan let her pull him out of the sleeping bag. Grumbling, he put on clothes, then led the way to the hut.

"Ssh," he warned, turning to her at the threshold. But there was no need for quiet. Old Mr. Colman was not inside.

The children were staggered. Evan couldn't believe that Mr. Colman would go without saying good-by. Claudia kept thinking of how she had meant to tell him that she thought she'd seen his crow. "Maybe he didn't plan to be out overnight," she suggested. "I mean, wasn't he just going to check his traps?"

"That was . . . day before yesterday."

Claudia fetched the bronze man and held it out to Evan. Now she wanted him to feel better. It was no good unless he cared.

Almost without noticing, Evan took the proffered hilt and led the way to the bar. It was already submerged. He stood there dispiritedly, as if content to wait for the next ebb. He might have fallen asleep on his feet if Claudia hadn't started pushing and insisting.

"It's too cold."

"Please, Evan, it's the last time." But she couldn't make herself charge him up with horror tales about the dun-colored pony. She just grabbed the hilt from him, held onto his hand, and led him into the freezing water.

It had never seemed so cold. Evan said so. Then he said it wouldn't work anyway.

"Why?"

"Because the old man's gone."

"But we have the hilt."

"Because of the grownups. Everything's different now."

Claudia clenched her teeth. "We have to try."

"What if we get stuck out here? The tide's coming."

257

"Evan, please," was all she could reply. They were slithering on the treacherous rockweed. In the peculiar darkness of the cloud-cover and mist, there was no way of telling where an edge of granite waited to slam their shins or knees. Finally they had to feel their way with their hands, the water clinging to their sleeves like weights.

Just as they reached the other side they heard the voices. They hesitated there at the base of the turtle's tail, each of them listening for familiar tones, each separately concluding that the speakers were unrecognizable.

They heard, "I am certain, yes. This was the place. Here did I chant my lay to summon Fergus mac Roich. Here at this stone they raised for him."

Another voice spoke quietly: "It is told that he was drowned. Have you heard that? That he was tricked and drowned by the King of Connaucht and that afterward the sea burst over his mound?" The voice paused. "Yet some claim it happened another way. I know that all the bards of Erenn have taken part in the quest for the whole true story. I hope that we scribes, on whom the duty now falls, will complete it."

The children approached the voices. They were so baffled and curious that they paid no attention to the noise they made as they groped blindly along the turtle's spine. It wasn't until one of the speakers whirled and pointed in their direction that they stopped short.

The man who faced them seemed to be the taller of the two. The other, who was kneeling beside a large boulder, was covered from head to bare toe in a whitish robe. Beside him was a bundle. The children could not see what it contained.

At the other's sudden gesture, the kneeling man also looked around toward Claudia and Evan, but with no sign of alarm. "You see figments of your pagan dreams. It is early yet, and we are alone."

"Early. Three days have you fasted here on your knees. I tell you, scribe, Fergus will not come for you if he would not answer the poem I composed to summon him."

"Mine is not the power that commands. I and my brother scribes are charged with recording these ancient tales, so that they may live forever in the retelling. If you did not regard the craft of writing as unfit for this great purpose, and if you had not abused your power, you bards might not now be left with such paltry fragments of this history. I have the blessing of the saints. I will keep my fast and hold my vigil here."

The bard kept glancing nervously toward the children. "Yet do I fear what I sense, a presence above the mound."

"He must mean us," Evan whispered.

"Your fear comes of ignorance and error."

"But it may be the huntsmen of Donn within the mound of Fergus. It is said that on certain nights they ride forth from the dead."

The scribe shook his head. "That is the old magic. It is finished."

The bard was pacing nervously. His eyes darted first toward the stone, then back to where the children remained frozen, watching and listening.

The scribe spoke in reassuring tones. "An ancient fable, that of Donn, Lord of the Dead. A remnant of the false belief."

The bard regarded the scribe in amazement. "You really have not fear of what may issue from that mound?"

"I fear no spirit of the ancient heroes."

"What if it is the huntsmen of Donn who ride upon you as you kneel there, feeble from your days of fasting?"

"It is Fergus I await."

The bard drew a breath. "Well, I have brought you to the place. I have watched beside you these long days and nights. I will take my leave while there is yet strength to stay ahead of the demons of the hunt." He hesitated. "You will not come with me?"

The scribe bowed his head. "I thank you for your guidance and wish you the enduring power of poetry and grace." He kept his head low while the bard turned on his heel and quickly disappeared.

What followed was a long silence. Then Evan whispered again: "I'd like to ask him how long it's going to take."

Claudia mumbled groggily. "Does this mean Fergus is dead? The way they talk about him . . . ."

Evan's answer was sharp. "It means everything we were in before happened ages and ages ago. Maybe a hundred years."

"But is he really dead? I mean, at the time of these two?"

"You ever heard of anyone living more than a hundred years?"

"Maybe it's less time than that. You don't know."

"Or a lot more."

Claudia considered this possibility. Her mind was whirling. How could she have missed Fergus after all her striving and watching? How could she still be herself, and crouch within sight of his grave? "I don't feel any different," she murmured. But she did. The leaden sensation of the past days had been a kind of going away, she supposed, a giving-in.

"I wish we could talk to that guy," Evan went on. "He doesn't even know we're here."

"He's concentrating on Fergus. It's funny we can understand what they said, though. Evan, that must mean it's more or less the same period." She tried to take comfort from this conclusion. She wished Evan would agree with her.

But Evan was simply growing restless. He kept changing his position, fidgeting with the bronze hilt. "Let's go back," he whispered finally.

Claudia shook her head.

"Nothing's happening."

"Oh, go then. You don't care. You don't even care—" She cut off her reproach about the dun-colored pony. What was the point of keeping Evan against his will?

But now that he was free to go, he hesitated. "What if it's those hunters of Donn?"

"What if I don't believe in them?"

"Fergus believed in Donn. Remember about the bull, Donn Cuailgne?"

Claudia really didn't know what she thought any more. But this silent, kneeling scribe had spoken with such quiet authority that she believed Fergus would come to him. "You go," was her answer. She was beyond argument. She felt Evan placing the hilt in her hands. She let it drop. "I don't need it now." She felt angry at his desertion, not scared.

A moment later he was back. "Claude. Don't . . .

261

don't try to cross back if it's too deep. I can get them to bring the dinghy around."

All she could feel was disappointment. She had thought he was changing his mind and would stay.

"Claude, did you hear me?"

She nodded, not caring whether he could make out the gesture or not.

TWENTY-THREE

For a long time she watched the scribe while the scribe watched the pillar stone before him. She felt herself dozing. It was good to let her eyes fall shut. She jerked her head up just as it was beginning to touch the cold wet ground. Suddenly she was wide awake. The scribe was no longer kneeling beside the stone. He was moving slowly, trancelike, toward the water. She slid down the cliff edge and followed until he came to a halt.

Mist curled around him, enveloping him in a web. She crept closer, her eyes fixed on the threads of moisture that wound themselves around him. It was a strange effect. He looked a little like a fat cocoon. She stared at his bare feet. They were the only part of him that seemed real any more. The mist was expanding. Soon she too was surrounded by the smooth gray essence, but now the scribe was clearer, and so too the other figure that slowly, silently appeared at the edge of the water.

Claudia was spellbound. As he emerged, standing in a craft that resembled an oversized walnut shell, he seemed to be suspended in the same web of mist. Yet she could see every detail of the man, his splendid cloak finer than the purple, its cloth with threads of gold shot through the woven green and blue. His face was unaltered, except that now it wore a look of unconcern, as if all care had been taken from him. Only, strangely, his beard and hair seemed to drip, as though he were risen from the sea. Although the scabbard was missing from his side, he carried the hilt before him as he stood facing the scribe.

"Welcome, Fergus."

"I trust that welcome, but I may come no closer."

"You may trust it, for I am charged with the task of committing to this book all you remember of your people and their history."

"I have not heard of any book. The bards set laws and histories onto the great wheel of memory and it spins ceaselessly from generation to generation. My people mark the names of heroes in oghams upon their pillar stones, and sometimes ogham phrases are cut on bronze and iron. The blade that joined this hilt had ogham marks, and they are still words on the wheel of my memory."

The scribe stooped down to his bundle and brought out a stiffly covered volume. He opened it to the first page. "Here have I begun with the story of Macha who was made to race against the horses of the king. This is the writing of it."

Fergus smiled. "That is in our ancient tales. The twins she bore gave our royal seat its name and our people a long and difficult penance." He was looking with interest at the scribe's book. "Your marks have many running shapes, like wavelets on a gentle sea. That is writing?"

The scribe started to hand the book to him, but Fergus pulled back, holding the hilt before him, bringing the scribe to a halt.

"You fear me then," said the scribe in quiet wonderment.

Fergus shook his great tangled head. "I am bound to the law of my ancestors, to the word of Donn, Lord of the Dead. I may not ever return to this land. If I but touch the earth of my ancient home, it will be as if I had lain in it for hundreds of years."

"Still you have come."

"I have followed this sword since it was given me by Cathbad. When it was broken at the grave of my fosterling, the blade and scabbard were buried with him to lead him to the Otherworld. I was to maintain his holdings, but when I was making ready for this, Ailill feared my going, thinking I might seek vengeance on the treachery done to the Hound. And so I never reached the land of my people. My charioteer was cut down, and I, with only my hilt, left for dead and cast adrift in this coracle."

"When was this?"

"I cannot tell how far it was to the Island of Mists or how long I have dwelt there. The hilt took me there, as it brought me here to you. Now I know the way westward without my sunstone; I will not journey from that land again."

"Then before you return will you tell me about the Ulidian heroes while I write in this book?"

"If you put it down with care and commit it to the holding of the most powerful druid, so that these heroes will live as long as the wheel of memory may spin."

"This book will be a record of all you say to me, Fergus. Others will copy what I have written, and with care, for that is how we are trained. The druids you would depend on are fading from this world."

"You must have great power to be taking their place."

The scribe returned Fergus's smile and seated himself

265

on a rock. "I have used all the power of my faith to call you forth with my fasting, and I feel emptier than I might easily describe. I am only a vessel that you must fill." He brought out a quill and a container into which he dipped the quill.

Fergus again smiled. "But of course your power is great. How else would you make your mark on that skin with a mere feather?"

"I use a dye." The scribe turned the brittle pages to show Fergus more of the writing. "It is different from our practice tablets where we cut our words into wax."

So Fergus began to relate the tales of Ulidia. Some of them were new to Claudia. Not all related to people she had seen or known. The telling was slow and careful, the writing continuous and painfully precise. It seemed to go on for a long time. Sometimes the scribe would raise his hand in a silent plea, and Fergus would pause and let him rest. Sometimes the scribe questioned Fergus closely and mentioned another version handed down by the bards.

Once Fergus broke off to reflect on those storytellers who would come after this writing. "They may not have your love of truth."

This made the scribe laugh. "There may be some more thorough than I without the slightest faith in the truth of this history. There will surely be storytellers who pass it on without knowing that they do. Each in his way, willing or unwilling, is a vessel like me. Let us hope that much will remain of what you are pouring into me and I spilling onto these vellum leaves."

The scribe had filled one book with beautiful writing, each new tale commencing with a letter resembling the scrolls on the missing scabbard. Had Fergus mentioned Claudia yet? She strained to catch her name as Fergus retraced his depiction of the fleeing harps. But she was at the mercy of her sleepiness and Fergus's steady drone.

"Now go back," the scribe interrupted. "Where was Ailill at this time?"

Such a question would prod Claudia into a momentary alertness. But soon she would subside again into drowsy pleasure at the voice, the tale, the feeling of being witness to the preservation of both.

It was always at the next query that she would awaken to a sense of what was missing. What about me? she wanted to demand. She willed Fergus to regard her, to recall.

"There are things I have left out," Fergus was confessing. "It was many years and many lives."

"Think again," prompted the scribe. "Were there others who conspired with Ulidians?"

What about me? Claudia insisted, invoking her image into the picture that Fergus drew.

"There was a bondsmaid . . . ," Fergus began.

Claudia sat bolt upright. She wanted to fling her arms around the scribe who was writing, who must be writing, though the letters were weird and foreign: "There was a bondsmaid . . . ," and looking up now, waiting for Fergus to continue.

"You tire?" the scribe observed. "You have stood all through this long telling."

"It is almost finished," Fergus responded.

"And the maid?"

Yes, echoed Claudia with her mind, the maid?

"A foolish thing. I pitied her, but I doubt any other

267

did . . . ." His voice trailed off as he reflected on her role.

"Oh, no," Claudia moaned.

The scribe looked up as if he could see her. She cowered in silence, startled by the directness of his mild eye.

"She was not important," Fergus concluded, "yet I could not help but think of how she had been caught up in circumstances she could never comprehend. Her folly brought her death."

All at once Claudia grasped that he was talking about Loche. Even so, relief was quickly replaced by anxiety. Had he forgotten her entirely?

"And many others, some more important, some less. I cannot tell of them all. Your hair would turn white before you had completed this writing."

Again the scribe urged Fergus to reveal everything within his memory. Fergus ran a hand through his heavy mane. He paused. "There were visions," he added haltingly, "and creatures made tame by strange happenings." He drew something from under his cloak. "I recall some of those things when I have this in my grasp. Yet maybe they were imaginings." His fingers rubbed the object. "There are those who touch you . . . . No ointments will heal those marks. Beltane. I had no joy of the coming of that sun. Through the bitter winter one creature, I know not who or what, carried this for a time, carried it for me, and was lost."

"The sunstone?"

Fergus nodded.

"And will you reveal its secret to me now before it too disappears?"

Slowly Fergus shook his head. "It may not disappear

until this hilt rests once more with blade and scabbard."
He seemed to be taking stock of the scribe. "You seem to
have a certain strength. Would you follow the sword of
Culann?"

"It is the secret I would carry, not the sword."

Fergus gestured toward the book. "Put that away from
you; make no markings with the dye."

The scribe set one vellum manuscript down beside the
other. Then, like a child, he held out his hands to show
that they held nothing.

"Came you here unarmed?" asked Fergus, suddenly
struck with the appearance of the scribe. "Are you like
the bards then, safe from attack, free to travel across all
boundaries, exacting your tributes?"

"Mine is a different brotherhood from that of the
bards. I have nothing, own nothing, not even this which I
have written down from you. I am a vessel, that is all.
And when this work is completed, I will go from here at
last to seek solitude in the pathless sea. I would live out
my life away from all I have known."

"Then let this gift and giver go to you who have nothing, for it will take you beyond all known bounds. And
let you pass it on when you are ready to send it from your
knowing." Claudia saw him bend over the side of the
coracle. "Only with water," he instructed. "Then the
bead floats in its place in the hilt." Holding the hilt out
flat, Fergus turned in one direction, then another.
"There. It points across his arm, there across the other
arm, and now to the leg. This is the magic of the sunstone
contained within the bead. Wherever you are, when fog
blots out the sun and clouds drive off the stars, this small
bead will tell you what your eye cannot see. It remem-

269

bers. You may set your course according to its pointing. It will not mislead you. It is as constant as the sun itself which keeps its course across the sky even when it is hidden from all human eyes."

The scribe was shaking his head, stepping back, stumbling. "I am only a scribe," he protested.

"Carry it," Fergus urged him. "Carry it for all those who are in the ancient tales you have been setting down with your crab-step writing." Fergus turned the bronze man over, catching the bead and draining out the drops of water from the hole. He lifted the thong from his neck and slipped the bead into place on it. Then, stretching to set it over the head of the stout, hesitant scribe, Fergus leaned out, reaching, with the hilt extended; the coracle rolled, and he stepped firmly onto the beach.

Claudia cried out, "No!" She couldn't hear the words of the scribe; she could only see him grasping the bead, transfixed, staring at the spot where Fergus, tall and confident of bearing, had just set foot.

It seemed as though masses of gossamer tentacles had seized Fergus, the fingers of the mist closing into a fist of white opacity. A vague fluttering stirred within that grasp; and then a stillness fell as when a captured moth beats out its life with failing wings. The mist parted its fingers and hung weakly over the edge of the water. Only the coracle remained, bobbing a little now that its burden was gone.

The scribe seemed uncertain, then suddenly reached for the coracle, which was beginning to slip back into the deeper water.

Without thinking, Claudia lunged after him. She was sure that if he touched that ghostly craft he would be lost.

270

If he were, then so too would be the history he had written down and the secret he had committed to memory.

The water was an icy clamp, squeezing the breath out of her. She forgot history, forgot the secret; all she knew was that this earnest, clumsy scribe had no business out in the deep water.

The sea held her back, but it slowed him too. His garments dragged at him and made him stumble. She opened her mouth, but no sound came. Her voice seemed frozen. The man was floundering, unequal to the cold and current. The coracle floated just out of reach. "Come back," she gasped. "Boat," he babbled. "Damn boat." Diving forward, she grabbed him. When she toppled him, she herself followed, dumped face-first into the water. She struggled to her feet and drew him back toward the shore.

"Damn," he spluttered, "damn." He tried to throw her off, but she had a firm grip on at least one of his layers of clothing.

She was so intent on getting him out that she scarcely noticed the ashen mound there where he had left the shore to plunge after the coracle. It was like a small gray heap of dust over which a whitish vapor seemed to hover, thin and transparent in the flat darkness.

They skirted this little pile as they regained the land. Once they were past it, groping for a safe dry place to rest, she caught sight of it again, saw, even as she turned to the shivering man beside her, how one of the thousand tongues of water reached out gently, delicately, and started to lick it away.

271

TWENTY-FOUR

MUCH later they were hunched side by side on a driftwood timber glowering at each other. He seemed unaware of his physical condition, only disconsolate over the loss of his boat. She was furious because she hadn't saved the scribe from a ghostly coracle at all, had merely kept Mr. Colman from rescuing his own double-ender when it had drifted off after he had landed here by accident.

He'd been set by the current, he told her, after some engine trouble over by the Reach. It had kept him out all the day, so that it was past dark and the fog patches sudden and thick by the time he made Thrumcap Island. "First time I come in I near fetched up to the other side where you have your fire. Had to pull off, free of the rocks, and then on the second try I landed just short of my cove." A spasm of shivering seized him and silenced him for a moment. Then he went on. "I've sat out a night like this before, but I never had the tide float my goddam boat off. Made fast it was too." He sounded hoarse and shaken. What he couldn't get over, he kept telling her, was someone interfering with him hauling it back.

"We won't have to wait till low tide to get across," she offered, hoping to make some kind of peace with him before having to face the humiliation of being rescued by her family. "My brother will get the others. They'll find your boat," she added with more conviction than she felt.

"Better find it soon, else it'll fetch up on some rock hereabouts."

"Oh, they will," she assured him. "Just as soon as Evan gets them."

"Boy here? Thought I heard talking."

"Yes, Evan and I—" She stopped. "You heard talking? Did you see anything?"

"Couldn't see your own whiskers on a night like this."

"But I mean were you in the Other Place? Were there . . . people?"

"Nothing but a pair of old hens clucking about . . . ."

"About what?" she pressed.

He shrugged. "The wits were out of them, you could tell."

"Did you see . . . a man in . . . in his little boat?"

Colman nodded slowly. "Damn oak tree, the size of him."

"Listen!" Claudia leaned toward him. "You have to remember it all, everything, even if you don't understand the language." She was shouting with excitement. "You're . . . you're a vessel."

"My boat," he retorted, indignation bursting out from his incomprehension. "My crow."

She understood that he was charging her with more than interference, with carelessness, loss. He had been wronged.

She was forced to consider his furtive visits to a place he had not once dared to enter fully. All he had heard

273

there had been meaningless to him. It was like being deaf, the deafness merging into a blindness toward everything he saw and could not see. For this old man the Other Place could not be mystery, only chaos. Yet he had been drawn to it through the years, always apart, always alone, and in his own way always searching.

"My crow," he repeated emptily. He coughed.

"But I saw it. I was going to tell you." She wanted to reassure him, to give him something—hope, a reason for caring. "I'm sure I saw it. It may be back in the hut right now. It was . . . the other night." She faltered. "I think it was your crow."

He was just sitting, absorbing, maybe afraid of believing.

Her voice rose. "Did you hear me?"

The response to her shout came from the water. "Where are you, Claude? It's thick as hell out here." Voices floated in across the point. They reached her before the chugging of the engine could be heard. She could tell that Rebecca was arguing with someone. Then Tim warned, probably from up forward, "That's it, Phil; we're right against the rocks." Phil's answer sounded calm, controlled.

"Mr. Colman's here," she yelled over to them.

"We know," Phil called back to her. "Becca told us. We've got his boat."

Now she could see the looming mass that was all of them on the sloop. "Maybe we can wade out to you. We're already wet."

"No, we're deeper than you think. Stay put."

"How come you're wet?" Evan wanted to know.

Claudia swallowed and stole a glance at Mr. Colman.

"His boat got loose and he tried . . . I tried . . . . It was too deep for him."

"Heroic." That was Rebecca.

"Are you all right, dear?" Mother.

"Quick thinking," Phil responded.

"Mr. Colman doesn't think so," Claudia murmured. Louder, she said, "I knocked him down."

"Tim's rowing in for you two."

Claudia turned back to Mr. Colman, who was muttering to himself and shivering. She started to help him up, but he was heavier out of water and still resisting her. She could hear Evan demanding to come. She told Mr. Colman that Evan was coming. He began to swear again, but he staggered to his feet.

As soon as Tim beached the dinghy, she drew Evan off to show him where Fergus had been. But she couldn't find the little heap, and even the rounded boulder shaped like a stooping maiden barely showed.

"What is it?" Evan asked. "The hilt?"

"No, the hilt's safe. I left it up on the cliff where you gave it to me."

"Come on, kids," called Tim. "The old guy's pretty cold."

Evan frowned. "What is it then?"

"There was this sort of pile of . . . something." She had to show him with her hands. "Where they were standing. Right around here. Fergus. He wasn't supposed to touch the shore. He wanted the scribe to take the hilt, the sunstone. Maybe . . . there might be something—I don't know what—something left."

Walking in small circles at the edge of the rising tide, Evan began to look. He whispered to Claudia, "The

275

grownups think we came here to get Mr. Colman. See, Becca figured it was him coming in on the other side and lost. She guessed you heard him too and knew where he'd headed and went after him. She did all the talking when we woke up the others."

"They're not mad?"

Evan laughed softly. "They're proud of us."

"Hey, you two," Tim called again, "the old man's nearly out of it. Let's get going."

"Wait." Claudia was amazed to feel tears on her cheeks. "I just have to show Evan something."

"Problems?" yelled Phil from the boat.

"We're on our way," Tim shouted back. He came toward them and stood watching Evan's methodic search. "I don't see anything. There's nothing here."

"Like ashes," Claudia told him. "From a fire."

Tim was returning to Mr. Colman. "You made a fire?"

"Made me a fire there, sure. Had it going nice till the damn boat floated off and she knocked me down. Every damn thing wet. Matches. Everything." To demonstrate, he wrung out his cap.

"It was just a fire," Tim called back to Claudia. "Now come on."

Claudia splashed over to the dinghy. Bringing her face close to Mr. Colman's, she yelled, "It was not. You know what it was. Big as an oak. You said that. You can't deny what you saw. You're a vessel too. A vessel." He didn't even draw back; he seemed hardly to recognize her. Suddenly she was hugging him and whispering, "It's all right, it's all right." She didn't know what she meant. He smelled of sea water and peat, guano and sour milk. His skin was shriveled and icy. She held onto him with all her might, as though he were really drowning and she mustn't let go.

"Get that child out here," Phil shouted. "Right now."

Claudia felt Tim yanking her back and shoving her onto the stern thwart. Then he called Evan, who was circling the shallows now, ankle-deep, like a heron at its feeding.

Suddenly Evan bent way over, fishing for something. He brought up an object from the water, examined it briefly, and ran to the dinghy. Leaning as he climbed aboard, he swung around past Tim, who was trying to set an oar in place, and nudged Mr. Colman, thrusting his find into the old man's hands.

"What was that about a vessel?" came Susan's question. "Is Claudia hysterical?"

"Vassal," Rebecca corrected. "She can't even say it right. And can't even pull off a rescue without turning it into one of her stupid stories."

Claudia caught a glance from Evan. They began to laugh, rolling from side to side and pushing each other. Tim had to tell them to cut it out and quit rocking the boat, but they couldn't stop. In another minute Tim was laughing too.

Only the old man in the bow sat wrapped in silence and remoteness. Clutched in his lap was the soggy cap, and next to it, face down, its encrustations still shiny black from the water, lay the bronze man.

AUThOR's NOTE

THE first manuscript containing an account of some of these people was probably written by an unknown scribe in the seventh century, not more than a century or so after linear writing was introduced into Ireland. This was a period generally referred to as the Dark Ages; but the monasteries that flourished in that time were havens of learning and art that never succumbed to the darkness.

The scribes who composed the earliest written legends were trying to preserve for all time what the bards with their disciplined memory and oral tradition had kept alive for centuries. Some of these versions contain attempts at symbolic authentication in foretales in which the ghost of Fergus is called on to relate the stories of Ulidian heroes.

These heroes (some considered semi-divine, like Cuchulain, the Hound of Culann) inhabit the world of Iron Age Ireland, the Erenn of the legends. The period cannot be pinned down precisely, but refers to the centuries just before and after the birth of Christ, an era of great migrations among the Celtic peoples of Europe and northern Britain and Ireland. It is believed that the Sidh represent earlier inhabitants of Ireland who, under pressure from the invading tribes, literally went underground and appeared to their successors as spirit-folk of the mounds.

The *Tain Bó Cuailgne*, the Cattle Raid of Cooley, which tells of the struggle between the men of Ulidia (Ulster) in the northeast and the men of Connaucht in the west, is the major tale of a group of legends known as the Ulster Cycle. The warrior society it reflects conforms to the few written observations that have survived from the Romans, and is consistent with archaeological evidence in Ireland, Britain, and Gaul.

Many of the names that occur in the Ulster Cycle have counterparts in Anglo-Saxon myth. Queen Medb, whose name stands for mead, becomes the British Queen Mab (present-day name is Maeve); and Fergus's sword, named Caladbolg in some accounts, evolved into Excalibur, the more famous sword of King Arthur. All of the Old Irish names in these tales act as a kind of geographical narrative or topographical key to that land, many of them still alive in the names of rivers and mountains and valleys, even of bogs and cooking places.

That earliest written version of the *Tain* is lost, but it was probably copied, perhaps many times, and parts of the original text may still exist in surviving manuscripts which, though written in the Middle Ages, use language forms of much greater antiquity.

One such manuscript, the Book of the Dun Cow, contains an incomplete version of the *Tain* based on one dating from the seventh century. On translucent leaves set between covers made of the hide of a dun-colored cow, an eleventh-century scribe laboriously copied from what may have been the earliest written version of the *Tain*. This manuscript is still intact, though the ink is badly faded near the margins and some of the parchment is tattered or has even crumbled away. It is one of the most treasured books in the Library of the Royal Irish Academy in Dublin. Other versions exist in medieval manuscripts like the Yellow Book of Lecan and the Book of Leinster.

We cannot know what that first seventh-century scribe thought or felt about the Iron Age Celts whose way of life was already so different from his own, but we do know what one later scribe declared at the end of his copy of the *Tain*. Casting his blessing on all who would faithfully transcribe, without any changes, what he had written, he added: "But I who have written this history, or rather fable, do not believe the things which appear in it. For some are the deceptions of demons, others poetic imaginings; some are believable, others not; still others were written for the delight of fools."